OMEGA'S RUN
THE MOON FORGED TRILOGY: BOOK II

AJ Downey   Ryan Kells

Second Circle Press

Published 2016 by Second Circle Press
Book design by Lia Rees at Free Your Words (www.freeyourwords.com)
Cover art by Cover Your Dreams (www.coveryourdreams.net)

Text copyright © 2016 AJ Downey, Ryan Kells

This is a work of fiction. Names, characters, businesses, places, events and incidents are either the products of the author's imagination or used in a fictitious manner. Any resemblance to actual persons, living or dead, or actual events is purely coincidental.

All Rights Reserved

ISBN: 978-1530253692

Dedication

To the people who make all my books happen behind the scenes. Jennifer, Melanie, (for this one Hannah), Gabrielle and most importantly, Lia. Thanks for all the effort you do. No one gets to know about you guys nearly enough. – *AJ*

To AJ, without whom these books would never have gotten off the ground. – *Ryan*

The Moon Forged Trilogy

1. I Am The Alpha

2. OMEGA'S RUN

3. Hunter's End

Contents

Chapter 1	*1*
Chapter 2	*7*
Chapter 3	*9*
Chapter 4	*20*
Chapter 5	*25*
Chapter 6	*30*
Chapter 7	*36*
Chapter 8	*43*
Chapter 9	*50*
Chapter 10	*62*
Chapter 11	*71*
Chapter 12	*83*
Chapter 13	*90*
Chapter 14	*106*
Chapter 15	*111*
Chapter 16	*118*
Chapter 17	*123*
Chapter 18	*133*
Chapter 19	*138*
Chapter 20	*149*
Chapter 21	*156*
Chapter 22	*177*
Chapter 23	*186*

Chapter 24	*199*
Chapter 25	*203*
Chapter 26	*218*
Chapter 27	*226*
Chapter 28	*234*
Chapter 29	*244*
Epilogue	*255*

About the Authors

Chapter 1
Remus

I wasn't sure how I ended up in New Orleans, to be honest. After being banished from my pack, marked as an Omega, and sentenced to death if I ever returned to Washington; it wasn't like I had anywhere important to go. The Big Easy seemed as good a place as any to hit up. Within a month of leaving the Washington Territory, I had ridden half way across the country and taken up residence in the Crescent City.

Being alone can give a person time to reflect, time to think about their life, time to think about the path they've taken and what brought them to where they are. Time to follow the trail of decisions that led into each new turn in the road. I'd been doing a lot of that kind of thinking in regards to myself and my own situation lately, for sure.

Our father'd been ruining the pack. If we hadn't done something, everyone would have been up to their necks in trouble before they had even known anything was wrong. I still didn't know how Markus hadn't realized how bad things had gotten. Was I the only one that could *see it*? Was I the only one with enough sight and the brain matter to back it up, to recognize the writing on the wall?

Every year things got harder and harder for wolf-kind. The Hunters' technology was getting better. Their methods to identify us, more accurate. Soon there would be no way to hide, no place that would be safe. The only choice was to find a way to cooperate with them, or wipe them out.

Killing one man, even if that man *was* my father, to secure a strong Alpha, was a small price to pay in the face of that. Although, William was right, too. It hadn't been the right play. At least not the way Romulus, and yes, even I, had decided to go about it. There had been other avenues that I could have chosen, made my brother consider, but for reasons I won't go into now, we'd chosen the avenue we did.

End result?

My father was dead. My twin was dead at my adopted brother's hands, and William was the new Alpha of the Pacific Northwest Pack along with his mate, the daughter of the very hunter who we'd helped to kill our father.

Yeah; the convoluted mess makes my head hurt too.

I grunted quietly and my attention wandered from my churning thoughts to just getting the job at hand done. The cheap hotel room stank of the sweat and bodily fluids of the many patrons to visit before us. It smelled even stronger of sex and fear as I pressed the whore I'd met further into the mattress. She was doubled over the bed, legs spread wide with one of my hands tangled in her hair as I drove myself into her mercilessly over and over. I'm sure anyone that might have been in the adjacent rooms were hesitant as to whether the sounds coming from her throat were moans of pleasure or screams of pain. It was probably a bit of both, to be honest.

"Oh, *fuck*," she whined and I did nothing to hide my sneer. She was weak; she was vapid, and she was greedy, but she was clean, both of drugs *and* disease, with a huge set of tits and a relatively nice ass.

Speaking of, I pulled out of her grasping cunt, ignoring her frustrated moan, all thoughts of my insane life driven from my mind by my lust. Before she could react, I shifted position and drove my cock as far into her ass as I could. I grunted again, not surprised to find that the bitch had already lubed it up some before we'd even started. She bucked against me and I held her down, pushing forward until my heavy balls rested against her sopping pussy, every inch of my dick buried in her tight little asshole. That had to hurt some, but that just made me harder with the kind of mood I was in.

The fucking we'd been doing thus far had me primed, and I spent only a few minutes longer on her, every thrust into her body punctuated by a guttural moan from her and a loud slap as the cheeks of her ass smacked against me.

The growl that slipped from my throat was purely animalistic as I crested the wave I'd been surfing for a while and I came, firing several shots of semen into her, holding myself balls deep inside her ass until my cock stopped twitching. As I started to soften I pulled out of her, leaving her ass gaping. She moaned quietly, theatrically, something she must have thought was incredibly sexy. She reached back and grasped her cheeks with her hands, spreading her ass even further until my cum started leaking out of her. A cheap porn quality move that did nothing for me, in fact, it did quite the opposite.

Disgusting slut, I thought to myself.

"Hey! What the fuck?" she cried a moment later when I grabbed her by the arm and hauled her to her feet. I scooped up her clothes with one hand and shoved them into her Pamela Anderson boob job, hauling her toward the door the whole while.

"You're done here," I growled, ignoring her as she struggled against my grip. "Get the fuck out."

"Where's my money you fucking douchebag?" she shrilled and I laughed.

"I don't waste good money on a no good whore," I explained. I jerked open the door and shoved her through it, still butt naked and holding her clothes in her arms. She glowered at me, dull brown eyes glaring daggers and opened her shockingly red painted lips to scream at me when I slammed the door in her face.

I turned, ignoring her muffled screaming and pounding on the door and looked at the mess of a room. Single queen sized bed and a dresser with a cheap TV resting on it. A single ceiling mounted light with a lazily rotating fan hung in the center, and a single door across the room lead into the bathroom. I sniffed at the air and made a face at the stench. Mold, mildew, sex and desperation, with underlying rodent activity. If moral decay had a smell this would be it. *No wonder I was here.*

"Clean up and get out," I muttered to myself as I moved for the bathroom, "This place reeks without the distraction."

By the time I finished showering the door had been kicked in and there was a group waiting for me. I walked out naked, toweling my hair, and ignored their presence as I went about getting dressed.

Four of them, counting the whore I had already thrown from the place once.

"Came back for another round?" I asked her as I zipped up my pants. The jeans were several sizes too large to actually fit me and only the belt I wore kept them from falling right back to my ankles.

"You owe me some money, Mon Ami," the first of them said with that Cajun flare coloring his voice. The bitch was sitting on the end of the bed she had so recently been bent over. Standing next to her was a mountain of muscle and bad hair, wearing imitation biker gear in an attempt to look intimidating. Two more slabs of meat stood by the door in similar attire and wearing expressions indicative of single digit IQ scores.

"I don't owe you a fucking thing, Jack," I sneered and grabbed my keys from the dresser. Keys went into my pocket and the only thing left was my bag by the bed, a large military knapsack I'd had for decades.

"You had a slice of my little cherry pie here," Cajun drawled, running the backs of his fingers down one heavily reddened and swelling cheek. Her face hadn't been that way when I'd shoved her out the door, so that was likely the result of her telling her pimp that I didn't pay.

"And no one gets a slice o' da' pie wit'out payin' me my money."

I snorted. He was trying to sound threatening. Trying to be scary. And to a normal person he might have been successful, but neither the gun he held in his other hand, nor the muscle by the door, did anything to scare me. It's difficult to scare someone who doesn't have anything left to lose.

"Look, I just had a halfway decent fuck, and I'm in a halfway decent mood, which leaves me feeling charitable. Not something that happens too often." I stared the pimp in the eye and told him: "So, I'm going to give you one chance to leave here with all of your limbs intact. Take it now and we can all leave healthy. Push me? And you *won't* be leaving alive, get me?" I growled the last for the gomers by the door, there were probably too many words involved for them to catch my meaning otherwise.

There was silence for a moment, and I started to think I would actually get out of there without having to destroy anyone. As usually happens though, these idiots didn't know when they were outclassed and in over their heads.

With one sharp word from the Cajun his muscle rushed me. I sighed once before I reached out and grabbed the first man's wrist in a tight grip. I spun to the side, turning and pulling on his arm until he left his feet with a startled cry and slammed into the wall head first. He was out before he hit the floor.

I turned back to the second man, grabbed him by the head and yanked down at the same time that I jumped up, my knee crashing into his face so hard that the front of his skull caved in completely. He was dead before his buddies knew it and my pulse began to race as the scent of blood flooded the room; rich, red, and vibrant. The suddenly lax muscles of the body released, and the man gave off the rank odor of piss and shit as his bladder and bowels voided in death.

I stalked across the floor, stepping over the twitching corpse, moving purposefully toward the idiot that sent him and his friend to their deaths. The Cajun's eyes were wide and the bitch was screaming, something that did little to calm my growing anger. As he raised the gun that he had, I reached out and slapped it with a negligent backhand that shattered several of his fingers, the bones snapping with spindling cracking noises as the gun flew to land somewhere on the far side of the room.

"I gave you a choice," I growled. The sound that came from my throat was entirely inhuman and came straight from the place of nightmares. "Live, or die. Thank you *so much* for choosing death, I needed to hurt something." I grabbed his left arm between his elbow and shoulder and pulled as hard as I could. The muscles in my chest and shoulders bunched tight and with a sickening tearing sound, his arm was ripped clean from his shoulder.

He fell to his knees and just as he opened his mouth to scream I shoved the tattered stump of his own arm into it, effectively gagging him. He fell over and lay on the ground, shock setting in as he bled out across the shitty carpet and I turned to look at the whore. Splattered in her pimp's blood and staring at me with a wide eyed look of vacant terror on her face.

"No one will believe you," I told her smirking. I shot a little salute in her direction, holding two fingers to my temple before I grabbed my bag and walked out the door.

My bike was parked at the far end of the lot and I quickly stowed my shit, lashing it to the rear carrier with a set of bungee cords. I shrugged into my jacket, ignoring the way it brushed against the Greek letter Omega that was burned into my chest, a parting gift from William.

The bike roared to life, engine rumbling and throbbing beneath me. I pulled on my helmet, heeled up the kickstand and roared off into the night, humming a cheerful little ditty to myself as the miles fell away under my wheels. It was time to head north.

Chapter 2

Ava

I watched the television as I slid bullets into a fresh magazine. The volume was off, but I didn't need to hear. The room was awash in the alternating flashing red and blue lights from emergency vehicles on the local eleven o'clock news. A pretty reporter, mixed race, spoke into the microphone, lips moving with a sense of urgency as the black closed captioning boxes scrolled up from the bottom of the screen, the white type rolling along to fill them.

Words like 'brutal attack', 'several men', 'blunt force trauma' and 'no eye witnesses' flitted along before new ones appeared in their place. It was the same story everywhere we'd been.

I'd nearly had him in St. Louis. Missed him by an hour in Huntsville. Fucker moved around a lot, leaving a trail of bodies in his wake. Scum of the earth? Yeah. But they were still worth more than his sorry carcass. I slid the magazine home and pulled back the slide, jacking a round into the chamber. I moved with the practiced ease and precision that all Crusaders were trained with and it felt good. Calm, and full of assurance. I popped the magazine back out of my weapon and topped it off before sliding it back home with a satisfying click.

He wouldn't be getting away this time. Failure wasn't an option. I slid my weapon, a Glock 23 with an attached tactical light, into the holster along the outside of my thigh. The attack on the news was just outside New Orleans. I'd been here a couple of days already on the hunt. If he was willing to draw this kind of heat from the mundane authorities then he was moving on, and if he was moving on, then so was I. I picked up my riding jacket. A Joe Rocket with Kevlar lining and slipped it on, zipping it midway up my chest.

A final check of my riding boots and I snatched up my knapsack and helmet, heading for the door. I made sure my credentials as a licensed bounty hunter hung in plain sight from the bead chain around my neck. Made the gun, not so much less *noticeable*, but more understood.

It really *was* my day job. When I wasn't hunting one of *them*, I spent my time getting paid tracking down your good 'ol, garden variety, human criminals. It kept me sharp for the hunts that mattered. The hunts like this one.

I checked out of the roadside motel and pulled on my riding gloves before I mounted my bike. She was a satiny black Buell Lightning and had never let me down. I had a guess as to which highway he would have taken out of the area. I put my helmet on and fired my baby up, pulling out of the lot smoothly, leaning into the turn that would take me out and toward the highway.

If my calculations were right, if I had gleaned his pattern correctly, he would head north again. I made to follow.

I'll get him, James. I promise. I thought to my brother, the familiar fractured ache of his loss giving a dull throb in the center of my heart. He'd gone down in a hunt last year, and it *still* felt like just yesterday.

I was well rested, I was primed and I would ride all night and into the next day to close the gap between me and my quarry. Remy Dulcet didn't know it yet, but he'd met his match with Ava Martine. I would catch him, it was only a matter of time and time, for him, was growing really fucking short.

Chapter 3
Remus

New Orleans to Chicago. I jumped onto the I-55 north, transferred onto the 57 north, and managed a ride that was just shy of a thousand miles in a little more than a day. I stopped as little as possible and didn't feel too bad for it afterward. A normal human would have fallen asleep at the handlebars or would have been in so much pain from the ride that they barely would have been able to move.

I checked into a motel near the Loop in downtown Chicago and crashed for a couple hours before I got up and headed out. Even I could admit that I had spent long enough wandering like a lost puppy. I didn't know what to do with myself. I didn't have anywhere to go since I was made Omega, and for the past six months I had done nothing but wander the country, fucking and fighting whenever the opportunity for either presented itself.

It was time to stop wandering and figure out a plan. I had centuries ahead of me if a Hunter didn't get me first, and I couldn't spend the next few hundred years just doing the same nothing.

Less than three blocks from my motel was a seedy dive bar. One of those hole-in-the-wall type of places that seem to crop up in every town in every country in the world, no matter the population. Live in a small town in the middle of nowhere? There's a seedy dive bar somewhere. Just the way of the world.

This particular dive, while still maintaining the sterling reputation of dives everywhere, at least sported nine foot pool tables instead of those crappy coin operated ones you'll see in most bars. And this bar also had something else. A regular that I was particularly interested in speaking to.

It'd taken me two months to track the fucker down. Four months after my banishment, I woke up one morning in an alley in Los

Angeles with a hangover the likes of which I had rarely experienced. That was when I decided that I needed to do something and not just wander around aimlessly. I may not have a pack anymore, but I at least still had a will to live.

I pushed open the glass door and entered a dim, smoke filled, interior. I wrinkled my nose in disgust before I could even think to hide my reaction. A wolf-kind's sense of smell was considerably stronger than a human's and even a human non-smoker would have been sent packing from this place by the rank odor.

Chicago had joined the rest of the country in instituting a smoking ban inside public buildings and businesses. Of course some places, like this dump, either chose to ignore such things or managed to get themselves grandfathered in as a private establishment or club as an end run around the new law. I found myself wishing that the man I was searching for had more of a tendency for frequenting a less, *fragrant*, bar.

There was little that I could do about the situation though. Beggars can't be choosers. So, I pushed down the urge to vomit and took shallow breaths through my mouth, tugging at the hem of the plain t-shirt I had thrown on beneath my jacket. I hated wearing shirts. Some might call it vain, an excuse to show off the muscles I had put a great deal of work into building. In truth, I simply didn't like being constricted and the garment was nothing more than a hindrance if I needed to change in a hurry. It made me uncomfortable. But even dives still required their patrons to be fully dressed. No shirt, no shoes, no service… so I was forced to stick to the inane conventions created by a human society that I didn't belong to in any way shape or form. A society I had never even been a part of having been born this way, rather than Moon Forged.

I'd stopped just inside the door and though it was glass, it was almost completely obscured, inside and out, with stickers and posters of various kinds and for various things. Skate logos, bands, book stores, bumper stickers with sarcastic sentences scrawled across them in spidery script and garish colors. You name it, it was plastered to it; so much so that when the door had closed, very little light filtered in from the outside, despite being just before sunset.

Not that it mattered much, my eyes adjusted quickly to the dimly lit interior.

The man I was looking for was already here at a billiard table near the back of the hazy room. He had his back to me, but I couldn't mistake that slight frame for anyone other than Cruz. Jeremiah Cruz was the Alpha of the Chicago pack. They held the whole city and had done so for a good thirty or forty years. They didn't have the kind of territory that my former pack held, but they had plenty for a pack of six to be dealing with and Cruz was the man to thank for their success.

"Remus Reese," he said as I walked up behind him. "I'd recognize that smell anywhere. What brings you into my territory?"

"It's Remy," I rumbled, startled to hear the name I had been given at my birth. I hadn't heard it in half a year. "Remy Dulcet. I'm not here to hunt, or out for your territory, Cruz," I assured him. "I just want to talk."

"Yeah? About what?" He leaned over the table, lining up a shot. With a smooth motion of his arm he sent the cue ball rolling across the table to sink the seven ball into the far corner pocket.

"I find myself in a difficult situation… I need a pack."

Cruz shot up from the table and turned to face me, his eyebrows already reaching for his hairline as he gave me a wide eyed expression of pure shock.

"Remus Reese, the golden boy of the Pacific Northwest was driven from his pack?" he asked incredulously. "What in the hell happened up there?"

"It's a long story that I played too much of a role in for my liking."

His eyes narrowed and I could tell I was losing him.

"You come to me, looking to join with my pack because you heard we took an Omega in a while back, didn't you? Well, just because we did it once, doesn't mean we'll do it again, especially if you won't tell me what got you the boot in your ass in the first place."

He was right, as much as I hated to admit it. He had no reason to believe anything of me and if I didn't come clean there was no chance at all he would even consider letting me join with his pack.

So I laid it out for him. The pack dying, falling apart under my father's flawed leadership. He had once been a great Alpha, but time had whittled away at his sense and he began making stupid decisions. Decisions that would have destroyed the pack if he had been allowed to continue as its Alpha.

Over an hour later we were sitting at the bar, beers in hands as I finished my tale. I'd spared no detail in the telling either, figuring if I wanted a shot at this, I'd better go for broke.

"So William branded me Omega after he killed Rom and his mate destroyed Lucinda. The fucking cunt deserved, it she was the biggest cunt in the pack." I'd actually been pretty fucking proud of little Chloe for pulling that one off. You'd probably never hear me say it out loud though.

Cruz nodded and chugged down some more of his beer, signaling the bartender with his free hand for another as he drained the last of it. He slammed down the glass and turned to me.

"I'll agree with you there. We've been hearing rumors about the Pacific Northwest pack out here for a while. A few locals even kicked around the idea of trying to horn in on your guys' territory."

I cocked my head to the side slightly at that, giving him a questioning look. "And what stopped them?"

"You and your whack job of a brother. May he rest in peace," he added the last almost as an afterthought while a guilty look stole across his face. I waved it away. Romulus really had been off his nut so I couldn't blame Cruz for what amounted to a reasonable reaction.

"Also, your numbers up there." Cruz continued, "There aren't very many packs that stand the remotest possible chance of going up against your people. If they tried to get into your territory you guys would just roll right over 'em, like the Nevada pack you all disappeared a few years back."

That certainly got my attention. I'd had no knowledge that a pack from Nevada had attempted to break into our territory. If that were true, and the pack wasn't responsible for defending our borders against them, then what'd really happened? Yet another secret father had kept.

I shunted that machination aside, returning my focus to Cruz as he picked up his fresh beer and continued talking.

"Based on what you're saying, I'll agree. Your old man needed to go. But to bring the *Hunters* into it? To bring the Hangman *himself* into it? You realize he's one of the highest ranked members in the states right? Got some contacts in New York that've speculated he might even run the entire damned western hemisphere of their organization... and you picked *him* to get involved?"

He shook his head in disbelief, "Man, that's a degree of poor decision making so bad that I'm not even certain they've invented a scale to measure it yet. If it was just getting rid of your Alpha, that's one thing. I can see that, I can understand that, could possibly even forgive the patricide aspect to it. But getting the Hunters involved with it is going beyond the pale, Son. I can't let you join our pack with that kind of a stigma hangin' over you. The rest of 'em will always be wondering when you'll bring the hunters to our door next. It would never work. I'd be fighting off challenges for my title every full and probably every new moon too."

My fingers tightened around the handle on my beer mug. I was grateful that I hadn't been holding the glass by the body or it might have shattered in my grip. As it was, the cracking sound of the thick handle fracturing under my fingers warned me early enough, that I made myself let go before anything shattered or broke completely.

It had been a long shot, honestly. But I'd had to give it a try, and I couldn't blame him. Jeremiah was a good Alpha. He protected his people and he protected their territory. We talked for a few minutes longer but after he finished his beer he clapped me on the shoulder, a gesture that did nothing to ease the pain in my chest and left me there. Still, as alone as I'd ever felt before, it was worse now that the last chance I could think of had walked away and left me in the dirt once again.

I had little to do after that, so I spent it drinking and playing pool. It was nearing midnight before she showed up and it marked the beginning and the end of all things for me. A chaotic mess that made the issues with my former pack seem like child's play.

I leaned over the table, jacket draped across a nearby stool with the cue held in my large hands. A hard tap and the cue ball was sent rolling with just the right English on it. I could feel it. The second the ball moved, I knew exactly where that shot was going to go and I straightened up to stare at her across the table. The ball's momentum carried it halfway across the nine foot table before the spin I had put on it took over and it curved around a cluster of balls to strike the one ball, sinking it gently into the corner pocket right in front of her.

Long, wavy, dark hair hung past her shoulders and a pair of gleaming, pale, jade colored eyes studied me from within a heart shaped face. She had a great body, encased in a short dress of a dark material. A Joe Rocket biker jacket hung perfectly on her frame.

"Nice shot," she said, her voice coming to me from across the distance of smoke filled bar and alcohol consumption. I blinked, somewhat blearily at her for a moment before I shrugged and leaned on my cue.

"It's not that difficult, once you get the trick of it." I didn't want company. I didn't want to be bothered. But... she was attractive, and she smelled wonderful, like jasmine, bright and floral with a hint of something sharp beneath it. I breathed in through my nose as subtly as I could, taking in the scent of her as it wafted across the table toward me. Over the stink of cigarettes and alcohol she was a pleasant enough change.

I came around the table and I noticed a pair of long, well-toned legs, half covered in knee high black boots. I stopped right in front of her, my chest almost bumping into her and she looked up at me through dark lashes. "You want to back up so I can shoot, Sugar Tits?" I asked and she laughed, a deep, throaty kind of laugh that made you think of dark rooms, sweat, skin, and the slick, slapping sounds of frenzied sex.

She backed up obligingly though and I leaned over the table to line up my next shot. "Was there a reason you decided to come interrupt my game?" I asked.

"Well, I see a tall, good looking man, all alone and playing with himself and I just can't help but wonder... what's made you into such a sad sack?" she drawled casually and I snorted, unable to help the small laugh. She was funny, and hot, I'll give her those two, but that didn't mean I was going to give much else.

"None of your fucking business."

She shrugged, an action that did some very interesting things to some portions of her anatomy that I did my best to ignore. I wasn't in the mood, as much as my body disagreed, based on its reaction to the sight.

"True, but my boyfriend stood me up and I figured why waste this dress that I picked out special, just for tonight? That, and you're definitely better on the eyes than him so..." She trailed off suggestively and I glanced up at her after dropping another shot. She was leaning over the table, jacket hanging loose around her and giving me an excellent view down the front of her dress, enough to tell by the way her tits hung that she wasn't wearing a bra.

"So, what? You think you'll hit on the only guy in the bar that's alone and make your boyfriend jealous?"

"That was sort of the idea. But I wasn't thinking of hitting on you."

"What do you call this then?"

"I call it asking you directly, take me to a hotel and fuck me until I can't stand up straight," she said and winked at me.

It was an enticing offer, I'll be honest, but for some reason alarms were going off in the back of my head. Something I couldn't quite reconcile with the beautiful woman that stood in front of me.

I've learned to trust my instincts over the decades though, and right then, my instincts were telling me that she was bad news. It wasn't the boyfriend. I could take down any boyfriend, no problem. Even without the prodigious strength I was gifted with as a Blood Born wolf-kind, I still had more than enough muscle mass to make me an intimidating and formidable opponent. Plus, I had more combat experience than most people.

I just couldn't put my mental finger on what was bothering me about this bitch. She was still staring at me, her jade green eyes almost looking into me, and another alarm bell started ringing in my head.

"Sorry, Sweetheart," I said and dropped my pool cue on the table. I'm afraid I'm going to have to decline." She blinked, startled and for a second I thought I saw a flash of anger burn through her eyes, but it was gone as quickly as it came and I couldn't honestly be sure it had ever really been there in the first place.

"Well," she said with another distracting shrug. "You can't blame a girl for trying." She winked again and turned to saunter away, a distinctive sway in her hips.

"You're a fucking moron, Remy Dulcet," I grumbled to myself and turned back to my solo game of nine ball.

I finished the game and downed the last of my beer in record time before I grabbed my jacket and headed for the door. With nothing else to do I decided to head back to my motel to crash for the night when I felt a finger tap my shoulder.

I was tired. I was buzzed. I was a little depressed too, to be honest. So I was more than a little surprised when I turned and found the hottie from the bar standing behind me. I was even more surprised when she pressed the barrel of a gun under my chin.

"I tried to be nice," she said with mock sorrow. The glinting humor in her eyes gave away how much she was enjoying this. "I really did try to get you out here without threats." She paused and her head cocked to the side slightly. "Well, honestly I guess it would have ended in a threat at this stage either way so..." she shrugged again.

"I knew there was a reason I didn't like you," I muttered, anger starting to build in my chest. "I couldn't really smell the gun oil over all that cigarette smoke. But I must have caught enough of it that I didn't feel right about you."

"Well you're an animal. What do I care how you feel?" she snapped. The beautiful jade of her eyes suddenly became as hard and cold as the stone they so closely resembled. Shit. I was starting to realize just how dangerous this chick was. Bad news didn't even begin to cover it.

Somehow, I didn't feel too upset about getting killed. I didn't welcome it, but somehow I wasn't as angry as I thought I would be.

"So are you going to put this dog down or not?" I snapped after we stood there for almost a full minute with the gun digging into my flesh. "If not, I've got other things to do."

"You're not going to die here, Remy Dulcet. Mathias Young extends an invitation. He wants to talk to you."

I wasn't afraid of dying. I wasn't afraid of fighting. But *that* put a tingle of fear into my spine. I wanted nothing to do with the Hangman; he had proven himself to be nearly as insane as Romulus was, and that information was the galvanizing force for what I did next.

My hand came up and slapped her hand to the side. Her finger jerked spastically and the gun went off, a bullet whizzing past my face so close that it burned a line of fire from my jaw all the way to my temple. I staggered to the side, my left ear ringing loudly from the explosive sound of the gunshot going off practically right next to my head.

I grabbed her by the jacket, spun hard and tossed her as hard as I could. Admittedly, off balance and with my head ringing like a church bell, 'as hard as I could' meant that she flew a yard or two and rolled expertly across the ground coming up on her feet like an experienced acrobat, gun whipping around to point at me again.

I was already running down the street. My balance was fucking shot and I swallowed back a wave of nausea that was, thankfully, already starting to recede. With every step the pain in my ear faded as it healed. The pain in the side of my face, however, failed to get any better. In fact it seemed like it was getting worse.

Fucking bitch was actually using silver coated bullets! The pain was only going to get worse as my allergy kicked in. I wasn't one of those wolf-kind that could shrug off the touch of silver. I reacted badly to it, and I could already feel the side of my face swelling up and my vision in my left eye starting to get blurry as it began to swell shut.

Yeah, this wasn't going to be good.

"You're not getting away, fucker!" she yelled from a half a block behind me. "Out of the way people! Move!"

Vision gone in one eye and the entire side of my face feeling as if someone had just poured a vial of acid across it, I bounced off of something hard, my right shoulder catching it and spinning me around like a top before I fell hard to the concrete, rolling awkwardly back to my feet and continuing to run.

How the fuck did I let a damn human get the drop on me? I was a Blood Born. One of the two most powerful wolf-kind of the Pacific Northwest Pack. *Only I wasn't a member of the pack anymore.* I had let depression get the better of me. I had let it dull my edge, and now I was paying for it.

I shoved people aside, bowling others over entirely as I ran down the street and blearily, out of my good eye, I caught sight of a fire escape running from the ground floor all the way up to the roof of a nondescript five story building. I dodged down the alley towards it. The beginnings of a plan started to form and I leaped for it, covering a dozen feet in a single bound and ignoring the startled screams of the idiots below me. I wasn't sure how far back she was, but I grabbed the ladder and started climbing. Another gunshot rang out behind me and a spark flew into my face as the bullet ricocheted off the metal hand rail.

Below me I could hear her boots pounding on the rungs of the ladder and I ran as hard as I could up each floor until I tumbled over the corner of the building onto the gravel covered roof.

"Where the fuck do you think you're going to go now, numb nuts?" she asked, panting slightly as she came over the edge of the building behind me. "You *do* realize you're on top of a roof, right?"

I looked back at her and laughed, a choking wheeze as the silver started to affect my throat. It wouldn't kill me, but I really wasn't going to be happy for the next few days.

"And you *do* realize I'm wolf-kind right? I'm not as trapped as you think." I broke into a shambling sprint running directly away from her and right toward the edge of the building.

The street below was five lanes wide, counting sidewalks on either side. I didn't have the slightest clue what that distance was in feet and I'm glad I didn't because I might not have attempted what I did if I *had* known.

I heard her curse behind me as my foot hit the edge of the building and I launched myself into the air. The gun went off once again and a searing pain exploded in the back of my right thigh. The controlled leap turned into an awkward fall as I left the roof of the five story building. I flew across the street and crashed through the third floor window of the next building over in a spray of broken glass and shattered wood.

I tumbled across an empty office space and crashed into the far wall. Something popped in my back, I had officially lost all vision in my left eye, and my right leg burned horribly. A bit of blood touched my lips as something inside my body protested its current treatment. Outside I heard a frustrated scream and I laughed, coughing up a bit more blood as I slowly struggled to my feet.

"Tell Mathias Young, he can shove his invitation up his ass!" I yelled and stumbled out of the office and into the rest of the building.

Chapter 4

Ava

"Oh you can tell him yourself, asshole," I muttered under my breath before raising my coat sleeve to my lips.

"It's the building across the street from my location, capture him as he comes out; don't be afraid to hurt him a little." I pressed a finger to my ear and waited for a response, the earbud in my left ear crackled to life.

"Copy that, Ava." I took a deep breath and let it out slowly as my heart-rate began to calm. I watched with detached interest from the rooftop as the front doors burst open at street level and Remus "Remy" Reese looked up, a smug grin on his face, twisted though it was in pain.

Aw, poor baby.

The van raced up and when Reese turned to lope up the sidewalk, he turned right into one of my guys who unloaded not one, but *two* police issue Tasers into Reese's chest. He stiffened, like a board and keeled over right onto his back where two more of my team waited. They caught the monster in their arms and pulled him into the van. The panel door slid shut, the engine revved once and pulled away from the curb to the blare of traffic horns.

"Package has been acquired, and is sufficiently detained," came through my earpiece a moment later.

I smiled and said, "Copy that, I'm en route."

I took my time coming down the same way I'd come up and when my boots hit the broken asphalt of the alleyway I breathed a sigh of relief. I cracked my neck back and forth and rolled my shoulders before heading back to my bike. The safe house wasn't far and then it would be a transfer to a Crusader facility after that, but first? I needed to get that slug out of his leg, pronto. So safe house and a little impromptu kitchen table surgery before anything.

I caught up to the van easily and trailed it out into the Illinois country. Every once in a while I would check on the package the van contained but according to my guys, he was out like a traffic light and showed no signs of stirring. Vitals were stable though, so there was that. I didn't need him dying on me. That wasn't the mission this time.

We pulled up to the farmhouse and Jordan got out of the front passenger seat.

"Jesus Christ he's a big bastard!" he cried and I leaned my bike onto the kickstand and hit the chinstrap on my helmet.

"Quit your bitching, you pussy!" Harper called from the back of the van. I laughed. She was just as bad as me sometimes.

Donnell shut the driver's side door and came around the front of the van.

"Shut the fuck up, the both of you. It's going to take all of us to get this monster inside." I nodded.

"Kitchen table," I stated and everyone froze and looked at me.

"Seriously? We should just take him to the facility and let *them* handle it," Logan said as he hopped out of the back of the van behind Harper. Mason followed Logan and my team was assembled. I shook my head.

"All of you knock it the fuck off, get his ass out of the back and in the kitchen, and make sure the fucker is chained down face first. I have to dig out that slug or there's a good chance he's not going to make it to the facility. Mathias would be fucking pissed if he dies and none of us are exactly his golden children. Not after losing his daughter. So seriously, move it or lose it!" I lectured, barking the last and they moved it. I went into the house before them and to the medical locker stashed in the corner of the kitchen.

There was a bunch of grunting, cursing and wheezing as they brought the tranquilized man... *creature*, I corrected myself automatically, in through the front door, past the living room, to do what I'd commanded.

They dropped him face first onto the rustic kitchen table and chained him at wrist and ankle to the eyebolts set in the floor.

Reinforced steel chain. The eyebolts were set into the foundation of the house beneath the floors, driven into the concrete by a good eighteen inches. It would hold a couple of elephants in place. One of these bastards, no matter how big, wouldn't be any match for the restraints.

"Need an assist, Av?"

"No, as long as he's secure," I stated.

"Yup," Mason declared, leaning up from the final shackle. I checked the restraints myself anyways.

"Cow," I heard Harper utter.

"Call me names all you want, Sweetie. Better to be safe than dead."

With a few extra grumbles and a gripe or two, the team went out front to the porch. They did, however, leave the front door open to keep an eye on things.

This was going to suck for the monster. It was going to suck hard. I pulled on a pair of latex gloves then pulled on two more. Double gloving was standard operating procedure with these things, even after discovering that their disease wasn't a blood borne pathogen.

I snapped the top off of the ampule of ammonia and went around to the front of the table where his head was at, but before I could bring it near, his head snapped up and he glowered at me, snarling and snapping.

"Oh, good! Don't need that!" I threw it into the sink and heard it plink into the garbage disposal.

"Listen up, mongrel. I'm going to dig that slug out of the back of your leg. It's going to hurt, a whole fuck of a lot, but you need to stay awake for me and tell me if I got it all. You copy?" I demanded and raised my eyebrows. He snorted, a derisive sound.

"There's not much you can do that I haven't already dealt with, just get the fucking bullet out."

I got up on the table and sat on his ass, mostly to pin him down as best I could. This worked best when they had a reminder that they needed to hold still.

"Ride 'em cowgirl," I commented dryly and he snorted. He was cool as a cucumber when I started digging for the bullet. He grunted a few times, made a choked noise and the table groaned where he gripped the corners.

"Break my fucking table I'll put another bullet in you on principle," I muttered.

"You're a cold bitch aren't you?"

I wrenched the pliers a little deeper into the wound, digging a little unnecessarily hard for the bullet I'd put in him, he grunted and bucked slightly beneath me.

"I don't know, you tell me."

He barked a bitter laugh and I grasped onto the offending object and pulled it out, mostly intact, dropping it into a dish waiting on a cart beside the table with a hollow clatter.

"Get it all?" I asked.

"Give it a minute, let the burning settle and I'll tell you," he grated.

I wiped at the sweat on my brow with the back of my wrist and breathed out. A moment later, he grunted again as if satisfied.

"I think you got it, now get the fuck off me."

I laughed some and slapped him on his ass, it was a nice one as far as the male physique went; too bad it was wasted on him. I got off and bent at the knees a bit when I hit the floor. I turned around and met smoldering dark eyes and raised a brow.

"Glare at me all you like, it was your dumb ass that got caught, not my fault you underestimated me."

He jerked at his bonds and growled and I gave him a sardonic little smile.

"Not done yet, Fido. Might want to save it until *after* I've finished. Wouldn't want this to be more unpleasant than it needs to be now would you?"

"Fuck you, Hunter bitch."

"You wish, buddy, it ain't never gonna happen."

I set to work fixing him up. We knew wounds made with silver took longer for the mongrels to heal and as far as wounds went, the one I'd dealt him was a bad one. Hell, his reaction to the graze was one of the most spectacular I'd ever seen. The side of his face looked like hamburger with how raw, red, and lumpy it was with swelling. It was to the point I debated using an epi pen.

"You breathing okay?"

"What do you care?"

"Personally, I don't, but Mathias does and what Mathias cares about, I better damn well care about too. So do me a favor and answer the fucking question."

Resolute, glowering, silence filled the space between us and I rolled my eyes. If he were being that fucking ornery, he wouldn't need the epi shot, but I slid a pen into my jacket anyways. You never knew and it was better to be prepared than not.

I used everything at my disposal, the medical training I'd received coming in handy. Granted it wasn't much better than your rudimentary combat medic training plus a touch more, but it would get him to the containment facility. They'd possibly take the care to get him fixed up right. I didn't know what they did with them after I brought them in, and it wasn't my problem. I just hunted them down, killed them when it was called for and brought them back alive when it was ordered for me to do so.

"Donnell! Mason!" I called out, both appeared in the safe house doorway. "Get him back in the van." I ordered. For some reason I wanted this particular mission over and done. It probably had a lot to do with the way this one was looking at me. A fire in his dark eyes that smoldered, a calculation to that dark stare… *control.* He had an eerie amount of control for one of these creatures to the point it was unsettling.

Yeah. I wanted this mission done, because this one almost scared me with what he could and might do if we slipped up. I didn't want to leave anything to chance. It wasn't my style.

Chapter 5
Remus

My leg felt like it was on fire, worse when she dug the bullet out but I refused to let her see my pain.

Do not show pain. Do not show weakness. Your chance will come, be patient, wait; watch for it.

These words passed through my head like a mantra while she dug around in my leg for the bullet and continued as we talked after. When she slapped my ass it was all I could do not to jump. I hadn't been expecting that at all and it startled me, so focused was I on everything else.

Rom would be ashamed of me for getting caught so easily. Father would be ashamed. Hell, even William would have mocked me for how easily they'd brought me down, how easily *she* had. How had I sunk so low? Had my instincts really dulled so much that I couldn't smell a hunter coming? I should have recognized the scent of gun oil around her, or the stink of silver. I should have *known*.

"What do you think they think about?" A voice asked and I blinked, coming out of my thoughts to find two men standing at the head of the table.

"Chasing rabbits or something?" One of them asked.

"Yeah but they're not dogs all the time, right?" The first voice asked coming from the man on my left. He was tall and willowy, whipcord muscle over bone with barely an ounce of fat on him as far as I could tell. His partner was exactly the opposite. Short and stocky with a rounder middle but no less strong for it. I could tell by the way he held himself that thick middle was all hard muscle beneath the fat.

"You two geniuses do realize that I can hear you, right?" I growled caustically and Whippy, as I mentally dubbed him, looked at me and nudged his buddy.

"Look, it's like he's trying to talk. Isn't it funny how they try to act like human beings? I mean, don't you think? Like monkeys at the zoo or something."

Tubby grunted. "Yeah, but monkeys only throw their shit at you. This guy'll rip yer head clean off and eat your heart if you give him the chance." I rolled my eyes. This was how it was going to be, I could just tell. I hoped we didn't have too far to go to get to this containment facility that they were talking about. I really didn't want to put up with them any longer than I had to.

There was no reasoning, or arguing with that kind of stupid. It just wasn't possible. All I could do was wait for my chance to get away. Statistically it was going to happen. I just had to be ready for it.

These fuckers moving me from the table to the truck would ideally be the most likely time to get away. I would be on my feet, and though I still felt woozy and my leg still hurt like hell, I was stronger than both of them combined. I could force my way out of there.

Right?

Wrong.

They disconnected the chains that held me to the floor and helped me to my feet. The second I started to try to run, and I do mean the very *second* there was a loud snapping sound, several points of pain bloomed on my back and a loud crackling noise filled the room as I pissed myself and my body started to flop around like an epileptic carp. I jerked and spasmed as the four contact points from the two tasers fed who knew how many volts of electricity into my body and all my muscles seized up and refused to cooperate with my mental commands for movement.

"Dammit, Ava," Tubby growled. "Now we gotta carry his heavy ass again."

"Would you rather tell Mathias that we lost him? Would you rather have that *thing*," she kicked at my leg. "Come back and rip us all to shreds? You can deal with having to lug him to the truck." She kicked me again, a sensation I was barely aware of in the deepening haze of darkness that enshrouded the edges of my consciousness.

"Now hurry up and move, I want this mission over and done..." Anything else she said was lost to me as I finally fell unconscious.

The next thing I knew I was laying on my front on a cold slab of metal and there was a sensation of motion that made me want to hurl. Thick, heavy chains were wrapped around my body, crossed several times from shoulders to ankles and I lifted my head only to realize that I was in the back of a cargo container on a semi-truck. Whippy and Tubby stood against the doors that opened on the back end and sitting on a stack of wooden pallets next to me, was Ava.

Her smoky jade green eyes regarded me intently and I glared right back at her. "What?" I snapped.

She shrugged, an action that did little for me this time as she was dressed much more practically than she had been the night before. She still wore her Joe Rocket jacket, but beneath that, she had on a simple black shirt that clung to her curves with a tactical holster and her gun tucked into it under her left arm. The shirt was tucked into a pair of black tactical 5.11's, the waist cinched tight to prevent them from falling off her slim hips. Her pockets bulged with who knew what items and the cuffs of her pants were tucked into a pair of shiny black combat boots and bloused.

"I was just wondering how long you were going to sleep. It's not like we've been that hard on you. We're practically babying you, compared to some." She smirked, her full lips turning up in a truly distracting way, but I crushed that under an ocean of rage and glared at her. Pretty she might be, but she was a royal fucking *bitch*. Yet for some reason, that wasn't taking away from her beauty any for me. It really should have, but it wasn't. Maybe being electrocuted had fried something vital in my noggin.

"So proud of yourself. Kidnapping and terrorizing innocent people just for who they are. You must find yourself compared to the SS a lot, right?" I didn't have to pretend to be pissed off, chubby aside, I was pretty fuckin' pissed too.

She glared at me. "We can't be compared to some lunatic despot trying to wipe out an innocent people. Your kind murder for fun."

I looked her evenly in the eye. "Humans kill for sport; my people do not."

"You mean you *animals* don't. Isn't that the quote? Animals don't kill for sport, only human beings do? I've heard that thrown around before by people trying to discuss morals and philosophy."

"And yet you didn't listen to them? Good move, Sugar Tits." I grinned at her when she suddenly flushed just slightly and crossed her arms over her breasts.

"So is that why you wore a skimpy dress when you tried to capture me?" I asked, abruptly changing the topic. I needed to keep her off balance if I wanted to try and get anywhere in this game.

"Tried?" she snorted. "I *did* capture you, you dumb ox. I thought even you would be able to recognize that. Guess I gave your intelligence too much credit."

"No, *you* didn't. I escaped *you*. Your *team* brought me down. Without them I would've been in the wind."

She glared at me for a moment but obviously couldn't think of an argument so she changed the subject. "What'd you mean about the dress?"

I smirked. "Well, since you're obviously forced to wear such an ugly, and simple uniform on the job I'm not surprised you'd dress up a bit when you got the chance. It must feel nice to get to pretend to be a regular woman now and again–" I was cut off as her hand whipped around, grasped the gun in its holster beneath her jacket, drew it, and pistol whipped me across the face all in one smooth motion.

My head jerk to the side and I saw stars for a second. I turned back to her, blood smeared grin firmly in place and spit out a fragment of back tooth. "Hit a nerve did I?"

"Shut up, or I'll tase your ass again. And this time? I'll keep doing it every hour on the hour until you're either a vegetable or until we get there," she hissed in a low, dangerous voice. Whippy and Tubby exchanged nervous looks and shifted on their feet where they stood by the door. They obviously weren't so sure about that, but Ava was just as obviously in charge. They couldn't exactly go challenging her authority in the field.

She was their Alpha. I almost laughed as the thought occurred to me but I bit it back and laid my head down, letting my throbbing cheek rest against the cold metal. The ceiling above me was nothing but fiberglass, letting the natural daylight through and the sound of the truck hummed through the metal against my chest.

In no time I was lulled to sleep. My body needed to heal. It needed to repair the damage and I really needed to eat. I was so hungry. I hadn't eaten in a while. But my exhaustion overcame the hunger and out I went, despite my best efforts to stay awake.

Chapter 6

Ava

Hours passed. I sat still with my arms crossed my over my chest and my legs crossed at the knee. I knew I was glowering at him, that my scowl had done nothing but deepen as the miles rushed past beneath the wheels of the truck and the daylight came and went.

Donnell huffed a clipped laugh, which he quickly silenced when my cold, furious gaze snapped from our quarry to him. Donnell held up his hands and wouldn't meet my eyes and I couldn't say that I blamed him. I had a certain… reputation. Because I was a woman, because I was lithe and was somewhat blessed with a halfway decent rack, men automatically assumed I was both weak and only good for my mouth or my cunt. To remedy the misnomer, I had cultivated a certain amount of ruthlessness among the Crusaders.

If a man wanted to think with his dick around me, I wouldn't hesitate to use it to drop him. I fought with calculated and underhanded maneuvers. When someone wanted to whine about such ridiculous notions as 'fair', I was pretty quick to point out that the dogs we were up against didn't give two shits about what was and wasn't fair and neither should we.

All these animals cared about was kill or be killed and the systematic destruction of the human race. The Crusaders had spent thousands of years protecting humans from these creatures. I belonged to a sacred order charged with the protection of humans against extinction. Thus far we had been exceedingly successful, but there was always a danger of these animalistic bastards going feral or rogue. Of biting or breeding to the point they turned the tide to where they could outnumber us. Spreading their disease, their epidemic of rage and lack of control.

"You should try to get some sleep, Ava. It's out and we've got a good few hours before we get there." Mason interrupted my thoughts and I glanced up the length of the dimly lit shipping container we travelled in.

"You sleep, I've got this," I told both him and Donnell.

Donnell snorted and settled back against the pallets, "Suit yourself."

I returned my gaze to the broad back of the sleeping giant, chained to the stainless steel table, bolted in the center of the cargo container. It was so damn freakish how human they looked. It could sometimes be easy to forget what they changed into. The strength... the claws... the *teeth*.

I didn't close my eyes. It only made the vision of my brother's sightless staring more vivid. The blood staining his pale skin, his throat reduced to so much raw, bloody meat. Below his throat had been much worse. The creature, Romulus Reese, A.K.A. Roman Dulcet, had sunk claws into my brother's chest, gripped his ribs, had fucking pulled him apart while he'd screamed. They'd ripped out his throat last, to silence him.

And now, one of them was here in front of me, and I had just dug a slug out of the back of his leg... saved him from a slow agonizing death that he richly deserved.

"Do it." The voice was a derisive sneer.

"Ava, come on! Seriously? Don't go 'own fucking program' on us now."

"Come on, *Ava*, pull the trigger," the creature taunted.

I pressed the barrel of my Glock into his back, between his shoulder blades.

"You'd like that, wouldn't you?" I asked him.

"Ava..." Mason's tone was equal parts nervous and warning.

Just to keep my people on their toes and to prove to the animal that I wasn't playing I lifted the Glock from where I was pressing it against him, instead pressing it against the bandaged wound in the back of his leg.

"How do your healing abilities stack up? Huh, Big Boy? Think if I blew your leg off at this close a range with a couple of silver rounds you could heal it?"

He grunted and gave a strangled laugh, "Think that I'll beg you not to? That I'll cower, and say *'please don't?'*" He snorted like it was both the funniest and most absurd thing he'd ever heard. "You got another thing coming, Babycakes. Pull the fucking trigger, see if I care…" I pistol whipped him in the back of the head behind the ear but he was a tough bastard and didn't go lights out. Instead he laughed. A harsh, half barking mad sound that sent a chill down my spine.

Defiant to the last… I guess we had at least one thing in common. I holstered my gun and returned to my stack of pallets and jumped back up, resuming my earlier post while Remus, A.K.A. Remy laughed until tears leaked out of the corners of his eyes.

I ignored him, while the rest of my team back here in the semi's cargo container shifted uneasily in their seats. Eventually he and I settled into a defiant locked stare. His dark eyes smoldering and impossibly deep. Hatred radiating out of them and spiraling all the way to the very bottom. What do you know? It looked like we had something else in common.

The remaining hours dragged on impossibly long in the back of the semi's cargo container after that. Our captive had closed his eyes again but I doubted very much that he slept. I was growing weary from the constant uncomfortable jostling but I would be damned if I would show it. Finally the truck pulled up and stopped. Voices shouted back and forth and the semi lumbered to life, lurching forward, pulling into a smooth turn before stopping again.

The animal was alert alright. Eyes open and pinning me where I sat. Wheels turning, almost visibly, as he thought through what was happening. The loud, even, backup tones sounded from outside the truck as we backed into what I knew was a loading dock. The distribution center we used as a cover was still an active one for the American Red Cross, but we'd dug *deep* and the tunnels beneath it ran quite a ways out. We still had a ways to go, about an hour's worth of a ways to go, *under*ground.

First things first, though. We had to safely get Fido down there. I didn't much feel like leaving anything to chance. The intelligence sparkling out of those deep dark eyes of his was two points past terrifying.

"Get me the tranquilizer kit," I ordered.

The wolf-man's gaze splintered with rage before simmering down to flat and unfriendly. Interesting. This one had some serious control then. But, then again, the dossier on the twins had stated that Remy had always had the cooler head. Roman was the bat-shit one. It'd also stated the two were damned near inseparable and it was assumed that Roman was dead when Remy started showing up around the country flying solo.

I never took my eyes from his as Harper shuffled around us, digging through a pack by another ratchet strapped stack of pallets to find the small zippered case containing the Azaperone I needed. It was an elephant tranquilizer... literally, and one of the few tranqs effective for longer than twenty minutes when it came to these things.

I took the case from Harper as the big rig shuddered and hissed to a stop. The brakes fully engaged. The sound made the wolf-man wince and that made me smile, a nasty quirk of my lips that made Harper shift uneasily beside me. Again, Donnell wouldn't look at me, and I really didn't care. My eyes were kept steadfastly on the very still, very *real* threat in front of me.

Even strapped to the stainless steel table like he was with reinforced, heavy steel chain, I couldn't be one hundred percent sure that he couldn't or *wouldn't* break free.

I unzipped the sleek black leather case and laid it open. Vial of drug on one side, a row of capped hypodermics on the other held in by black elastic. Irony of ironies... I hated needles, even when I was shooting up one of these damned beasts.

I set the case on the nearest stack of pallets and slid the ampule of tranquilizer free, swirling the yellowish liquid in the glass vial. I judged there was enough, even for this big fucking brute; I set it to the side. Next I slipped one of the needles free. Uncapping it, I raised and upended the vial. Plunging the needle through the rubber stopper made my skin crawl but that sensation was about to get worse when the needle met flesh.

I measured out a dose of the tranquilizer and stopped the precision pull of the plunger on the syringe. I flicked my eyes back to the obsidian stare Remy Dulcet had fixed on me and looked him up and down one more time. Compressing my lips into a thin line, I drew more tranquilizer into the needle. I didn't trust the initial math and it was better safe than sorry with how quickly these bastards metabolized this crap.

I slid the needle free of the little bottle and stepped in Remy's direction. He snarled at me and jerked against his bonds. The metal groaned, and my heart seized up hard in my chest at the sound.

"Jesus!" Mason cried and leveled his assault rifle in the general direction of the wolf-man's head.

"Hold your fire!" I snapped.

"You better fuckin' kill me," Remy taunted, "I break this shit, I'm tearing you in half first, then I'm gonna fuck your boss 'til she fuckin' *bleeds*."

"Charming," I said dryly.

The look on the animal's face was savage, but beneath that, a very real, very unsettled emotion slid behind his eyes. He didn't like being out of control of the situation and the drugs in my hand promised that and so much more: total helplessness. I could almost sympathize with that, but not enough to not dose him.

"Just a little pinch," I soothed mockingly and he growled and snarled again, he jerked at his chains and metal screamed but I wasn't afraid. I should have been, but I was a woman of action. I stepped forward and plunged the needle into the nearest bit of exposed muscle and flesh at the beast's shoulder and with a surety I didn't exactly feel, smoothly depressed the plunger at the back of the syringe.

I didn't watch the elephant tranquilizer go in, all that golden liquid disappearing. Instead my gaze was locked on the wolf-man's, a mixture of hatred and pleading in his eyes that I found curious, before the sharpness faded, his eyes unfocused and the snarl left his lips. His eyes fluttered, his head drooped and without thinking about it my hand shot out as his head fell into it. I kept him from cracking that handsome face into the stainless steel table and I honestly couldn't tell you why.

"Ava, come *on*. Mathias is waiting and there's no telling when this douchebag is gonna come out of it." I took a step back from the table and looked up at Logan, back lit as he was from the lights behind him. I hadn't even heard him and Jordan roll up the truck's back door.

"Right," I uttered and hit the catch locking the wheels into place with my booted foot, disengaging the brakes so we could roll him freely. The boys pulled the gurney over and heaved Remy's dead weight up onto the ramp after releasing some of the chains we'd used, bolted into the floor to hold him in place during the drive. After he was released from the truck floor and we'd ensured he was strapped down with the reinforced nylon, more to keep him from sliding off the gurney than out of concern he would wake and try to escape, Donnell pushed and Mason pulled and the table rattled over the diamond pattern of the industrial dock plate. I walked alongside the gurney, handgun at the ready, maintaining dual focus. One foot in front of the other, don't trip, but also, making sure Remy stayed knocked the fuck out. He so much as twitched, I'd put another round in him so help me fucking God...

No one was going to die on my watch. My brother James shouldn't have died, but then again, that hadn't been on my watch. *Cocky son of a bitch.*

"Ah, the prodigal daughter returns..."

The voice was smooth and rich and I glanced up at the sound of it, my lips pressed down into a thin line.

"Good to see you too Mathias," I lied, because it wasn't. It really wasn't. However long the both of us lived it would never be good to see him. Because Mathias Young had been the man to send my brother to his death.

Chapter 7
Remus

Waking can be many things. It can be a slow and gradual process… One where you rise gently from the depths of sleep into an ever increasing state of wakefulness until you find yourself conscious, rested, and alert. Or, it can be the groggy awakening after a night of too much drink or too little sleep.

It can also be abrupt; brutal, *painful*.

I experienced all three. There was a terrifying sensation, that teetering on the precipice about to fall for just a moment. Then the balance tilted and over I went. My eyes shot open, my arms flailed out trying to grab something, anything, to catch myself to stop the fall. But it's not the fall that hurts, is it? It's that sudden stop at the end that usually does it. And this case was no exception.

There was a loud clatter and my abused body met a solid surface with enough force that I tasted blood in my mouth and stars bloomed across my vision as my head bounced off the concrete floor. Pain flared in my leg from my wound, and a low groan escaped me despite my best efforts to contain it. Barking, mocking laughter erupted from behind me followed by a rattling noise and I rolled, pushing myself over with my hands just as a loud clang echoed through the space.

The door slammed shut with a degree of finality that I am sure I will remember for the rest of my life. My vision was blurred, body sluggish, still feeling the effects of whatever drug it was that fucking bitch had shot into me. But it was rapidly wearing off, and by the time I managed to scramble awkwardly to my feet I was feeling stronger and clearer by the moment.

"I must say, you are a difficult… *man*… to locate." The word man was said with a distinct sneer and I glared, turning my head just enough to spit to the side, but not enough to break eye contact.

"Mathias Young. I really could have gone the rest of my unnaturally long life without ever seeing *you* again," I snarled and he shrugged, completely unfazed. He stood at parade rest, his feet shoulder width apart and his hands clasped together at the small of his back. Black, military issue combat boots covered his feet, laces perfectly straight with a pair of BDU pants bloused at the tops of his boots. A black, button down shirt was tucked into his pants and the butt of a pistol could be seen protruding from beneath the edges of his calf length black overcoat.

Steel grey eyes peered out from beneath thick, bushy eyebrows gone grey with age. A short cut beard covered the lower half of his face and his hair stuck out in all directions. Kind of reminded me of a lion's thick mane. He had a distinct grace to him, even standing perfectly still. Somehow, the predator in me recognized the predator in him and I am not ashamed to say that I felt cowed by it. I did my best not to let my fear of him show though. It would only increase the already substantial power that he held over me.

"It seems to me that you would want to meet with me, after that unfortunate business with your father."

I snorted, not even trying to hide my disgust. "'Unfortunate business'" I sneered. "You mean setting it up so you could murder my father? He may have been acting strange the last few years but I've been starting to think that I overreacted in thinking we needed to remove him from his position as Alpha."

He shrugged again, as if he hadn't a care in the world. "Be that as it may, with how that situation ended, and with you being ostracized from your pack, one would think that you would be compelled to seek out some kind of ally in this world."

"You are no ally of mine," I snarled and fought the urge to leap at him. With the metal bars between us and the distance he stood from my cage I would never be able to reach him. Didn't stop me from wanting desperately to tear his throat out though.

"We were, at one point, working together."

"My father was bringing the pack to ruin. We just want to live and raise our families. He was going to see us destroyed at the pace he was going..." I trailed off and bit my tongue. Damn I was tired. I would never have run off at the mouth so much before but obviously exhaustion and weakness were getting the better of me. I tasted blood in my mouth but refused to let up.

"You can't honestly expect us to believe that you fucking animals just want to be left alone in peace. That's why you filthy mutts attack innocent people? That's why you kill and hunt people, just for the fun of it? Left in peace you'll get stronger and your numbers will grow until you can kill every last one of us at your leisure."

I couldn't believe it. Seriously, that was how the hunters saw us? That was really what they believed? I stared at Ava, completely dumbfounded and confused all at once. How does someone come to believe such vitriol about a people she knows nothing about? How doesn't she see the comparison to basic racism and bigotry? How can the human race be so damned blind to their own atrocities but so quick to point out others?

I was so fucking glad I was never human to begin with in that moment. In fact, I was pretty sure it would have killed me.

"You don't have the slightest understanding as to what you're talking about," I growled, ignoring the way a trickle of blood escaped my mouth and ran down my chin. "Wolf-kind are nothing like that. And you humans kill yourselves more than almost anything or anyone else."

She glared at me and I saw a hint of steel growing in Mathias' gaze. I was bothering them so I grinned, a blood filled rictus, and pushed forward. "The Romans conquering the Druids, The Crusades. The Spanish Inquisition. Slavery in the American Colonies. The Salem Witch Trials. The Holocaust... Do you really need any more than that to tell you that humanity is the real monster here?"

Ava growled, a sound worthy of any wolf-kind, and surged forward, hand darting beneath her Joe Rocket jacket but Mathias' hand shot out, quick as a snake and grabbed her by the shoulder, yanking her back to stand next to him.

"Touched a nerve, did I?" I taunted and winked at her causing her cold mask to crack with unadulterated fury.

"Leave him," he ordered. "I'll come back later, Remus. Perhaps then you will be more willing to discuss your future with us."

I glared at him as he turned and left without another word, Ava following sullenly behind him. Before she left, she shot a glare at me over her shoulder; her eyes burning with the kind of hatred I had only ever seen before in the gaze of my brother Romulus.

The door shut behind them and I sank to the ground, sitting cross legged with my elbows on my knees. My leg protested the action and I held back the pained groan that wanted to escape me. There was no way in hell I would let on how much I hurt. My leg throbbed and burned, my stomach growled ceaselessly and I could feel myself slowly growing weaker from it. At my best guess, it had been roughly twenty-four hours since I last ate anything, maybe a little less.

I wouldn't last for much longer without turning feral and getting crazed. Was that his plan? Did he want to drive me to starvation so the wolf would come out? Why? It didn't make sense. Unless he wanted to use that as some sort of proof to his hunters that I was the dangerous animal they thought me to be.

That still didn't seem to fit though. It was too straight forward, too simple a thought for what I knew of Mathias Young. His actions always held deeper meaning. Plans within plans, hidden behind layers of agendas and everything he did was shrouded with misdirection. I was never much of a chess player, but Mathias seemed to be a master of the game.

I felt, though, that I might just have a possibility open to me. A weakness in the Hunters' armor. For a moment. Just a moment, when Mathias grabbed Ava by the shoulder, I saw a look of open revulsion cross her face. Naked hatred and disgust. Before her poker face slid back into place and she was able to hide the seething turmoil I now knew raged beneath. If at all possible, I needed to try to use that because it told me one important thing.

Ava hated Mathias. Almost as much as I did, and the enemy of my enemy might just be my only friend if I could spin it right. If not I was as good as dead.

I looked around the room, taking in as much as I could. Dark stone walls surrounded me, and the interior was lit by way of recessed lighting in the ceiling behind round panels of, what looked like, bullet proof glass. The room was square and at my best guess, roughly fifty feet by fifty feet. In the center of it, a single steel cage open on all four sides, the bars thicker around than my wrist.

That struck me as interesting. Even as thick as the bars were it wouldn't be impossible for me to break free. I would be able to tear my way through with a minute or two's worth of work, even injured and half-starved. So what the hell was going on? What good was a cage that I could escape?

I jerked up and winced at the throbbing stab of pain that ripped through my thigh at the sudden action when a scraping sound caught my ear. The door leading into the stone room containing my private cell was heavy wood with metal bars blocking a small window in the center at about head height. I lifted my head and sniffed at the air as quietly as I could. I didn't want to give anything away.

Two guards, at least. Standing outside the door in the hall. I could smell the scent of gun oil on both of them. That explained it. If I tried to escape there was no way I would be able to without making a significant amount of noise. Those guards probably had orders to turn me into Swiss cheese if I tried it. So, they put me in a cage I can escape but leave the guards to encourage me to be a good little doggie and sit in my time out. That or they thought to tempt me to try to escape, just so they'd have an excuse to shoot me. In self-defense, of course, but in all reality, for their own amusement. These bastards were special, for sure.

I thought about it some more and finally had to shake my head. *Sick motherfuckers, every last one of them. Even her, especially her… Even if she was a stone-cold fox.*

"A trap within a trap, within a dungeon," I muttered and leaned back against the bars behind me. I groaned and stretched my leg out in front of me, feeling the unaccustomed weakness and pain in my limb. For a man that has never suffered injury for more than a few hours before healing up entirely, this was absolute torture. I wondered briefly how humans put up with it without going crazy.

I looked down at the ground and snorted at the irony. There, on the floor was a single red cross with equidistant arms on a perfectly square background of pristine white.

"Alright," I sighed and looked up at the ceiling, trying to ignore the burning agony in my leg that I could feel expanding through my body. "We've always wanted to know where it was the Hunters originated from. If you survive this, Remus, you just might have something to bring back to your little brother. If he doesn't kill you just for showing your mug."

* * *

"Look alive, you son of a bitch!"

I jerked awake and the motion sent shards of pain ripping through my body, a wave of nausea following right on its heels. I moaned and my eyes flickered open. Hunger gnawed at my belly just as exhaustion gripped me and tried to smother me beneath its weight.

"To what do I owe this great pleasure?" I grunted and pushed myself up to a sitting position. At some point I had fallen asleep and slumped over onto my side.

"Mathias says you need to eat something," Ava sneered and dropped a metal tray laden with food heavily to the floor. Half of it splattered onto the ground and even more slopped over the edge when she kicked it forward and it slid through a slot at the bottom of the bars. "Personally I think you should starve to death. It would be entertaining to see you suffer."

I ignored the food despite my nose doing its best effort to overwhelm my mind with the enticing aromas of meat, potatoes and creamed corn. "Oh." I sighed. "You really wouldn't want to see that," I drawled with as much casual laziness as I could muster. "There aren't many things more frightening than a wolf-kind in a state of feral hunger." I caught her eyes with an intent gaze of my own and let that steep for a moment before I continued.

"You are right about one thing, Babycakes," I said and winked at her which only caused her to scowl further. "Monsters we aren't, but we *are* animals. And when you starve an animal it becomes mad with hunger, and even more dangerous. You wouldn't want me out of my mind with hunger and rage. It would only end with blood... probably yours."

She glared at me a moment longer before she turned and stalked out of the room, the sound of her boots striking the stone floor was drowned out entirely by the door slamming shut behind her. I waited until her footfalls had receded into the distance before I dove on the food, scooping up all I could and even reaching through the bars as far as I could reach to collect that which had spilled on the floor, desperate to ease the yawning ache of hunger.

Chapter 8

Ava

"Play it again."

"Ava…" Mason's voice was full of uneasy chiding as he drew out my name, but I really didn't give a shit.

"Again!" I snapped.

Lines appeared on the screen as he wound the footage back and instead of lunging forward for the food splattered across the floor, the monster lurched back. I watched myself enter the room and the footage stopped and began to roll forward again. There was no sound, I didn't need to hear what was being said. I was there and it replayed in my mind's eye over and over again.

"This ain't going to bring James back, you know." Mason said softly. I brought my arm up, bent it at the elbow and snapped it back and felt it connect solidly with Mason's nose. I felt a satisfying pop through my thick jacket sleeve. Mace yowled, his hands flying off the control panel to cover his face.

"Goddamn it, Ava!"

I glanced back over my shoulder at him and raised an eyebrow, keeping the rest of my expression cold and flat. No one knew better than I did that James wasn't coming back. Mace's eyes watered and he pulled his hands away from his face to see them stained with blood. Of course all I could see when I looked at my own hands was my brother's blood from where I had tried to press his insides back where they'd belonged.

I turned back to the monitor, jaw set in grim resignation. I wanted to kill it. I wanted to kill it so badly, but *Mathias* stood in my way, and truthfully I wanted to kill him too, for sending James practically solo, after those mad dogs.

"Leave us," his rich, melodic voice wafted over from the control room's doorway. Speak of the devil, or in this case, think of him...

Mason pushed back from the desk and sniffed, glaring at me contritely. I gave him blank face; gave him nothing. Sometimes, like now, I felt a little bad for being so rough on them but it was for their own damn good. So they wouldn't end up like so many of the others who'd gone before. So they wouldn't end up like *James...*

"Resent me all you like, Ava. You know I did what I thought was best."

Don't trust Mathias, Baby Sis. Something's up. I can feel it.

I pressed my lips into a grim line and tried to school my face into a neutral expression.

"I don't," I lied, and at the angry expression on the older man's face I quickly changed tact... "I mean, I do... he was my twin brother, my only blood and family I had left, I understand but..." I crumbled a little on the inside and went for broke, and told the truth.

The truth will set you free, little sister...

"I miss him." I whispered into the lengthy silence and felt the tears spill hot and salty slick down my face. Mathias' face hardened.

"I have a job for you," he said imperiously and I nodded once sharply. I hardened my heart, drew it all in and stuffed it down. Locking my emotions back in the deep, dark footlocker in the deepest recesses of my soul where no one, not even Mathias Young with his prying eyes and manipulations could reach.

"Sir, yes sir." I said calmly.

"There are reports that one of them has gone rogue in New Hampshire, I want you to follow up. Find out if there's any truth to the rumors, and if there is, take care of it."

"As soon as I can conceivably muster the team." Mathias gave me a pointed look, but I didn't break stride or falter in my speech patterns at all. "The hunt for this last one took a lot out of them. I would like to be here for whatever you have in store for the bastard. I think I've more than..." he cut me off, expression stern.

"You leave tonight, tomorrow morning at the latest. With no delays, am I understood?" he demanded.

Why the rush, you old buzzard? I thought to myself.

"Sir, yes sir," I uttered again. You didn't defy Mathias Young to his face and get away with it unscathed. There were a lot of rumors where the old man was concerned, the thing was, I knew they weren't just tales. Mathias Young was the definition of ruthless.

If he were feeling generous, you'd live… minus a few parts, but you'd live. Rarely, if ever, was Mathias Young generous. I'd been one of his prize foot soldiers. My brother had been too before he'd become a prized pain in the ass. That had eventually lost James the pinky and ring finger of his left hand. Mathias had taken them a year or two before James had died… That was when I'd started to nurture a dislike, if not a downright hatred for the old bastard.

James hadn't questioned Mathias' orders again. He'd done what he was told. Ever since the night Mathias had maimed him, James had looked at me different. With a glint of something undefinable. I was sure some kind of threat had been made against me, but James would never speak on it. I couldn't deny the effectiveness of the tactic. Had our roles been reversed, had it been I who had been threatened with James' well-being? I would have folded like cheap origami.

Mathias looked me up and down, a calculating glint in his eyes before nodding once, as if to himself and grating out: "Dismissed."

I snapped to attention, saluted and made to go past him when he caught my sleeve. *Jesus for a man his age he's unnaturally fast.* I looked him eye to eye from inches away and kept my stoic mask in place.

"Do as I ask, Ava," Mathias said to me but it was what he said *without* words, what he said with his intense gaze that got my attention and sent a tingle of fear down my spine. His eyes held a weighted 'or else' as well as a myriad of other unspoken horrors in their steely depths.

"Of course," I murmured and nodded. Mathias forced a smile and leaned forward, placing a kiss on the crown of my head.

"I miss him too, Child," he lied, but it was too late to placate me. He'd pushed too hard. I bowed my head so he wouldn't see my rage. I closed my eyes so he wouldn't see the fire in them and I did my level best to nod solemnly.

That one little white lie sealed the deal for me. Utterly. Completely. *Fuck him*. Fuck Mathias Young and his bullshit wild goose chase in New Hampshire. I was suddenly like one of the things we hunted. I was on the scent. Mathias was hiding something and I was going to find out what it was.

"Go on, now," he said and released my sleeve. I nodded and attempted to look sufficiently cowed, before slipping out of the control room and up the dimly lit hallway to the knight's quarters.

For a quasi-military organization, we didn't have barracks precisely. The underground rooms were small, but comfortable. Simple. No more than cells, really, that locked from the inside rather than the outside. The underground facility was old, very old, but had undergone a series of retrofits throughout the intervening years to make it both more habitable as well as more functional to our cause. Hence, what had once been cells to hold prisoners for interrogation, had been refashioned into quarters for the men and women dedicated to eradicating these demon spawned creatures.

This far underground, there were no windows or really any ability to tell what time of day it was. We relied on artificial lighting to keep us up on what was arcing across the sky up top. That was why the halls were so dimly lit now. It was deepest night, almost edging on towards dawn and I was feeling it, even this far removed from the sky. The lighted strips along the floors and ceilings would begin to lighten with the press of real dawn outside. I felt it in the form of a slight burning at the backs of my eyes. In the way of a bone deep weary that settled over my shoulders like an old cloak.

Mathias was a tough bastard that expected the rest of us to be just as tough, but at the end of the day, we were all simply human. In need of food, in need of rest, or we would make mistakes and making a mistake, out there, with *them*… often a mistake made under those circumstances was the last mistake any number of us could or would ever make.

I wasn't about to lose any of my team to some stupid, half assed mistake that was made because one of us was tired when we'd had the opportunity to rest. So when I slipped into the rec room to find the majority of my team lounging and awaiting the next set of orders or dismissal to their bunks, there wasn't any real decision to be made.

"Rest up, get a full eight hours, then gear up." I ground my teeth and willingly defied Mathias Young, "We leave tomorrow afternoon. Mathias wants us to check out reports of a feral rogue in New Hampshire."

My crew dragged themselves wearily to their feet. I glanced at Mace who glared back, not that I could really blame him.

"Did I break it?"

"No," he said, eyes sliding to the side and away from me. I fixed him with my gaze and he shifted uncomfortably as the rest of the team filed out around me.

"Good. You were right, and I'm sorry about that."

"You get more like the Hangman every day," he said with a one shouldered shrug and I flinched inwardly at that, though I refused to give any outward appearance.

"Dismissed," I said simply and he pushed past me and out the door. I closed my eyes and sighed out, softly swearing at the empty room.

I went over and fixed a cup of hot tea in the small kitchenette in the corner. It was just enough to make a drink; the mess hall was down the corridor and to the left in the sprawling complex. I wasn't really hungry. I wasn't even really all that thirsty to be honest, right now I needed something for my hands to do while my brother's nagging doubts and odd behavior played out in my mind.

James had found something out, something that had shaken his faith in the Order. He'd become agitated, withdrawn, then he'd become almost defiant… angry with the Order's council. Mathias being the head of that council didn't help. He'd begun to openly question things and finally had begun to openly question the missions that he and his team were being sent on.

It had become increasingly rare for James and me to be teamed together in the last year or so of his life. I had climbed ranks, come into my own, been entrusted with my own team, which seemed to rankle my older brother, who was only older by virtue of nine minutes. The joke between us was that he would always and forever be the one to lead the way. Which had been the case, for the most part until he'd found whatever he'd found.

My brother had become cagey. Dropping hints and whispers, never being forthright, but my loyalty lay with him. Had always lain with him, and even after death would continue to lay with his bones. James and I were the only thing either of us had had the entire time we were growing up and now… now I was alone and it was all because of that son of a bitch Mathias and the brother of the fucking animal we had caged in the lower levels.

I jerked my hand back and dropped the paper cup overflowing with hot water.

"*Shit!*"

I shook out my hand and gave it a cursory once over. Red and angry, I thought it would be fine, I ran it under cold water from the small sink anyways, the cool water soothing the sting of the scald.

I couldn't go out like this. I needed some sleep. I needed to regroup. *I needed to know what the fuck was going on.* Why Mathias was so keen on getting me out of the facility and back into the field. While quick turnarounds weren't unheard of, they certainly weren't commonplace.

It was customary to give a team a day or two of R and R after a hunt. Especially one as intensive as the one it took to track Remus Reese down. We'd been on his trail for *months*. Why the rush to get us back out there? Let alone for such a low level target?

My team was well beyond checking out rumors. Way past looking into a 'potential' rogue somewhere. We didn't do soft targets like that anymore. Hadn't in a long time. So why now?

No. Mathias was up to something, and I wanted to know what.

I turned off the water and dried my hands. I didn't bother cleaning up the hot water seeping across the polished cement floor. It was only water and would take care of its self. Instead, filled with equal amounts purpose and dread, I stalked down the corridor and to my quarters.

My need for sleep hadn't diminished despite my determination and the plan I'd formulated. I needed rest. I needed a full eight hours of sleep. I would need to be cunning and alert for what I'd decided to do. I would need to stay one step ahead of the master of the game if I were going to go through with it.

'If,' there was no if. I was going to and there would be no going back. I needed to know what was going on. I needed to know exactly why my brother was dead and the key to that knowledge lay in the mongrel in the cage downstairs. I needed to know what Mathias wanted from him and the only way to find that out was to defy Mathias and stick around.

I closed my eyes and let myself into my small cell, sending up a little prayer to my brother.

I'll find out just what the fuck is going on, James. I promise. Just do me a favor? Watch my ass, okay?

Chapter 9
Remus

It wasn't enough food. Not by a long shot, but it calmed the ache in my belly by just enough that it curbed the growing hunger that had nothing to do with food. Since then, no one had returned to my cell. No one looked in the window except the guards every fifteen minutes. I knew it was fifteen minutes because one of them was wearing a watch with a second hand and it was quiet enough otherwise that I could keep count by listening to the ticking.

Three hours had passed since she brought the food and left. A dozen checks between now and then... Three long, solid, hours of no contact or interaction with anyone. Of nothing but the inside of my stone room and metal cell to look at. I didn't mind much though. I liked my solitude. The conditions could've been better but I couldn't complain. I mean I *could*, but what would be the point? Especially when there wasn't a single person that would give a flying fuck about it. So I sat there, quietly, and considered the series of events that led me to where I was.

I was laying on the floor, in the center of my empty cage, with my eyes closed when I noticed him. I didn't know how long he'd been standing there and the fact that I didn't notice him come in honestly scared the shit out of me in a way I don't think I've ever experienced before. Not once in my unnaturally long life.

"Are you just going to stand there all day, or was there something you actually wanted to talk about?" I asked after another several minutes of silence. "I mean, I know I'm pretty, but I never thought I was your type, Mathias."

"Your sense of humor was moderately charming, even a touch endearing when we first met, Remus," he said with an exaggerated sigh. "It has long since lost it's... patina of novelty. I have grown tired of it and would rather speak plainly, if you feel yourself capable of it?"

"I am capable of things that you would find yourself unable to believe, old man," I growled quietly and finally opened my eyes. I sat up to find him standing calmly, arms clasped behind his back at parade rest, which was per usual for him. It was the same stance he had held the night we first met. When Romulus and I reached out to him to help remove our father as Alpha.

"Such disgust on your face when you look at me," he said and I snarled at him. "For one that came to me seeking help in murdering his own father..." he shook his head in a mocking display of disappointment.

"You kill our kind with impunity. I would have preferred not to take my father's life but it was the only way to remove him as Alpha while preserving his dignity... his legacy, at face value anyways."

"Dignity?" Mathias seemed startled. "You can't kill a person, even one such as your kind, and leave them with their dignity. Death and dignity don't go hand in hand."

"There's no way to remove an Alpha from position without killing them. And if I challenged him, I would have had to tell the pack about the trouble he was causing. My father was pack Alpha for *centuries*. He was *loved* and *respected*. I wanted him to die with that respect still intact." I didn't raise my voice. I didn't yell, or rage, as much as I dearly wanted to. I had learned enough about Mathias Young that such displays of emotion were only going to make things worse with him. I wondered how his daughter, Chloe, ever survived long enough to eventually bind herself to my little brother. She was a rather emotional creature the last I remembered. But then again, she had been through quite a bit in a relatively short amount of time.

"That makes you better?" he sneered. "That makes you not a beast killing his own family? Because you wanted to preserve his dignity and honor? Some false *legacy* that was purely a flight of fancy?" Mathias scoffed before continuing. "Wouldn't giving him the chance to face you or your brother in battle be more dignifying than getting strangled in his own home by a hunter that *you* let into the house? Don't you remember, Dog? *You* contacted *me*.

"You told me that he needed to be removed. You made promises in return for my help, then you failed to deliver. You or your brother were supposed to be the next Alpha of your pack and you were supposed to give me some of the... less reputable members in return."

"Why?" I demanded. I hadn't asked before because I hadn't intended to go through with our part of the agreement. I had no intentions of handing over any of my people to him and the rest of his butchers. "Why would you want some of my kind anyways? Just so you could kill us? I mean, what other possible reason could you have?"

He gave me a long look, steel grey eyes piercing like knives, before he finally spoke again. "My reasons are my own, and you would have been better off if you or Romulus had become Alpha and kept your part of the bargain. If you had simply given me a few here and there, the rest of your *people* would have been spared." He said the word 'people' as if it left a nasty taste in his mouth. "Now I'll simply have to do what I should have done years ago... when I first discovered that your pack was residing in Washington. I'll simply have to wipe them all out. *Take* the ones I want instead."

I was frozen in place, fixed by the words now resonating inside my head like an echo through a dark cavern. Years? He had known about us for *years*? Why hadn't the hunters come in force? Why hadn't they picked us off a long time ago? What had kept them waiting for so damn long?

"How did you find us?" I asked, scarcely able to believe what I was hearing.

"How did you think your father managed to keep such a large territory for so long?" He shot back. "Did you really think that your pack was so feared that others wouldn't try to encroach?

"Washington is a great territory the perfect location for your kind to hide in. There are many places in this country that have such remote wooded areas, but the others are all fiercely fought over. Areas of Colorado, Utah, and Montana wage a constant war to defend their borders. Bloody battles are fought to take and to keep those territories. Your pack hasn't been involved in many of those battles to protect your borders, now have they?" His tone was mocking and I felt as if I had been hit over the head.

"The Nevada Pack," I muttered, thinking of what Cruz had said back in Chicago.

"Father stopped protecting our borders a long time ago, didn't he?" I demanded, suddenly furious. "He let you guys patrol around our territory and do the hunting for him. That way the pack was protected, and you got to pick off wolf-kind for your own purposes."

He nodded, a slow grin stealing across his lips.

"Ahhhh, finally. Understanding dawns like the morning sun over the horizon," he mocked. "It took you long enough. I'm really rather disappointed in you, Remus. You were supposed to be the clever one."

"I couldn't care less, Mathias. You've got some explaining to do. Why would you want to attack my pack now after protecting it for who knows how long?"

"The arrangement I had with your father, Declan, was no longer adequate." He shrugged and started pacing back and forth on the other side of the bars, just out of reach of my long arms.

"When I first entered into the arrangement with Declan, the Northwest pack was attacked fairly frequently. There was a steady stream of new specimens for me to work with. But over the last few years, the other packs learned the futility of even attempting to encroach into the Washington Territory. My men did their jobs a little *too well* it seems. The rest of the packs of you rabid dogs were too scared to even try to go near Washington. I found my need for new specimens severely outweighed the supply available, things needed to change."

"You sick fucking bastard," I snarled. "You contacted Romulus. Didn't you? I always thought *he* found *you* somehow but no, it was the other way around, wasn't it? You reached out to him. You got in touch with him and offered to help remove our father as Alpha." It was suddenly so painfully clear. The Hangman was well known for never leaving evidence behind except the damage to whatever body he'd dropped. He should never have left his weapon when he'd killed our father.

"Why did you leave the garrote?" I asked suddenly, and he blinked owlishly. "There's no reason to do that unless you're trying to draw attention to yourself. We knew it was going to be you. We arranged for you to meet with our father under a pretense of peace. No one else in the pack knew but us. So leaving your weapon... that was only to draw attention. Wasn't it?" I frowned, turning over his actions in my mind. "You wanted to draw William's attention. You wanted to force a fight for Alpha figuring we would kill him and eliminate that potential threat."

He shook his head and I frowned again. "Your brother is little threat. Simply a minor roadblock in the grand scheme of things."

"If it wasn't about removing William from the table..." I felt feverish. My mind whirling faster than ever, struggling to piece together the puzzle that was Mathias Young. I considered what I knew about him. What the pack knew, and what I had discovered since first meeting him. Cold blooded was an apt description for the old man. Cold, methodical, precise, and manipulative. Manipulative to the nth degree. There hadn't been a scale invented to measure the level of manipulative villainous shit this man was into…

"Chloe," I blurted out before I could stop myself, just as the thought occurred to me. The fucked up horror of it blossoming in my mind, flickering to life like a tongue of flame licking at the edges of dry paper, ready to consume everything else.

"You're doing something down here, capturing wolf-kind instead of killing them, but even you have to answer to someone. Even you have superiors. They don't know what you're doing, do they? And you were counting on William kidnapping your daughter. In fact you wanted him to kill her so you could garner sympathy from your superiors."

He didn't move. He didn't blink or shift his weight. His breathing remained exactly the same. But somehow I knew I had hit the nail on the head. His lack of a response, his total stillness was telling in and of itself.

"You are some piece of work," I breathed, shaking my head in shock. "You would sacrifice your own *daughter* just to advance whatever fucking agenda it is that you've got going on? You sick fuck!"

Alright, I'll admit that I lost my temper a bit there. I surged forward rolling to my feet and lunging across the cell to hit the bars with a loud crash. A moment later the door burst open and the guards rushed in, rifles aimed at me but they didn't fire as Mathias calmly held up a hand toward them.

"What the fuck is wrong with you!?" I roared and shook the gate as hard as I could. The metal creaked and groaned under the force and the guards shifted nervously.

"You call me a fucking animal but you would just throw her to the unknown like that? Like any other pawn on your fucking chess board!"

He took a step forward, his face showing nothing and just as I reached through the bars to try to grab him the pain hit me again. My body stiffened and jerked and I hit the ground muscles locking in spasm, uncontrollable, and I went down like a felled tree.

My teeth ground together and I pissed myself as I lost all control over my body. Pain screamed through my injured leg and I was pretty sure that the half-assed healed wound in it tore open during the spastic seizure created by the two leads buried in my chest. Mathias held a professional grade Taser, likely with some modifications to it, in his hand. He held down the trigger, pumping who knew how many volts of electricity through my body for what felt like hours rather than mere seconds.

When he finally let up, all I could do was lie there and twitch, glaring at him with an impotent rage that stoked the fires of the beast within me. The wolf didn't like not being able to sink its teeth into our tormentor, and I agreed with it whole heartedly.

Since my banishment from the pack, I had survived only because I didn't have anything better to do really. However, as of that moment, I found a new reason to survive. I vowed to myself that one day, one day soon, if I could help it, I would tear Mathias Young's throat out with my own teeth – human or wolf, it didn't matter so much right then. I'd take either, so long as I got it done. This fucker needed to die. For father, for Rom, for William and even for little Chloe, but especially for me.

"Glare all you like, Kid," he rumbled in that deep basso voice of his. Forget that I was at least a century older than he was.

"You're caught. And you're not getting out of here. I have plans for you. Do you have any idea how long I've been trying to capture a Blood Born with your level of control? You're right. Things haven't gone exactly according to plan, but I can say that this might be even better in serving my cause."

He leaned down until he was crouching close to the bars on the other side of the cage. So close, I could have easily killed him, but when I tried to move he pulled the trigger on the Taser again and sent a surge of agony running through my body that left sparkles flitting through my vision and put me in a state of barely hanging on to consciousness.

"You're right, Chloe was never supposed to survive," he whispered. "You fucking dogs can't even kill one little bitch right. I shouldn't have expected anything more from a useless fucking animal like your lunatic brother. He was much more open to the idea of being the new Alpha and letting me take the weaker members of your pack for my experiments. Now, with William as the Alpha, I will have to take different measures when it comes to finding new test subjects. You, hmm, you are just the beginning."

I snarled and tried to say something but I must have bitten my tongue when I was spazzing because all that happened was some blood leaked from my mouth. I wasn't able to get out anything more than a garbled gurgling sound before he smiled brightly at me and pulled the trigger on the Taser again.

This time he didn't let up until I blacked out.

* * *

I jerked awake, my eyes snapping open only for me to groan and close them again against the bright, searing light that beamed down on me from overhead. I felt cold metal around my chest, arms, waist, and across my thighs and ankles. I was strapped down pretty solid... not that I wouldn't be able to tear my way free. Few were the restraints truly capable of holding me if I didn't want to be held.

"Before you decide to tear yourself loose from there, I would like to warn you; any attempt to do so will end badly for you."

"Why is that?" I asked of the disembodied voice.

"Because, you're wearing a collar that will deliver a rather hefty electrical charge, should the man across the room over there press the button on the remote he's holding. I've told him to go ahead and hold the button down for as long as he likes if you so much as even twitch."

As soon as she said something about it I realized I could feel the collar around my neck. Thick and bulky, a metal contact, warm from my body heat, resting just over the pulse point in my neck. I really didn't want to find out what would happen if the dude sent a jolt through there. Even my healing might not be up to the job to fix that much juice to the brain.

I squinted my eyes and turned my head, just about the only part of me that I could actually move, to look at the bitch standing next to me. She was kinda hot, honestly. Tall, leggy, blonde; wearing a smart blouse and one of those business type skirts that made a guy want to bend her over the nearest desk. She wore the smart little secretary's number up under a white coat, like the kind doctors and scientists wear.

"Ya know," I muttered hoarsely and paused for a moment to clear my throat. "I always did kind of have a medical fetish. Be gentle Doc, I bruise easy." She smiled and laughed, a deep throaty kind of laugh that made you unable to think of much else but sex.

"Mathias did warn me that you had an... unconventional sense of humor," she said. "But, strangely appropriate in this case, I guess you could say."

"Why for, Doc? You gonna wrap those pretty lips of yours around my cock?"

She shook her head, a mocking rendition of a regretful expression on her face.

"Oh no," she said. "As fine a physical specimen as you may be, I won't be *personally* acquiring your semen."

I blinked. Really not the answer I was expecting to hear. Semen? What the fuck was going on. I lifted my head as best I could and looked around the room. It looked like your average medical suite at just about any hospital. In the corner was the guard she'd mentioned, leaning against the wall with his arms crossed over his chest and in his hand, a slim silver remote control. He looked extremely bored with the entire goings on.

As flippant as I tried to be, it was all I could do to hold my shit together. I did *not* like hospitals or hospital settings or needles or doctors or... you get the idea. The strange fluttering in my chest told me just how much I didn't like it. The fear that I rarely felt clawed at the back of my mind.

I was strapped down to one of those tables they use with the stirrups on it. You know, the kind for women when they're getting their lady bits checked out. Not a position I ever thought I'd find myself in, that's for sure.

My legs were spread wide, feet strapped into the stirrups and I was as naked as the day I slithered out. I couldn't see past the metal chains across my chest but I could feel something stuck to the skin around my groin. The slick caress of wires or cords draped across my leg. The looker of a lady doctor came around to stand between my legs and smiled brightly, adjusting her latex gloves. She held up a silver probe of some kind and lubed it up.

"Might want to breathe. This can be a little uncomfortable if you're not used to it." She wheeled over a stool and dropped out of sight. I growled and she laughed.

"Need I remind you my friend stands at the ready to fry all your synapses? I don't really need you alive for this part. Sperm is viable up to three days after expulsion or death. Did you know that?" she spread my ass cheek to one side and pressed the wand thing in her hand at my back door. I snarled and something was shoved inside my ass.

That fear I was feeling? Yeah it ratcheted up a few more notches and I knew I was starting to look a little wild around the eyes when the deranged hottie stood back up and moved next to me. I tried, I really did, but I couldn't force the emotion back any further than I already was.

Sweat was starting to stand out on my face and chest and I fought the urge to wrench at my restraints. I wasn't sure what would be worse, whatever she had planned or the electricity that would course through my neck if the guard decided to play 'Ooo, ooo, ooo what does this button do?'

"So what exactly is the plan here, Sweetheart?" I asked, unable to keep the nervousness out of my voice no matter how I tried. Honestly, I didn't give a fuck. Yeah, it'd just give them more satisfaction to know that I was scared but fuck it, I was honestly *scared* and there's no hiding that.

"Well, you're a 'Blood Born' mongrel. And Mathias wants to examine all aspects of your physiology. We've already taken samples of your blood, hair, urine, even some spinal fluid while you were out." Was this bitch for real? When she'd said blood born she'd made a face like she'd smelled something bad along with little finger quotes in the air with her latex gloves before stripping them off and donning another pair.

"So you've got all the bits that make me tick, what the fuck are we doing here?" I snapped. The fact she knew so much about us to even know the term 'blood born' made me freak out even harder on the inside.

She grinned and turned to pick up something off a table, a little plastic thing, it kinda reminded me of a really thick condom with a tube attached to one end. "Have you ever heard of electro-ejaculation?" she asked and I was forced to shake my head, my heart sinking in the center of my chest. I hadn't heard of it, but it sounded pretty fuckin' shitty. I didn't really want to find out exactly what she had planned anymore.

"Well, to quote Saunders Comprehensive Veterinary Dictionary... it is a 'method used for the collection of semen for artificial insemination or for examination'." She reached down and grabbed ahold of my flaccid dick, slipping the condom thing she was holding over the end of it. The tube I saw ran to a machine standing next to her and I immediately felt some pressure, like the suction from a vacuum or something.

Dread surged through my veins and made me seriously rethink whether I should be trying to bolt right about now. Mind made up, I tried like a son of a bitch to get my body, paralyzed with fear as it was, to pitch, thrash, or otherwise do what I needed it to do to get me the fuck out of here – brain melting surge of electricity or not. I stared at the crazy cunt in her efficient little lab coat and realized I was seriously nothing more than a fucking lab rat to her crazy ass. She continued talking as if I wasn't staring at her like she'd sprouted a second head.

"See what we do is provide electrical stimulation by way of electrodes applied to the lumbar sympathetic nerves. This promotes semen emission. Further electrodes applied to the pelvic splanchnic, and internal pudendal nerves, are used to promote erection of the penis and ejaculation. Most of these are contained inside a probe placed in the rectum." She smiled sweetly at me and I stared into her eyes. The lights were on but nobody was fucking home in there. She didn't feel one way or the other about what she was about to do to me... I'd seen the same look a thousand times and more out of my twin brother's eyes. Shit. Shit, shit, shit, shit, shit! Resignation sank in, and with it something akin to courage but not.

"And people talk about Alien abductees being victims of anal probing," I muttered. "You are out of your goddamn mind, you understand that right?"

She gave me a thoughtful look, tapping her lower lip with one bright red fingernail for a moment before she shrugged and smiled. "I don't really care. Again, Mathias wants us to study all aspects of your physiology, and since he *is* the one who signs our paychecks, we will." She clapped her hands together like a giddy little girl for a moment. "And you know what else? Human men need some time after they ejaculate for the body to build up seminal fluid again. Usually about half an hour or so, give or take. I wonder how fast you'll recover, not being human and all. I've actually been dying to find out."

She reached over my head and did something, pressed a button, flipped a switch, I have no idea. But a moment later I felt a mild current run through me. I bit my tongue again, determined not to scream. Strangely the pain I was expecting didn't come. It didn't exactly feel *good*, but it wasn't the agony I'd been expecting.

"Another little fun note about this is that it *can* actually be a rather pleasant experience. If we were to gradually increase the current to the point where it would cause release, you could potentially really enjoy yourself." She smiled at me and reached back over my head again. "But we don't want you to enjoy yourself do we? Oh, no we don't. So we're just going to crank this sucker all the way up and enjoy all those pretty screams that you're going to give us."

I gritted my teeth and took several deep breaths. I was determined not to give her the satisfaction. I wasn't going to scream. I wasn't going to scream.

I was not. Going. To. Scream.

She twisted her wrist.

I didn't scream.

My world vanished into a haze of white hot agony and I fucking *howled*.

Chapter 10

Ava

Eyes sightlessly staring, I gazed into the absolute black of my bunk and lay perfectly still. It was the exact opposite of what my mind was doing. On the inside it seethed and twisted, the thoughts roiling in on themselves, looping back around, strangling my ability to sleep.

Mathias was up to something. The sudden bullshit mission to New Hampshire felt all wrong. My gut told me he wanted me and my team out of here in one seriously big damn hurry. Why? Everyone had a motive for everything they did. That was a given, so what motive did Mathias have to pitch us onto a wild goose chase halfway across the country?

The short answer? Remus Reese AKA Remy Dulcet... it had to be. Remus was the one point my mind circled around and there wasn't any way I was going to sleep. There wasn't any way I was going to find out the deal with Mathias' peculiar obsession when it came to this particular werewolf bastard if I kept my ass in bed either.

I sat up abruptly and was met with the soft clicking and ticking of the motion sensor light coming on. The small, former cell, lit gradually as the energy efficient lights warmed up.

Nightmares happened a lot on this crusade and sometimes even in my regular line of work. Part of the remodel of this facility had been to equip each room with a set of motion sensing lights. Sit up beyond a certain point, the lights came on; like now. They were on a timer, if you lay down, went still, they'd switch off in a few minutes time. I'd never really appreciated the lights, until James...

I got up and splashed some cold water on my face from the sink above the John and mechanically went through my morning routine. Brush teeth, dress in my tactical chic. Lace boots, blouse pants, check weapons, clean anything that needed cleaning, strap them on and finally with nothing left to do, I swung into my modified Joe Rocket and with a peculiar feeling, zipped it up despite how warm it was in the facility.

James had bought the coat and had one of the tailors, loyal to the order, retrofit it with pockets on the inside to hold plates of body armor. James had gifted it to me right before he'd gone out on his last mission.

Trust me, Ava. Just in case...

I'd argued with him. Kevlar didn't do shit against knives or claws, and he'd given me a pointed look, his green eyes so like my own, glassy with a poignant mixture of love, regret and pleading. He'd crushed me to his chest and kissed the top of my hair before letting me go for the last time. The moment had held a substantial amount of weight. Heavy, like gravity had suddenly increased, weighing us down from the inside out.

James had never been one to express affection or love physically like that. It'd been weird, and I'd found out why hours later when my team had been dispatched to pick up survivors. Except there hadn't been any survivors. We'd really just been dispatched for body recovery.

A rectangle of folded leather sat on the small ledge above the sink. A wallet; old and well-worn, but in good shape. I flipped it open, looking at the driver's license inside belonging to Remus' alter ego Remy Dulcet. Six foot six inches tall and two hundred and thirty pounds according to the laminated cardboard rectangle. He had answers. He might not know it, but he had them. Without thinking I closed the wallet and stuffed it into an inside pocket of my jacket.

I snugged the zipper up the last few inches and drew and replaced my guns in their thigh holsters a few times to get the feel with the bulkier coat caging my body. Three guns, one on each leg and the third beneath my arm and I felt icy inside. As still as the night; quieter than death. I felt like the ground at the beach, when the wind blew and the sand shifted. I even looked up briefly to see if there was any movement above my head.

I resided in that quiet few inches between the solid earth and the shifting chaos and I felt calm; *ready*. My decision had been made and I was willing to find answers… at whatever cost. James was already dead, and I had nothing left to lose.

I slipped out into the silent hall and breathed out. Squaring my shoulders I put on my resting bitch face and went calmly in the direction of the nearest route that would take me lower. Down to where the containment cells were located.

It'd surprised me that Mathias hadn't put the beast into one of the maximum security containment cells, but rather one he could easily escape, with a couple of guards he could probably just as easily overpower. Granted, no matter how smart he was, he wouldn't get far in this rat maze of floors and tunnels and what-have-you, of the facility we were in.

Truthfully, that was what had surprised me the most. That the dog hadn't even *tried* to get out of his kennel. None of the others that had been brought in had so much as a sliver of the self-control this one did, not when they were hungry and these beasts were ravenous *all the time*. This was especially true of any of the others that had been classified as 'Blood Born.' They all seemed a little half cracked to begin with. Think along the lines of little to no self-control, violent, and bloodthirsty. Like that sadistic bratty boy-king on that one premium channel TV show everybody raves about.

I'd caught a few episodes with my team in our down time and didn't really understand how they could be so into it when we dealt in life and death and adrenaline all the time out in the raw and real world.

Anyways, that was the thing that had bothered James from the beginning. Why did Mathias even *want* to capture these things? What was the point in studying them? It wasn't like there was a cure for what they were. They were animals. The end. Not even enough there to make a long story short. You couldn't *get* much shorter than that.

My thoughts swirled around inside my head on the subject, chasing one another down rabbit holes and through warrens, one leading to the next, to the next, to the next; even as my feet did the same, one in front of the other, carrying me towards the monster's inefficient cage.

I halted several paces outside the crude wooden door set with the iron barred window that looked like it came out of every badly done dungeon movie you'd ever seen. There were no guards posted. *Why weren't there any guards posted?*

I crept forward quietly and the nearer I came, the distinct sound of male voices in earnest conversation became clear. Ah. The guards weren't on the outside because they were on the *inside* with Mathias and the beast. My heartbeat settled into its regular cadence. I thought they'd taken him. That he'd expired from injury or had already been executed. That I'd missed my chance.

"I could care less, Mathias. You've got some explaining to do. Why would you want to attack my pack now after protecting it for who knows how long?" Remus asked.

What in the absolute fuck? I thought to myself. *Mathias was protecting some of these bastards!?* I listened hard for a denial.

"The arrangement I had with your father, Declan, was no longer adequate."

I tasted bile at the back of my mouth. *Jesus-fucking-Christ, James. Is this what you found out?* I heard Mathias' boot heels click against the stone floor hollowly and I could imagine him pacing slowly back and forth in front of the cage. Looking down his nose at Remus. It was what he did with all of us when he was silently judging.

I'd seen him do it a thousand times in front of James. My brother had always been the risk taker, the more daring of the two of us. More vivacious, more intelligent, more inspiring... just *more*. And now he was *no more*, he was gone, and as Mathias continued talking I was beginning to get a clearer and clearer indication as to why my brother had been sent to his death, but not the big 'why,' the 'why' of it all.

The sharp crackle of the Taser going off made me jump, heart in my throat, my chest squeezed tight. The sound the contacts made went on for what felt like forever before ceasing, leaving a deafening silence in their wake.

"Take him to Helen. I want samples, and I want them all. After that, put him into maximum containment. Run the usual gamut of tests. I want to know why he is different from the rest."

I drifted down the corridor and, ghosted around the corner. The door opened, the two guards lugging the unconscious werewolf between them. I drifted down the corridor further and slipped into the alcove one of the other cell doors made.

Gritting my teeth I waited and my patience paid off. The elevator chimed, the guards grunted and cursed and a moment later the doors shushed shut and the elevator was underway. I waited for several uncomfortable heartbeats and dared look. All of them had gone, including Mathias.

I crept to the elevator bank and watched the indicator. Up, they went up. I worried my bottom lip between my teeth and contemplated my next move.

All roads lead to Remus... my mind whispered and it sounded like my brother's voice.

"James, you better not get me killed." I murmured to myself and hit the stairs. They'd stopped on the medical level, which only made sense. Helen was Doctor Helen Bradley, who patched us up whenever we got banged up on a mission. It was going to take me a while to get up to medical by the stairs from way down here, but the stairs afforded me the ability of looking like I was moving throughout the facility naturally. I rarely, if ever, took the elevator unless I was traveling with someone or in a hurry.

Deviations in normal behavior. It was one of the first things we were trained to look for. Naturally, it would be one of the first things I would avoid doing.

When I slid through the door at the top of the stairs, what little breath I'd had left was stolen away by the most horrendous sound... I can't even describe it. It tore through the air, reverberated along the walls and struck ice into my heart and through every vein. Pain didn't begin to cover it. Agony barely reached. I un-holstered my guns and strode up the hall, stopping dead, struck mute, outside one of the medical suite's glass doors.

The curtain had been left aside and what I saw... Remus Reese was chained to an exam table. Not just any table, but a gynecological examination – I gagged, hard. Shock and disbelief burning off, swept aside by a wildfire of anger and dismay.

I don't care what you are… *no one*, nothing, no creature deserved *this*. I hit the safety off my guns, sucked in a deep breath and committed to my course of action, knowing full well the consequences and not giving two fucks about them.

I shot the guard, right through the glass and then I aimed my guns at Helen.

She stood openmouthed, clipboard and pen forgotten in her hands as I stepped over the metal lintel of the shattered glass door, my ears ringing from the report from my guns in such an enclosed space.

"What in the absolute *fuck!?*"

"Ava…" Helen warned.

"No! No! No!" I cried, "What are you *doing* Helen!?"

"Now Ava, I need you to calm down…"

"Calm *down?*" I demanded. "*Calm down?*" my voice was rising but I couldn't keep it in check.

"Ava it's not what you think!"

"Not what I think? What the hell are you *doing* Helen!? Since when has the order been into torture?" I was seriously beginning to wonder who the animal was at this point as I gazed past Helen in her sharp white lab coat at the barely conscious nude man strapped to the table.

"Remus!" I cried, but his head simply lolled to the side, I tried again.

"Remus Reese!" I barked and his head snapped up with a snarl.

"Ava, no!"

"Shut the hell up Helen! You lost your voting privileges! Remus, get up!"

He snarled and broke the chains, ripping the wires and contact pads from around his groin area. I stared cold and hard at Helen in a bid to give him some privacy for the rest. He staggered over in my direction.

"Thanks, bitch," his voice was bitter and dry, hoarse from those unnatural screams.

"Where will you go, Ava?" Helen asked; her voice musical and a touch haunting. The half-smile on her face was totally insane and I couldn't believe I'd never seen it before. Her crazy. She'd patched my brother, my team, and hell, even *me*, up countless times... how did I never see it?

"None of your fucking business, but I'm out. After that, I am so out."

"He'll hunt you to the ends of the earth, Mathias will. You know he will."

"Just fucking shoot the crazy cunt." Remy growled. He was working a pair of green hospital scrubs up his legs but they were having a hard time making it all the way. The material straining around his powerful, muscular thighs. Too short, they rode high at the hems, around his calves, a bad parody of a pair of Capri's.

"Shut up, she's the facility's top doctor, and an excellent surgeon. I can't kill her." I was torn. So very torn...

"Better make up your mind, Babycakes, before it's too–"

I made a critical mistake, a rookie mistake and took my eyes off Helen for a split second, a rustle of fabric and Remy cutting off mid-sentence alerted me and training, muscle memory, took over. Compensating for my inattention. My finger twitched on the trigger and my gun went off and when I looked, Helen was going over backwards, crashing into the edge of the exam table and sliding to the floor a small pistol gripped in her nerveless hand.

Blood blossomed high on the white sleeve of her lab coat. A lucky blind shot, I'd hit her in the arm of the hand that had her gun in it. That was my fucking cue to leave. I shot a silent prayer of thanks to my brother for watching my ass and refocused, honing in on the monumental task at hand.

"Let's go," I bolted out the door with Remus Reese on my six and stayed on target: getting us the fuck out of here alive.

I bolted down the hallway and hit the button for the elevator. The doors opened and I sent it up and hit the button for the doors to close. Remy stepped forward and I pushed him back, out of the death box.

"Come on! This way!" I shot down the hall, around the corner and crashed into the stairs with the large werewolf loping along behind me.

"Damnit," he cursed and I holstered one gun and hauled him ineffectually along by one arm into the stairwell. Pushing him ahead of me.

"Faster, for fucks sake!" I barked.

"You wanted faster outta me you shouldn't have fuckin' shot me!"

"Hind sight is always twenty-twenty, quit your bitching and move your ass, level four!"

He crashed through a door and ditched right, plastering himself against the wall. I cursed inside my own head; you never follow your own breech! I guess he wouldn't know that being a civilian. I went through the door aiming one gun while bringing out the other. Nothing. I didn't let out the breath I was holding just yet, anyways.

"Jeep Patriot, third down the line." I holstered my weapon and he loped in that direction. I pulled out the key and hit the locks. Lights flashed and the headlights lit up out into the parking lot where the Jeep was backed in.

I was three quarters of the way there when the snarls and snapping raised the hair on the back of my neck. Remus popped up over the roof of the Jeep, standing on the runner to look behind me.

"Ava, *move!*" he shouted and came up with the shotgun from the passenger side holster, a sawed off deal. I threw myself at the driver's door and opened it as the boom of the shotgun blared through the garage, reverberating through my chest. A yelp and a whine, very dog-like behind me. I stayed focused and got behind the wheel, jamming the key in the ignition.

I turned it over, slammed the door and rammed in the clutch simultaneously. I slammed the stick shift into first. A wild romp on the gas, screaming tires, I popped the clutch and shot forward as the gun went off overhead one more time. Remus folded his impossibly large frame into the Jeep and slammed his door.

"Don't stop!" he bellowed and I dropped it into the next gear and picked up speed, short shifting and hauling ass up through the garage.

"Don't stop, Girl, go right on through them," he grated and I gritted my teeth and prayed they fucking moved. I shot straight at several members of my team who stood, guns pointed, stunned before scattering to either side. Too shocked to fire…

"Thank you James," I breathed and pulled out into the morning light. The fire of the sun a cleansing thing… burning the horror of what I saw away just enough to make the memory of it bearable.

I drove. I drove hard and fast and knew the only chance I had to get the answers I sought so badly was to get us off the grid. The good news? I had a place for that. The bad news? It was a ways away.

Here was to hoping we could make it and the beast beside me didn't rip my fucking face off before I got the full meal deal on what the fuck was going on.

Chapter 11
Remus

"Look, Babycakes," I snapped. "You hunt, I evade. It's what we do, and since we're evading, you might want to listen to me and get us to the fuckin' water!"

We had been arguing for about an hour. An hour where the hunters had undoubtedly been gathering their forces and sending teams after us, and with what I saw when we made our escape... I couldn't believe it. Wolf-kind. Fuckin' w*olf-kind*, working for the damn hunters. Worse, working for Mathias fuckin' Young! What in the ever loving hairy fuck!? How in the hell..? I couldn't wrap my head around it.

"What the fuck," Ava growled, a distinctly wolfish kind of sound that I'm pretty sure she wasn't even aware of doing. She had this bad ass bitch persona going on, and she had no idea that it was very similar to alpha bitch material. It was kind of hot, honestly.

I shook my head, banishing that thought as fast as I could and turned again to look behind us. "Would you quit fuckin' looking back?" she snapped and I looked at her. Her hands were tight on the wheel. Knuckles mottled white from the pressure of her grip. Her shoulders were tense and the skin around her eyes creased as she squinted through the glare of the late morning sun through the windshield. "If anyone sees the half-naked guy constantly looking back it'll look suspicious. Just stare front and center and *try* to act casual?" she ground out between gritted teeth. "God, you really are a fucking civilian, no tactical sense whatsoever."

I was a bit offended at that but chose not to respond in kind, simply turning back around in my seat.

"Look, wolf-kind can track by smell. If we want a chance at throwing them off, we need to get across water. They'll be right on our tails."

She snorted, and indelicate, mocking sound. "Pun intended, Wolf-boy? Seriously though, you think I don't know that? What the fuck does your kind have to do with it anyways?"

"You heard it, Ava," I said, purposely using her real name instead of one of my little derogatory pet nicknames for her. I needed her to focus on what I was saying instead of her irritation at my propensity for using condescension on her. "You heard them back in that garage. The last ones coming at us, those were wolf-kind. I don't know why or how but Mathias has my people working for him, or with him, I don't know."

She said nothing, just continued to stare straight ahead at the road so I pressed my point. "With wolf-kind on our tails we need to cross water to lose the scent. They'll have to spread out and cover more ground up and down the far side of the lake to try to pick up our trail again, and by the time they get there the trail could be cold and we'll have a good chance that we've lost them."

"Could?"

I shrugged. "It's hard to say how fast they'll move. They might get lucky and find the spot where we go ashore before the trail has a chance to really get cold.

"It's not really possible to track us when we're in a car doing seventy-five on the highway is it? Through the walls and with all the other smells in the air, I mean, that's impossible. Right?"

I shrugged. "Police dogs are capable of it. They can track a kidnap victim even if the victim is put in a car for a short time but the trail does go cold rather quickly. A wolf-kind's nose is even better than a police dog's, if we know what we're looking for, which we do. Match a human intelligence with the senses of an animal, it's what we are, Babycakes. The best of both worlds." She looked sideways at me for a moment, I guessed trying to decide if I was exaggerating or not. I honestly couldn't give two rancid monkey shits if she fully believed me, as long as she *listened* to me. It was the only way we were going to escape with our lives. And speaking of which...

"Why did you bust me out of there?" I asked. "Not that I'm

complaining, but what happened to change your mind on the whole torturing and experimentation thing?"

She made a disgusted sound in her throat and for a second I thought she was gonna hack one up and spit to the side. Instead her hands tightened even further on the wheel and she glared at the road ahead, as if daring it to do something to piss her off.

"I never signed on for medical experiments like that," she said, finally, after several minutes passed in an ever increasingly weighted silence. "I've been crusading for years, wolf-kind are dangerous and they hurt people, but they're still living creatures. You're supposed to put 'em down quick... painless whenever possible. Torture for information sometimes has to happen but that?" she shifted in her seat uncomfortably, "The order has been changing things up recently and I don't like what I've been seeing," she finished, and if ever there was putting it mildly...

I nodded but didn't say anything. We were in a fragile state of a truce at the moment and I didn't want to get her trigger finger itching. No matter how much the shit coming out of her mouth pissed me off. Instead, I turned and looked out the window, considering our situation and our best chance of survival.

"Where the fuck are we anyways?" I muttered, looking at the landscape passing by outside.

"South Bend, Indiana," she said, shortly.

"Indiana?" I was surprised. I hadn't realized we'd left Illinois. "Why the fuck did we go to Indiana?"

She was silent for another minute, perhaps struggling with the natural inclination to deny information to one of the creatures she had spent who knows how long hunting. Since we were officially in this together at this point, I was reasonably certain she would start to talk eventually.

"The facility we were holding you at is an American Red Cross distribution center. The underground portion is a secret from the majority of the Red Cross employees."

"Why a Red Cross Facility?"

"The Red Cross is a front for our organization."

My mind latched onto that information faster than you could

imagine. Finally, a chance to get into the details, get some information about the Hunters. I would never be able to rejoin my pack, but if I could take some of this to William, it might earn me some leeway. However, before I could do any of that, we needed to finish our escape.

"Head north," I said, changing topics abruptly and in her defense Ava simply nodded and rolled with it, without a hiccup or a stutter. She shifted mental gears with equal precision to shifting physical gears in the Jeep.

"What's the plan then, oh great evader?" Her tone was only slightly caustic and I ignored it in favor of keeping the peace. There was no reason to fight with her right then. I knew when to pick my battles, unlike my late brother Rom.

"We'll get into Michigan and ditch the Jeep. We'll steal another one or buy one if I can get access to my bank accounts. Then we'll turn west until we hit Lake Michigan."

"What happens when we hit the lake?" I grinned and suppressed a wince of pain as a flare of heat burst in my leg from the slowly healing gunshot wound.

"We're going to cross it."

To her credit she didn't flinch or swerve us off the road in her surprise, she just kept driving but she did glance at me out of the corner of her eye as her mouth dropped open in shock for just a moment before it snapped closed again with an audible clack of her teeth.

"Are you completely out of your damn mind?" she demanded. "It's mid-May, there's still likely to be ice on the lake. We might not actually be able to cross the thing without us getting sunk in the process."

"As long as there aren't any storms we should be good." I leaned over and looked through the window up at the clear sky. "I don't see any storm clouds, do you?"

"That's not the point, why the hell would we want to choose to go across the lake. It's dangerous, not to mention *huge*."

"Exactly why," I said and shifted in my seat, grimacing again as I moved my leg. "Goddammit, my leg is driving me nuts," I grumbled. She didn't have anything to say about that and just waited for me to continue.

"Look, crossing the lake isn't going to be a picnic. It *is* a big-ass lake, and yeah there probably will be ice on the water at this time of year. The hunters following us might agree with you that it's too dangerous to cross after us. And if they drive all the way around, or even if they catch a plane, by the time they get to the other side they won't have any idea where we came ashore. They'll waste time trying to find us and we'll have a better chance of getting away."

She fell silent, considering my argument for a minute.

"Actually, that's not a horrible idea," she admitted, finally. "Do you have a plan in place for what we're going to do once we get to the other side of the lake?" she asked.

I shrugged. "I hadn't actually gotten that far," I admitted. "My main goal right now is just to shake them off our tail," I gave her a pointed look that communicated she'd best keep it shut when it came to the unintended pun as I continued. "We'll figure out where we're going after that."

She considered that silently for a moment before she nodded once, sharply, and let out an explosive sigh. "There's an apartment," she said. "In Ashland, up in Northern Wisconsin. It belongs to me and it's completely under the radar so we'll go there after we hit the other side of the lake."

I shrugged. "Sounds like a plan to me." I was honestly getting too tired and felt too worn out to care much one way or the other.

She glanced at me and then hit the turn signal to pull us off the freeway.

"What're you doing?" I asked.

"You need some clothes and we need some food. Can't have you running around in some scrub pants that don't even fit."

I grunted. "Not gonna be doing much running around at all."

"Boo-hoo," she mocked. "Suck it up, Butter Cup."

I couldn't help the annoyed growl that slipped out of me. The wolf and I *did not* like being mocked. Not in the slightest. And considering *she* was the one that'd shot me in the first place, neither one of us felt particularly charitable on that front. She pulled into a parking lot of some large department store or other, I couldn't be bothered to see which one, and pulled smoothly into a space. "Look, stay here, I'll run and grab you some clothes and then we'll grab something to eat."

Without another word she opened her door and jumped out. I grunted and leaned back in my seat, my eyes slipping closed almost of their own accord. She was right. Clothes would be good. But honestly? I didn't feel particularly hungry. And *that* scared the shit out of me.

* * *

I jerked awake to find the sun was setting and we were driving again. Ava had a fast food cup in one hand and was just finishing off what smelled like a cherry coke. She set her cup in the Jeep's cup holder next to a second, full cup, and glanced at me.

"Morning Sunshine," she muttered and I grunted a barely coherent response. "What the fuck is wrong with you?" she snapped. You've been out for hours, I wasn't sure what to do so I just kept driving."

"Not feeling so hot," I muttered. That wasn't entirely true. I felt pretty damned hot, feverish in fact. My body was alternatively burning up and wracked with chills that set me to shivering uncontrollably.

"There's food if you want. I ordered a metric-fuck-ton of the stuff. Hope you like cold burgers and fries." The smell hit me then and I wretched, body convulsing as my stomach heaved attempting to expel the nothing in it. I had no idea when it was that I last actually ate or drank anything. I reached blindly and rolled the window down and stuck my head outside to rid myself of the smell of the food. Honestly I was tempted to just throw the bags out, but she was right, food was needed and it wouldn't do to waste it.

"What the fuck?" she yelped. "Remus, what's wrong?" Her voice was tight. Not with fear, not for herself at least. I could almost think that she was worried about me.

"Worried about me?" I said in a languid kind of drawl. I felt drunk, delirious almost. Something was severely wrong. Wolf-kind don't get fevers. We don't get sick, but this all seemed familiar. I couldn't quite place it but I was sure I had seen my symptoms in someone else before. If I could just concentrate...

"Not really. I need you alive. You've got information I want."

"Information on Mathias and his deal with my father, Declan Rees?"

"Among other things."

"Tit for tat," I muttered, letting my eyes close again as the cold air from the open window caressed my overheated skin. "Quid pro quo. I tell you something you tell me something."

"Like what?"

"Why is the Red Cross a front for the Hunters?"

"Not all Hunters," she said. "Just our... chapter... I guess you could say."

"Alright, then why is the American Red Cross a front for your Chapter?"

"Because our chapter can trace its origins back to the Knights Templar."

I blinked, completely unsure how to take that information. "I'm confused," I admitted finally. "What does you guys being Templars way back when have to do with anything?"

She glanced over at me again, a small smirk tugging at the corner of her lips. It was really kind of sexy, and distracting. I gave myself a firm mental shake to snap out of it.

"What's the universally recognized symbol for the Red Cross?" she asked and I frowned, feeling like my brain was trying to work through a layer of cotton batting.

"A red cross?" I ventured.

"A Red Cross on a white background. That was the emblem of the Knights Templar, genius. The American Red Cross was founded entirely as a front for our branch of the crusade. With it, we were able to create an organization capable of going all over the world without too much scrutiny and we could actually do some good and help humans in need while we're at it. It's a win-win situation."

That made some crazy kind of sense, so I nodded. Nothing more was said for a time until the sun slipped completely beneath the horizon. Ava left the freeway and a short time later left the main roads and rolled into a parking lot near an access point to the edge of the lake.

"Come on," she said after she parked the car and turned it off. "We need to find a boat. There's a dock about a half a mile up the beach, we should be able to steal something from there."

"Why not just drive the rest of the way there?" I complained and bit back a moan of pain as I shifted to get out. My leg told me in no uncertain terms how little it enjoyed the treatment.

"They'll waste some time searching around here for us and we'll stick to the asphalt as long as possible to avoid leaving tracks leading them right to the dock."

"They're not going to be lookin' fer tracks," I mumbled as a wave of dizziness swept over me and I swayed for a moment on my feet. One hand shot out and I grabbed ahold of the Jeep to keep from falling over. "They're gonna smell us and we'll just be losing time walkin' there."

"We'll see," she muttered tersely and came over to tuck herself under my arm, bearing some of my weight on my right side. "Don't get any fucking ideas, Werewolf," she growled but there was no heat in it. "It's not that I like you or anything I'm just trying to save both our asses."

I nodded but didn't say anything as we made our way to the dock she was talking about. It didn't take us too long, but definitely longer than it should have. Something was really wrong and I wasn't positive what.

The next bit is still a jumbled mess of images and impressions in my mind. The smell of water and fish, motion, the clunking of heavy footsteps on wood and then I was falling, unconscious before my body struck the ground.

* * *

"You know," I muttered hoarsely. "For a guy that has never had any health issues I seem to be in a lot of pain and dealing with more illness since I met you than I ever have in my life. It's been a fucking long one, too."

Ava chuckled somewhere off to my right and I finally opened my eyes to see the blackened night sky above me, clouds rolling in and out in waves to obscure the half moon and the stars blazing away more brightly than it's possible to see them in any city. The ground shifted beneath me and I could hear a sloshing sound. That's what clued me in that we were on a boat.

"Where are we? And what exactly happened?"

"We're on a boat. Not a particularly large one, a 40 foot yacht I was able to steal. Still, it'll get us where we're going if we're lucky." To my right and above me Ava sat in a chair. The chair was anchored to the deck and she had turned slightly so she could look down at me lying on my back on the hard wood with one of her slim hands still holding onto the wheel. In her other she held up a small glass jar with a metal cap screwed on tight and tossed it down to me.

The jar, which probably held baby food in its previous incarnation, landed on my chest and bounced and I was barely able to catch it before it fell to the deck. I held it up and shook it to see a few tiny pieces of metal rattle around inside it. Minuscule specks, no larger than a sliver or a splinter.

"What the hell are these?" I asked and looked over at her.

"Shards of the silver slug I pulled out of your leg. I thought it'd come out in one piece, but obviously it didn't; I missed some of it. That's why you were feeling sick, they were poisoning you. Your leg was infected and seriously inflamed and you passed out just as we got onto the boat, here, so I piloted us out onto the lake and let us drift for a bit while I checked you out." She turned back to the front as if dismissing me but continued to talk a moment later.

"I didn't see anything obvious so I checked your wound and that's when I figured out what had to be wrong. I'll tell you what, it took some serious effort to get those out of you considering I didn't exactly have proper medical equipment on hand or decent lighting, or a sterile environment. Of course, the sterile environment part doesn't exactly mean much to you–" she side eyed me, "…guys, does it?"

"Do I want to ask what you were just going to call my people?"

"Probably not," she admitted and shrugged. I threw the little glass jar with its offending contents high and out into the lake where it landed with a little splash. I pushed myself up to a sitting position and groaned quietly. Removing the silver had definitely helped with the fever and chills, and I was certainly feeling better, but I was weak, starved, and my leg hurt more than ever.

"You didn't happen to bring the food from the car aboard with us, did you?" I asked and a moment later a takeout bag landed on the deck right next to me with a low thump. I pushed myself back so that I was leaning against the metal railing that encircled the deck. I put my legs out in front of me and dug a cold burger out of the bag. I didn't care that it was cold. I was so fucking *hungry* I would have eaten a raw cow if that was all that was available.

"Tit for tat," she said and I looked up at her, my mouth full of food, with a questioning expression on my face. Despite myself, and despite the knowledge that I really *shouldn't* be finding myself attracted to this woman, I couldn't help but stare at her tits, in response to the words that came out of her mouth.

"Eyes up," she snapped and I blinked, snapping my gaze up to meet her eyes with as innocent an expression as I could muster. "I told you something about the crusaders, now you owe me some information," she continued as if nothing had happened.

I frowned, trying to remember what she had told me. Gradually the foggy memories surfaced and I nodded, swallowing the lump of food, I wiped my mouth with the back of one hand. "What'd you want to know?" I asked before I took another bite and she turned her chair again so she could see me more easily, her head swinging back and forth to me and to watching our course across the lake.

"Mathias said that he had an agreement with Declan," she said and I could hear a hesitation when she spoke my father's name. Obviously she had been tempted to say something else but changed her mind at the last moment. "What was that, exactly?"

"No idea."

"That wasn't our deal," she snapped, glaring angrily at me and I held up a hand in a placating gesture, waving her down.

"Look, I don't really know. Not for sure. But I can make a reasonably educated guess."

"Then guess," she growled and, again, I chose not to comment how just like a wolf-kind female she sounded.

"From what I've learned recently, it sounded like father had an arrangement with Mathias that he would have hunters patrol the border of our territory for any other wolf-kind attempting to encroach on our land. It sounded like Declan would allow him to take any trespassers that attempted to get into Washington and in return Mathias would leave the Northwest Pack alone. In essence, the hunters were protecting my packs' territory for us."

"But that doesn't make any sense," she argued. "Why would he make a deal with an Alpha? Mathias is well known for hating wolf-kind more than almost any hunter I've ever heard of."

"Considering the experiments he was doing, it isn't too hard to understand." She glanced down at me again, silently urging me to continue. "Mathias is obviously trying to figure out what makes us tick. Maybe how we live so long or how we complete our change. He wants to learn *something*, and it's difficult enough to hunt us when we're spread out all over hell and gone. With that arrangement he had a nearly sure trap. Wolf-kind were sure to occasionally try to breach our territory. It's a fact of life. Territory is important and Washington State has some of the best."

"So... what? He could just pick off other wolf-kind as they try to enter the state?" she asked and I nodded.

"Sounds about what the situation was."

"Why? What could he possibly hope to learn?"

"Like I said, why we live for so long, maybe? Why we heal so fast or how we're so strong? Maybe how it is that we change?"

"But we already know that. Wolf-kind come from ancient Druids in Ireland, before St. Patrick subjugated the Pagan people and converted them to Christianity."

That got my attention and I started so hard that I dropped the remains of my burger, the food slipping from suddenly nerveless fingers to drop to the deck with a wet plop.

"What did you just say?" I demanded sharply and her deep green eyes locked onto mine, staring at me as if she were just seeing me for the first time.

"Wolf-kind come from the ancient Druids. The first shifters were able to do so because of a connection to a wolf guardian spirit. The story goes that after St. Patrick converted the druids the ones that had already connected to the wolf went mad, started changing with the moon, and ever since, they've spread their madness and the hunters have been attempting to wipe them out because of it." She eyed me curiously. "Didn't you know that?"

I shook my head, eyes wide and feeling as if I'd just been hit over the head with a two by four. "No one I've ever known has any idea as to our origins. Wolf-kind have spent so long just trying to survive that a lot of our history's been lost." I spoke as if in a trance. Numb with the enormity of the information that had just been dropped on me.

The hunters *knew*, they knew where we'd started, *how* we'd started. How the first wolf-kind were born, or created. They knew far more about us than anyone had ever imagined, and the very notion of it at once thrilled me and filled me with dread. If they knew so much that had been lost to us, what else did they know?

Chapter 12

Ava

I'd blindsided him. Good to know I still had the ability, but it hadn't been my intention this time. He sat silent, staring off into space for a long, long while. His dark eyes narrowed and calculating. I had a hard time believing that the mutts didn't know where they'd originated, but no matter how good an actor he might be, no one was *that* good. You couldn't fake a reaction like that.

"Hey, Dingo." I nudged his hip with my foot, his eyes narrowed further and snapped to me.

"Fuck you," he growled and I smiled and knew it wasn't exactly nice.

"That's what you get for calling me 'Babycakes' all the time. 'Dingo…' I rather like that little nickname for you. With that appetite of yours I wouldn't put it past you, you know… the whole eating babie–" he snarled, his arm snapping out, one of his massive hands going around one of my ankles. He gave it a surprisingly gentle squeeze and we locked eyes.

"I have been trying pretty fucking hard to keep it civil, *Babycakes*," he looked at me, soul deep and I swallowed hard. We were perched on that razor's edge of violence and it could honestly go either way. If it went sideways I was pretty sure I was going to lose the leg. If I managed to get my gun out and on him, and actually *survive* the encounter, I probably would die from blood loss before I could get back to shore.

Me and my fucking mouth. I had always been the cool, calm and collected one. I was behaving more like my twin and less like myself every day. I closed my mouth and nodded slowly.

"Fair enough," I conceded and honestly, with the way he was looking at me, I indeed felt duly chastised. I held his gaze and refused to back down, to be the one to look away first and with a slight, almost knowing smirk, he conceded. His hand slipped from my leg, but it did so in a lingering caress, and I fought to suppress a shudder.

"I was thinking," I said, as much to change the subject from the intense interaction as anything.

"Yeah? About what?" He settled back against the side of the boat and shifted uncomfortably.

"We can't cross this lake, not in this thing. It's something like two hundred miles give or take to go north and cross to make landfall anywhere near where we'd need to be. There isn't enough fuel to go even straight across at over a hundred miles. This thing was still in winter storage."

"You got a point coming up anytime soon?" he grated and I guess I couldn't blame him for being in a mood. I tried my best to squash down the image of him strapped to that table of Helen…

Good Christ, what had I been a part of?

"Yeah, we're a mile, maybe two off shore. Is that enough to throw the scent?"

"Should be," he said eyeing me suspiciously.

"Good. I'm going to take us as far as I can, we'll make landfall where we can, steal another car or buy one or whatever and then we'll have to catch a legit way around or across."

He grunted noncommittally and we lapsed into silence. He finished the cold food while I piloted us carefully through the darkened waters, glad he'd been unconscious while I'd struggled to get the hang of this and get us out here.

When he'd finished making his way through the rest of the cold, fast food, he leaned his head back against the railing. I took the time to study his face while he had his eyes closed. He was handsome, strong featured, though his growth of beard really didn't do much for him. He looked scruffy and unkempt and disconcertingly feral. Deep, dark circles resided under his eyes and they almost appeared sunken despite the fact the rest of him appeared fit.

He had washboard abs and honestly looked like Michelangelo had carved him from flesh and bone. His definition was phenomenal and I had to bet he worked very hard at keeping it that way. He had gym rat written all over him, however, as pretty as he was for me to look at, it was proving to be somewhat of a distraction so…

Thwack!

"What's this?" he asked, glaring at the thick plastic of the bag between his knees.

"Clothes. I managed to stop and get you some while you were napping."

He grunted a scoffing laugh and pulled the items from the bag. Nothing fancy, a pair of loose jeans and a zip up hoodie. I finished 'em off with a pair of white jogging shoes. He'd look like a regular Joe walking down the street if we needed him to. Well, as long as he zipped up.

"Nice," he said almost appreciatively and I felt the need to nip that right in the bud. Wouldn't want my hard assed reputation to suffer.

"I read your dossier, remember?" I mused idly.

He grunted noncommittally and put his arms through the sleeves of the hooded sweatshirt, zipping it halfway up. His arms were so damned huge that the sleeves stretched ridiculously to accommodate them, but nothing tore at least. He breathed out a sigh of almost relief, his breath pluming the air and worked on unfolding and opening up the jeans, tearing tags and peeling stickers in a big damn hurry.

"You cold?" I asked, and he froze in place looking up at me sharply, a glint of something undefinable in those dark eyes of his.

"Yeah…" he drawled and unstuck, resuming his efforts to change into the denim from the ruined, too-small scrub pants. I averted my gaze and studiously steered us up the coastline, trying to keep the winking lights of the shoreline off to my left without losing them.

"I don't get cold," he stated after he'd gotten into the pants. He pulled on one shoe, then grimaced and looked like he was going to hurl when he tried to bend his bad leg to get the other.

"Hold up, tough guy. Let me help you."

"I don't want your help," he growled.

"Yeah, well you need it, so suck it up, Buttercup." I got up from my seat and knelt down next to him. He could glare at me all he fucking liked.

I knelt down and unlaced the shoe and eased it on for him before lacing it up and tying it securely for him.

"Good?" I queried.

"Good," he affirmed.

I resumed steering the stolen yacht, watching the fuel gauge and sighing after about another hour when it was at a point I figured we'd better head to shore. I glanced down at Remus who was huddled against the side pretty miserably. He looked miserable, and I was betting he was still feeling sick. I felt a slight tickle of remorse. It wouldn't do to feel bad for him but...

"How long until we get wherever you got us going, Ba–" he cut himself off, "Ava?"

I nodded, acknowledging his attempt to maintain a truce. He *was* trying harder than I was and that kind of sucked. I hated to be outdone.

"Depends on what kind of vehicle we can score. We're going to need a four by four of some kind, if we get lucky and score one at the get go, it'll save us some time, not having to switch vehicles and all."

He nodded, but the expression on his face was sour, "You good Wolfie?" I asked, momentarily forgetting myself as something very like concern thrilled through my veins. Alarm bells were going off in the back of my mind at his appearance.

"No," he stated simply, "Feel like I'm going to puke." I laughed without being able to help myself.

"Sea sick? The werewolf is sea sick?" I asked incredulously.

"No, I don't think my body is over..." he stopped, scrambled to his knees and retched over the side. Fuck. From everything we'd learned about their unique physiology, this was bad fuckin' news.

"You better get us to wherever we're going, Babycakes. If I'm going to die, I think I'd rather like it to be peaceful at this point. I'm tired."

He sounded a mixture of terrified and resigned and I couldn't help but feel a little scared for him myself. I nodded and realized he couldn't see it with how he was draped over the side, facing away from me.

"Sure, yeah," I said quietly and increased the throttle on the boat to get us ashore. Dragging him had been a bitch, he was twice my size and heavy as fuck and I didn't think there would be a dolly that I could roll him onto this time to make the going easier.

"You just gotta stay awake and help me as much as you can with mobility, you got it?"

"Yeah, I hear you."

I lucked out and there was a dock, a private one, but a dock none the less. We were making landfall in a residential neighborhood.

"I need a cane, or a staff or something," he declared when I cut the engine and got down onto the dock. I nodded and looked around, moving up the dock and into the back yard of the house we were at. It wasn't perfect but there was a broom with a thick handle up under the back porch of the upper middle-class house we were behind.

I dug it out carefully from the pile of random crap it was lumped into and whisper quiet, brought it down to the dock. Remy had managed to get himself over the side and was standing, weight mostly on his good leg, the one I'd fucked up dangling almost uselessly.

I handed him the broom and he eyed it. Nodding, he raised it and with a little more extra effort doing what should have been effortless for him, snapped the broom head off the handle. He pressed the broken end into the dock and bore weight on it a couple times, nodding.

"Let's move, get you around front. I'll get us something in the neighborhood and pick you up at the street." I whispered. He nodded and leaned hard on the stick, putting his good arm around my shoulders for support wordlessly. I worried that he was going to die on me before I got my answers as we made our way slowly and carefully up the lawn and down the side of the house.

The front of the neighborhood was nice too. I left him leaning heavily, panting and sweating, but shivering against a decorative outcropping of rock at the end of the driveway.

The neighborhood had that empty feel, the one that overtook everything in the middle of the night when the vast majority of the world was sleeping and you felt like you were the only creature stirring. I found a decent car in the form of a newer Land Rover, a few houses down.

Fuck, I would set off the alarm, and it was chancy, but…

I opened the small flap at the top of the collar of my jacket. James had worked several little Easter eggs into the coat aside from just the body armor and had shown me them all. Some of them hadn't made any sense to me, like the slim Jim he'd worked into the body of the coat beside the front zipper, but I was thankful for it now, just like I was thankful he'd taught me how to use the damn thing proficiently.

It wasn't exactly standard crusader training. The order had been around for ages and in that time, and with the American Red Cross as a front, we weren't exactly hurting for money and by default, vehicles. I slipped the thin steel from the coat and slid it expertly down into the crevice between window glass and the sheet metal of the white door.

I got it on the first try and lights flashing, horn blaring and alarm squealing I popped the handle, opened the door and simultaneously reached for my knife and up under the steering column for the wires I needed. A flick of the knife, a few severed wires later and the alarm was silenced. I stood up and looked around, heart in my throat and almost waited for lights to come on.

I didn't wait though, my training taking over, you didn't sit around and wait to be killed, or in this case caught; you moved your fucking ass. I retrieved the slim Jim, tossed it into the car and followed it up inside. A twist of wire, a couple of sparks and she started right up. I backed out of the drive and pulled up. Remus pushed heavily off the rocks and groped for the door, he hauled himself into the Land Rover and leaned heavily back into the seat.

"Used to have something like this… mine was black though," he muttered and I looked over at him. He was fading, fast and I didn't know what to do. I mean, I'd gotten all the silver out, what more needed to be done?

"You hungry?" I asked.

"No."

"Thirsty?"

"Yeah."

"You gotta stay awake for me," I said but when I took my eyes off the road and looked, he was already out.

Fuck. Fuck, fuck, fuckity, fuck!

Okay. I needed to get us someplace else, someplace off the grid and there was only one place I knew of, the apartment in Ashland wasn't a viable option at this point. It was too far. My brother's cabin, however… Shit. The thing was tiny, but completely off the grid. I glanced at Remus and sighed.

There was no choice. I needed to get him to the cabin and figure some shit out, I needed to know what he knew. For myself, for James, and to make my next move. I think I'd known the cabin was where I was going to end up. Hence my insistence on stealing a four by four or all-terrain vehicle. The directions to my brother's place most definitely included 'turn off the paved road' and required the extra vehicular muscle.

I got my bearings as quickly as I could, utilizing the vehicle's GPS unit, and no, not to look up specific directions, just to get a map of the surrounding areas. I may not be used to being the great evader, but it really was only a matter of tracking in reverse. If it was a trick I used to find 'em, it was something I avoided doing. I mean, it should do the trick. Right?

I certainly hoped so as I took a dubious look at my passed the fuck out passenger. I really fucking hoped so.

Chapter 13
Remus

"Please, tell me that somebody died in the crash," I muttered. "I can only assume a horrific crash or accident of some kind can be responsible for how entirely awful I feel."

Silence greeted that statement and I continued to lie there, wherever *there* was, for a while. My ears and nose didn't tell me much. Quiet. Dust. Wood. Ava. Not much else available in the air, and at best, I felt like a lump of lead. The motivation to get up or move around just wasn't there.

I tried to get a handle on the series of events that had led me to wherever the hell I was. The last clear memory I had, was getting into the Land Rover stolen by Ava. I vaguely had a recollection of getting into another vehicle at some point. The sound of doors opening, the irritating chime of the car telling us the key was still in the ignition, then the smell of leather and vanilla air freshener. Driving sucked, I could remember that much. Every motion of the car sent my stomach roiling and I couldn't have been more grateful that my stomach was too empty for me to throw up in the car.

"So, then what?" I muttered, the sound of my own voice barely recognizable to me. Rough and weak, it fit the shape I was in. Rough and weak seemed to sum up my entire world recently.

I thought more about what I could piece together from the few shaky memories I still retained. We changed vehicles at least once more, possibly twice, and eventually stopped.

"Come on, Remus," Ava had said repeatedly. "I need you to work with me, I can't lift your heavy ass up these stairs by myself." Stairs. Stairs sucked too. I don't think I liked stairs very much anymore. I had an impression, not even really a memory, of crawling my way up a steep set of stairs and then nothing but oblivion.

"Alright, so that covers the basics," I said aloud again. "Time to see where we are." I opened my eyes, finally. The ceiling above me was rough wooden planks, unfinished but sturdy. The walls were similar wood all around, as was the floor. It was a well-built looking structure, but it wasn't fancy. This wasn't like William's house, where everything was neat and polished. This was a house built for functionality. That was something I could appreciate.

The bed was a massive thing of solid wood and was piled high with several layers of blankets, underneath which I was buried. Digging my way out from under them took significantly more effort than it should have, and by the time I finally managed to push them aside and sit up, I was short of breath; a fine layer of sweat standing out on my skin from the effort.

The sweatshirt I had been wearing was nowhere to be seen, and my jeans had been changed for a light pair of sweatpants. A part of me wondered how much of an eyeful she got when she changed my clothes, but I mostly didn't care. Okay, that was a lie; I mostly wondered if she'd liked what she'd seen. I wasn't about to ask her though. We didn't have that kind of relationship, not at all. Still, if the roles had been reversed...

I reached out and snagged a t-shirt hanging from the back of a chair, squashing those thoughts as I pulled it over my head. It was chilly in here, I noted, before taking a look around the room.

Small was one word to use to describe the place. Not tiny, but it definitely wasn't roomy either. I didn't get the impression that it was a place that was well lived in. But it definitely wasn't an apartment, and I distinctly remember Ava saying we were going to an apartment. An apartment didn't have the rustic feel that this place had.

Where had she brought me?

The broom handle I'd been using as an improvised crutch was leaning against the wall, next to the bed, so I grabbed it and used it to help push myself to my feet. It took longer than I would have liked to get down the stairs, but I managed it, and only came close to pitching forward face-first twice.

The downstairs seemed even smaller than the upstairs because it was a living room, kitchen, and a small water closet of a bathroom all in a space the same size as the bedroom above.

Just as functional as the rest of the building. The door faced to the north and along the wall next to it, sat a low couch with a blanket folded carefully on one arm; a pillow resting on top of it. Ava was sleeping down here, obviously. I didn't have an explanation as to why she went through the extra effort of getting me upstairs, when she could have just dumped me on the couch. I mean, it would have saved her a lot of effort.

I sat down and looked around me. The place still had a slight residue of dust on a few surfaces but she had been making an effort to clean. Down here, the scent of cleaning chemicals was stronger than it had been upstairs and I pushed open a window to let some of the cool, outside air in, before sitting back down on the couch. That little bit of effort had me sweating, and pain radiated from the back of my leg and up into my lower back.

I didn't know what else I could really do at the moment, so I just waited, staring at the floor while I let my mind go back over what I had learned before passing out.

The Hunters knew how wolf-kind started. They knew how we became what we are, how it all started. I needed to get more information out of Ava, I needed to learn more that I could bring to William and the rest of my former pack. It probably wouldn't get me back into the fold, I didn't think there was any way for that to happen, but it was still information the pack should have. We should know more about ourselves than we did.

The sound of an engine approaching caught my attention and I raised my head toward the door. There was a quiet squeal of brakes then the engine stopped and a door opened. Footsteps outside echoed in my ears and the door slammed shut. The rustling of plastic bags then more footsteps heading toward the door.

When it opened, Ava didn't bat an eye to find me sitting on the couch instead of upstairs. She simply shut the door behind her, still dressed in her black boots, shirt, pants, and her Joe Rocket jacket. Grocery bags from a nameless store hung over one arm and she carried them over to the corner that served as the kitchen and set them down.

"Good to see you up and moving," she said without turning to look at me.

"Doesn't feel particularly good," I said.

"Not surprising. You've been out for a couple of days. Was starting to worry that you'd never wake up."

"Concerned for my safety?" I asked, surprised. "Not something I expected from you, to be honest."

"Not worried about you. I haven't gotten enough information out of you, and I really don't like playing nursemaid to a fucking invalid."

That got on my nerves a bit. "Oh, right," I growled. "Big bad hunter can't be a decent person and show a little compassion for another living being. That would just be beneath your hard assed persona wouldn't it?"

"Fuck you, asshole," she snapped and rounded on me.

I snorted out a laugh. "Thanks, but I think I'll leave taking it up the ass to you, Babycakes."

She growled, her eyes flashing angrily, and lunged for me. I'm still not entirely sure how it happened. One second she was in the air, the next I had grabbed for her wrists and twisted in my seat on the sofa. My leg screamed in pain but I ignored it and she let out a startled cry as I pulled her over. The next moment she was lying on her back on the couch and I was spread out on top of her, our faces so close that our breath mingled together.

She smelled of gun oil and jasmine, a far more feminine scent than I expected from her. The scents clung to her like a second skin and despite being pissed at her I was suddenly very aware of how close we were, the heat coming off of her body and the slow flush growing up her neck and cheeks.

"If I remember correctly, weren't you the one with a probe up *your* ass, getting your nads electrocuted when *I* saved *you*?" she snapped. I couldn't tell if she was turned on too, or if she was just pissed, but it was hot as hell. I pushed away with a pained grunt.

I sat up and dropped my head into my trembling hands. My arms and shoulders shook violently, and I couldn't make them stop no matter what I tried. What the fuck was wrong with me? Why was I shaking like a damned leaf over such a simple altercation?

When I felt a hand on my shoulder I jumped, I think. I couldn't be sure because I was still trembling so badly.

"Let's get you back up to bed," she muttered quietly and I wanted to pull away but I didn't have the strength.

I hauled myself to my feet, ignoring the hand she held out to help me, and carefully made my way over to the steep staircase leading up to the bedroom. I was sweating bullets by the time I got to the top, but I gritted my teeth and pushed the rest of the way over to the bed and collapsed onto it with a creaking of wooden timbers and a low groan of discomfort. I was a bit heavy for the bed, but it was a solid piece of furniture, so it held up admirably.

"Jeez," Ava muttered from the stairs behind me and I turned my head to look at her. "How much do you weigh, anyway?"

I shrugged awkwardly from my position laying on my back. "Last I checked I was close to four hundred pounds." Her mouth dropped open and I grinned at her. That was usually the reaction that I got when people heard that. She recovered quickly though and nodded.

"Right, I remember the doctors saying something about that before. It's how you people are so damned strong without being just ridiculously huge."

I arched an eyebrow at her and she shrugged. "Your abilities really aren't all that supernatural if you think about it. To be able to lift a car the way you can, your muscles would have to be extremely dense. Dense muscle equals large power from a smaller sized muscular structure. You'd be four or five times your current size to try to equal the kind of strength you have with typical human muscle mass."

"So the Catholic Church is the reason that we've been hunted for our entire existence?" I asked. "Why am I not surprised to hear that?" When in doubt, change the subject.

"That's not what I said before." She leaned against the wall next to the stairs and glared at me. "The Catholic Church may have converted the Druids to Christianity centuries ago, but since then the Crusaders have expanded far beyond the Church. After the Templars were nearly wiped out, we took it upon ourselves to go underground. These days the church doesn't even believe that wolf-kind exist."

I frowned and pushed myself further up on the bed with another quiet grunt so that my legs were no longer hanging off the edge. I was able to sit up against the headboard with a little extra effort.

"Alright," I muttered. "We need to sit and have a coherent conversation about this. You want information from me and I want information from you. Why don't we do that?"

She cocked her head to the side, green eyes peering intently at me for a moment.

"How so?" she asked, finally.

"You ask a question and I ask a question, rinse and repeat."

She thought about it for a moment longer before she straightened up and nodded sharply. "Sounds like a plan. Let's get you settled first. Do you need to use the rest room?" I almost jumped at the straightforward question and I thought about it for a moment before nodding, fighting back a blush that wanted to work its way onto my cheeks.

Without a word she stepped over and helped me to my feet. I didn't know why I was embarrassed. Using the bathroom was a natural part of the human or wolf-kind condition. Everybody poops, or in this case, takes a piss. There was no sense being uncomfortable about it, but for some reason her being in such close proximity had me flustered and that bothered me more than my mild embarrassment over my natural bodily functions did. See how circular my logic can be? It's infuriating at times.

I took care of business in a tiny water closet of a bathroom that I hadn't even realized was attached to the bedroom while she stood outside. I kicked my sweat pants aside after I finished and flushed and turned around, attempting to get a look at the bullet wound in my thigh in the small mirror hanging above the sink. A thick bandage, partially soaked through with old blood sat high on my upper thigh, just below my ass.

I needed to get a look at the wound and I needed to clean up too. I hadn't showered since before Ava's team grabbed me, and I was more than a little ripe. "I'm gonna shower really fast," I called through the door while stripping my shirt off over my head. With the shirt still partially covering my head I heard the door open behind me and Ava's voice.

"What was that? I couldn't hear..." she trailed off and I finished pulling the shirt off and turned to face her. The look on her face was priceless. Eyes wide and her mouth hanging open. Her eyes hadn't quite reached the level of my face, lingering more on the level of my chest and I could see the struggle in her face not to look lower. Her eyes flickered down toward my stomach and I grinned and cleared my throat.

She jumped, her head snapping up so her eyes met mine and I quietly repeated myself. "I think I'm going to take a quick shower. It's been a while since I had the ability, and I'd really like to get cleaned up."

"Ummm... yeah. Ok, you do that," she mumbled and started to look down but her eyes snapped back up again. "I'll go get something together for dinner and we'll eat. Talk after you're done?" She turned without waiting for a reply and beat a pretty hasty retreat after that. I couldn't help but chuckle quietly to myself. I didn't laugh nearly as loud as I wanted to, mostly because I was pretty sure that would have been the end of my life at that point, but I did allow myself a bit of amusement for a moment before moving on to the matter at hand.

Removing the bandage sucked, but I've dealt with worse, so I did so quickly and inspected the wound. A round puckered scab sat nearly in the center of my leg, angry and red around the area with what looked like a fading infection. I sort of remembered Ava forcing a handful of pills down my throat and saying something about them being antibiotics, but it was a vague memory at best and could have just been a fever dream. I refocused on the wound; the skin around it was angry as fuck and the veins were darkened beneath the skin. All together it didn't look good, not even a little bit, which was scary because if I were up, that meant it probably looked better than it had been and made me wonder just what Ava'd had to do to keep me going.

As for how the wound looked now? There wasn't shit I could do about it, so I shrugged it off and wedged myself into the tiny shower. It was barely wide enough for my shoulders. I carefully cleaned off, hot water pouring down my skin. I wanted to just stand there for a while, but I wanted to get some information out of Ava even more, so I cleaned up quicker than I wanted to. I shut off the water and climbed out, hanging onto towel rods and the sink cabinets so I wouldn't face plant. It was already rough enough that Ava'd had to help me in here.

I couldn't find any bandages in the medicine cabinet so I patted the area around the wound dry with a towel and redressed in the Sweats I had been wearing before. I left off the shirt though; it was too hot after the shower and the constant motion. Besides, I was about to get back into that bed and its layers of blankets, so I had no worries about being cold.

Ava was waiting for me when I stepped out with a couple of steaming plates, and I couldn't help but arch an eyebrow at her again.

"I wasn't in there that long," I said. "I'm surprised you're done already."

She shrugged unapologetically. "I picked up a couple plates of lasagna from a little place in town that I like. They were still in the car so I just warmed them up."

I nodded and limped my way over to the bed and climbed in. "I don't know how you fucking people do it," I grumbled, irritably and she frowned at me.

"What 'fucking people'?" she snapped and I winced and held up a hand in her direction.

"Sorry, no offense, I meant humans. I don't get how humans deal with healing so slowly. This is the longest I've ever been injured in my life and its absolute torture, I'm telling you!" I sighed in exasperation and slumped back on the bed, the blankets pulled down to my waist. There was a weird sound suddenly in the room and for a moment I looked around trying to locate the source.

It wasn't until I glanced in her direction that I realized where the sound was coming from and what it was in the same instant. Ava was laughing, and not laughing in a snide or condescending way. I'd heard that. She was really *laughing*. Honest, amused, laughter. Slumped in a chair next to the bed with her head thrown back, deep belly laughs pouring out of her slender throat, and I felt an itching in my palms as the desire to stroke the soft flesh of her throat came over me. Not to choke, or kill her, but to pull her toward me–

I squashed down that thought as hard as I could and reached for one of the plates while I waited for her to calm down.

"If you're quite done?" I finally spoke up after several moments of unabated laughter had passed. She looked at me for a moment, before going off into more hysterical peals of laughter. I sighed and shoved a forkful of food into my mouth. I had to admit it was good lasagna, and she had an even better laugh. The carefree sound of it made me feel a little better, and I gave myself a mental slap.

She was the *enemy*, dammit! Her entire life had been dedicated to killing my kind! There was no part of her that I should find endearing or attractive. I should be trying to get information out of her and then ditch her, or kill her. One or the other. Fucking hell, she wasn't laughing anymore.

I glanced up as the silence in the room suddenly registered and found her leaning forward in her chair, elbows on her knees with her chin cupped in her upturned palms. She'd taken off the jacket at some point, and was dressed just in her boots, pants and black shirt and the way the shirt clung to the curves of her body I found distressingly distracting.

"What?" I blurted out, surprised to find her staring at me so intently. It made me feel like a bug under a microscope.

"You're thinking."

I blinked, surprised by the odd statement, and beginning to feel that I would never be on an even keel with her. She had a way about her of making me feel off balance in all of our dealings and it really irritated the hell out of me.

"What?"

"You're thinking," she said again. "I can almost see the wheels turning inside that handsome head of yours. So why don't you go ahead and tell me what it was you were thinking about?"

I shook my head and shoved another forkful of lasagna into my mouth. I chewed quickly and swallowed down the still steaming chunk of food.

"Nothing doing," I said and she frowned.

"That wasn't entirely the deal, now was it? You give me information and I give you information."

"Except my thoughts had nothing to do with Mathias and whatever other information you might be looking for in regards to wolf-kind *or* the Hunters. So therefore, it doesn't fall under the conditions of our agreement. That being said, I'll kindly keep my private thoughts to myself, if you don't mind."

She continued to watch me, as if trying to catch me in a lie or something. Finally, she shrugged her slender shoulders and picked up her plate, leaning back in her chair and settling it in her lap. She took the fork in one hand but didn't start eating right away.

"So what *can* we tell each other?" she asked. "What more information is there that you need, and what more can you provide for me?"

I thought about that for a moment. To be honest it was difficult to tell exactly what we might have that the other could use. Information that would be useful, but at the same time, not endanger those we wished to protect. That was the trick. If I brought back information about the hunters to William, it had to be information that would be *useful*. Otherwise it was just a curiosity, but didn't help us to survive as a species any more than not knowing whatever it was in the first place had. So how could I get her to reveal secrets that would help us without her betraying her own kind?

"Well, how much are you willing to give me?" I asked and she frowned.

"How do you mean?"

"Well, you're a Hunter. That's obvious enough. I'm fairly certain you wouldn't be willing to give me information that would help my people wipe out sections of yours. That's self-defeating isn't it?"

"Not entirely." That got my attention. She would be willing to betray her own people?

"Wanna explain that?"

She was still frowning and started tapping the fork against the edge of her plate. It made an irritating sound, but I didn't call her on it, not wanting to interrupt her thought process.

"It depends on who's getting wiped out, I suppose. There are a few people back there that I *do* still like and trust. That I think might be able to see the truth behind what Mathias is doing. It might be possible to convince them that we've been lied to all along. But otherwise, the Templar chapter of the hunters appears to be rotten through and through. Helen certainly isn't any kind of saint, and Mathias needs to be dealt with more than anything else."

"Why are you so willing to kill Mathias?" I asked, curious. "He's been your leader for a long time, hasn't he? He's trained and taught you; mentored you…"

"And like I said, he also sent my brother to his death and told me that *your* brother is the one that killed him. Although, I'm not sure if he was lying about that, too… come to think of it."

"William?" I blinked. "William's never actually killed a Hunter. He's killed in defense of course, but never one we were positive was a hunter."

"Not William," she said, quietly, and the confusion I felt melted away. Romulus. She thought Romulus had killed her brother. I looked around us at the small cabin and thought of the neat and orderly arrangement. The attention to detail throughout the building and the dust that had still covered several surfaces downstairs.

"You said we were going to an apartment in Wisconsin." She nodded. "This isn't an apartment though." She nodded again, tears welling at the corners of her eyes that she didn't let fall. "This was your brother's cabin, wasn't it?" She didn't nod this time but her head lowered and I sat back and let her gather herself.

I could understand her hatred for me now. I still didn't agree with it, but I could understand it. If she had thought that Romulus killed her brother, a man that looked exactly like me, killed her only family... I could understand. How quickly she'd turned it around though... how she helped me. She must *really* hate Mathias Young.

"My brother is not part of the information you need to know. So I'd kindly appreciate it if we kept my private life, private," she said in a quiet mutter. I nodded, even though she still hadn't raised her head.

"We can do that," I said. "I didn't mean to pry but it does tell me a lot." I gave her another minute before I spoke up again. "What did you want to know?" I asked and she finally looked up and took up her fork again.

"What was the arrangement between Mathias, you, and your brother?"

I winced. "Not my finest moment, I'll admit. Declan had been running the pack into the ground. We knew that the pack was getting weaker and the internal politics were getting out of hand. We needed to do something, and Declan couldn't remain the Alpha. Something needed to happen, and neither of us could bring ourselves to directly challenge our father for the seat. It's frowned upon for a child to challenge his father for Alpha. It's seen as being power hungry. So, we thought we needed to find a more underhanded way, a sneakier way to remove him from Alpha. The only way to do that though, was through his death."

"So you arranged for Mathias to kill him?"

"We didn't know what we were gonna do. We couldn't think of any way to go about it that wouldn't directly come back to us. We couldn't think of a way to get around it. But then, one day, Romulus came to me and said that he had an idea, a possible way to remove Declan and the blame would fall on someone other than us.

"If a hunter killed Declan, then the blame would be directed elsewhere and we could take up leadership of the pack without looking like we were being power hungry brats trying to take over. We needed to be saviors, rescuing our pack from the chaos. We needed to *rescue* the pack, not steal it."

"So, how did Romulus get in touch with Mathias? I mean, how would a blood born contact *the* Hunter of Hunters in the first place?"

"I don't think he did," I said. "I got the impression that it was *Mathias* who contacted *him*. That was what I gathered from the discussion with Mathias before you came to the rescue." I shrugged helplessly, unable to really specify any further than that. I had always been known as the more level headed of the two of us. Between me and my brother, everyone had always commented that I had gotten all of the brains and control. It was uncomfortable for me to admit out loud that Rom had been the one to engineer just about everything. That I had been so much in the dark. No one, not even me, considered that Rom was smarter than we'd all given him credit for.

"So Mathias got in touch with the most insane Blood Born out there for... what? On a whim? Out of spite?"

"No. We've already established that he has plans for wolf-kind beyond killing them, like the Hunters have been doing for generations. Hunters have done nothing but hunt and kill us for a very long time now. So why would he suddenly change directions like that?"

She frowned and started working on her lasagna. We ate in silence for a few minutes while we mulled over our individual thoughts. I didn't know for sure about her, but my mind was spinning out of control and as hungry as I was, the fantastic food suddenly tasted like so much bitter ash in my mouth.

"The real twist," I said suddenly, "Is how he went about it." She shot me a confused look, urging me silently to continue so I set down my fork and organized my thoughts for a moment.

"Mathias was supposed to kill Declan. That was the agreement. Kill him and just make it obvious that it was a Hunter. Instead he killed Declan and left his weapon behind. He left the garrote." Her eyes widened at that and I bobbed my head in a nod. "Yeah, I know. He left The Hangman's signature behind like a big neon sign telling everyone that he did it."

"But why would he do that?" she asked. "It doesn't make any sense to advertise like that. It just puts him and his family in danger."

"Except he doesn't have any family except for Chloe. And he

doesn't feel anything more for her than he does for anyone else. She was always just another piece on his chess board."

"How do you mean?"

"I figured out that he intentionally put her in danger. Whatever he's doing with the wolf-kind. Whatever it is that he's up to, or trying to figure out, or whatever, he doesn't have the approval of the higher ups. He was planning on using her as his leverage against his bosses. He wanted William to kill her so that he could play her as the martyr, the victim, and play the sympathy card to get them to approve whatever it is he's already been doing under their noses."

Her eyes widened at that and then narrowed dangerously as her mind set on that new bit of information like a dog at a bone.

"Whatever he's doing he'll be in a ridiculous amount of trouble if the higher ups hear about it. So he's trying to find a way to get approval for his dirty experiments."

"That's the impression that I had," I said with another nod. "Mathias is dirty. We've gotta find out what it is that he's doing and out him to his bosses."

"I don't even know who his bosses *are*," she admitted. "I might be able to find out, but it won't be easy and it won't be quick either."

I gestured at my leg stretched out under the blanket. "Not like I'm going anywhere anytime soon. Here's the thing, Ava," I said, carefully using her name. "Mathias has proven himself to be both patient and methodical. We have to be just as patient in dealing with him, or we're going to screw everything up and tip our hand."

She frowned and chewed on her lower lip, a truly distracting action, so I looked down at the empty plate in my lap and set it aside, shifting my weight to try to get more comfortable on the bed. A sharp pain in the back of my leg caused me to bite off a curse and her head snapped up in my direction. Instincts honed by years of training had her running through the recent information and she glared at me.

"You didn't put a new bandage on your wound, did you?" she snapped and I shook my head.

"I didn't find any bandages in the bathroom so I just left it as is."

She let out an explosive sigh and set aside her own plate before she stood and disappeared quickly down the stairs. She was back within moments with a plastic bag from which she pulled sterile bandages, rolls of gauze, and tubes of a disgusting smelling antibacterial ointment, so vile, I could smell it through the tube and the intact safety seal.

"Roll over," she ordered, "Pants down." I arched an eyebrow at her again and her cheeks colored just a touch. "Your wound is too high up on your leg, you can't pull the leg up enough to let me get at it."

I nodded, slowly, a small smirk firmly in place but I didn't say anything. It wouldn't do to piss off my nurse, now would it? I tossed the blankets aside and pulled my sweats down, wincing several times before I had 'em low enough. She carefully stared at the ceiling until I rolled over onto my stomach.

The bed dipped slightly as she knelt on it, hovering over me. Her hands were cool against my heated skin, and I did my best to ignore the sensation. Chin resting on my crossed forearms, I kept my eyes firmly fixed on the wall in front of me and concentrated on not getting an erection. One thing most males would know is that if you're straight, and an attractive woman has her hands on you, your body is very likely to react no matter what your brain is telling you.

I closed my eyes; teeth gritted almost painfully, while she gently rubbed the ointment into my leg and pressed a bandage against the wound. She was in the process of reaching under my leg to pull the gauze around when her fingers briefly found the physical reaction I had been trying so desperately to hide from her.

She paused for the briefest of moments, her fingers exploring curiously for a moment before she realized what it was she was touching. I could tell when she figured it out because she yelped and jerked her hand back like she'd been burned and jumped to her feet.

"Alright," she said, speaking a bit louder than was really necessary. "Ummm... ok, you can finish with the bandage right? It's just wrapping and securing it in place. That should be easy enough."

She grabbed the trash from the medical supplies, stuffing everything back into the grocery bag it had come from. Then she grabbed the plates, and without looking at me, practically sprinted for the stairs.

"We'll talk later," she muttered and disappeared before I even had a chance to roll over. I stared at the stairs, and the empty space where she had been, then looked down at the offending erection that had sent her fleeing, red faced, from the room.

"Well, what am I supposed to do about you?" I muttered. With no answer forthcoming, I finished wrapping the bandage, pulled the blankets back over me and tried to settle down to get some sleep.

Chapter 14

Ava

I cleaned up a little downstairs and resigned myself to another night freezing my ass off on the couch. I flopped onto the leather and huddled, fully clothed, on my side beneath the thin throw blanket. With Remus at the height of his fever, I had piled the blankets on him so he could sweat the sickness out of his system. The generator would be shutting off shortly to conserve fuel, and James had never gotten to finish the cabin. The potbellied stove sat in the corner but the stovepipe hadn't been hooked up to the outside to vent properly yet.

I lay staring vacantly at the defunct stove, my cheeks stinging with the heat of my embarrassment. I couldn't believe I'd felt him up like that. I sighed out and closed my eyes. I can't even claim 'mystery solved' on what he was packing either. I'd seen for myself it was an impressive specimen of the male figure when Helen had him hooked up to that… that thing. My face flamed all over again, for a very different reason, as the white noise of the generator outside ceased.

I lay, breathing even and slow, hoping I would fall asleep before the chill seeped in and overtook me, but fuck my luck, it wasn't in the cards. I could feel the cold seeping in, and my mind wouldn't shut off for shit. All I could keep thinking about now was Helen, and what fuckery Mathias had her up to.

She'd never struck me as being, well, *insane*. I mean, she'd always been normal to me; to my team. I closed my eyes as if it would help banish the awful memory of the sheer glee on her face as she'd spun the dial on that switch and sent Remus shrieking. I'd seen a lot of shit. Put down a lot of animals in my time, in more than a few heinous ways, but I'd never seen anything like that and it was going to haunt me. I hugged myself and shivered for two fold reasons.

"Ava!" Remus' deep baritone called from upstairs.

"What?"

"Come up here," he ordered.

"Why?"

"Just come up here."

"Why, so I can make an ass out of myself again, or just so you can rub it in?" I muttered quietly under my breath.

"Wasn't planning on bringing it up at all, actually, but now that you mention it…"

I froze. I had muttered, below a fucking whisper, and there he was responding to what I'd said like I'd been speaking clear as day. I swallowed hard. The more time I'd spent with him, unconscious or no, the more… human, he seemed to me. It was becoming easier and easier to forget just what exactly he was.

"Ava,"

I cut him off, "What do you need?" I called out in a normal speaking voice.

"Just come up here… please."

I wasn't going to go, but the please caught me off guard and sort of suckered me into it. I sighed with mock harshness I didn't really feel. I was honestly tired. I'd been up, pretty much watching him, trying to help him get through the blood poisoning I'd inflicted on him with that shot, nonstop. I hadn't had more than a couple of hours of sleep at a time in days. It took a toll.

I dragged myself to my feet and up the stairs, stopping at the top.

"What?" I asked.

"Can you come here? I think this bandage has come loose and I can't quite get it."

"Really?" I asked plaintively in a sardonic tone of voice.

He looked right back at me, dark eyes neutral, giving nothing away before finally rolling them. I relaxed, marginally, and stepped to the bed.

He threw back the blankets and I reached out. Big mistake. I shouldn't have let my fucking guard down. He snagged me by the arm, lightning fast, and before I knew what was happening I was airborne and falling, swallowed by his massive arms as he tucked my back against his chest, the blankets falling in a heap over the both of us.

"What in the absolute fuck!?" I cried indignant.

"I'm never going to be able to crash listening to you shiver all night. Now shut up and go to sleep."

I struggled but he held me fast and I really didn't need to set him back on his healing time.

"Shh, relax Babycakes, you're safe. What's more, despite what my cock says, I'm not going to hump your leg or anything."

I choked, incredulous and started laughing as the image overtook me. A deep resounding chuckle reverberated through my back and chest.

I held still so I wouldn't hurt myself, or him, and waited patiently for him to fall asleep so I could slip away.

"It's not going to happen. You being all tense like that only serves to put my baser instincts on edge. You might as well relax and soak up some heat. It'd be nice if you kicked off the boots though. They're kind of digging into my shin the way I've got you."

"I always sleep in my boots," I said, and immediately wished I could take it back.

He stilled his slight shifting to get comfortable behind me and drew me back further into him. There went my hope that my dumb assed admission would get him to loosen up enough I could Houdini out of his grip. I know, I know. Wishful thinking with his speed and strength.

"Why do you always sleep with your boots on, Ava?" he asked me.

"I'd rather not talk about it," I snapped.

"You opened the door, Babycakes. Excuse the fuck out of me for walking through it. Might be a boon knowing a thing or two about each other in the long run though, don't you think?"

I scoffed and he pressed his nose into the side of my neck and breathed deeply. I froze.

"What are you doing?"

"You smell good. Like jasmine and gun oil. It's nice on you. Uniquely you."

I made an incredulous noise. Did he seriously just compliment me on my *smell*?

"God, could this be anymore fucked up?" I uttered to myself.

"Yep. You know, this is the first time I've even remotely had the upper hand in this little arrangement of ours. It's kind of nice. Gotta take the perks when they show up. I am now a firm believer in you might not get a second chance. You gonna tell me about the boots or not?"

I thrashed and he chuckled, I wasn't going anywhere and he knew it. I felt a hot flood of tears, an incandescent rage at myself for allowing it to happen. For being caught. I mean, I was sure he wasn't going to do anything per se, but it didn't matter. I didn't do helpless.

"Hey, easy. Breathe, Ava. Deep breaths. Nothing's going to happen here. I need the information you got and you need the information I got. It's as simple as that."

"Why you being nice all of a sudden?" I demanded acidly.

"I can taste the salt of your tears on the air. I can smell 'em. You don't cry. Something about this has set you off."

"Aren't you just so fucking perceptive?"

He snorted, "Wish I'd been a fuck of a lot more perceptive. I might still have a pack. I might still have my b–" he snarled and snapped his mouth shut, with a dull, audible click.

"Can I ask you something?" after we were silent for a time.

"What?" he snapped.

"Fine. I'll tell you mine if you tell me yours."

He was silent for a time before grudgingly, "Deal."

"James and I came up in foster care until we were both eight and the crusade found us. Some of the foster parents... You kept your shoes on in case you had to bolt from a perv, okay?"

"Ah, so that's it," he stated flatly. I frowned. I wanted to ask what the fuck he meant by that, but I was born at night. It didn't mean I was born *last* night. Yeah, him holding me against my will, in a bed no less, echoed back to some really bad shit. My brother and I had been lucky that they kept us together, but there was really only so much James and I could do both being fucking four, six and eight in the respective homes where we'd been saddled with pervy fuckin' foster parents.

"Ask your question, Ava."

"Do you miss him?"

He was silent and his grip on me relaxed, but I knew better than to test my limits. He was fast, even laid up.

"He was my twin. Of course, I miss him. I don't miss the fucked up shit he'd get us into. Rom was like a fuckin' mad bull in a China shop for the most part. He was real 'Hulk smash!' always doing shit without any forethought. Still, he was my brother, he was my twin, and when he died it's like I lost the other half of me."

We lapsed into a weighted silence.

"James was my twin," I finally confessed.

"You guys were twins?"

"He was older by nine minutes, but yeah."

More silence, and finally, he sighed out.

"Can we declare a truce?" he rumbled and I closed my eyes. It felt incredibly good to be warm again and my tiredness was breaking down my resolve to remain a bitch.

"You going to let me go?" I asked.

"Not tonight, Babycackes. It's cold, you're tired, and I really wouldn't be able to sleep with you shivering."

I sighed, and grated, "Yeah, okay, sure. Truce."

"What was that?"

"Don't pretend like you didn't fucking hear me when you fucking heard me whisper from an entire floor away, smart ass."

I could hear him smile, "Yeah, okay, fair enough. Truce tonight, but would you be willing to lose the boots if I solemnly pledge to defend your honor?"

"Don't push it."

He laughed, a booming shock of sound that suffused me with a different sort of warmth. I felt myself blush, was glad he couldn't see it, and I sighed out, closing my eyes and bedding down.

Probably only took a couple of minutes before I was out.

Chapter 15
Remus

Someone was going to die and it bothered me that I felt that desire. Seriously. She was a Hunter. I'd been over this a dozen times already. Not getting attached to the woman that tried to kill you just seemed like a rational and level headed rule to live by to me. But the story she told; the fear that obviously still clung to her… If she was as over it as she wanted to think she was, then she wouldn't still sleep in her boots.

So it'd left a scar. An invisible one, to be sure. But indelibly, there was a scar that her experiences had left on her person. And just the fact that she was afraid, the fear residing inside a person I had seen to be fearless, had me wanting to tear somebody's arm off so I could beat them to death with it.

For all her talk about not trusting me and thinking of me and my kind as nothing but animals, she'd fallen asleep pretty damned quick. So did she suddenly decide she trusted me? Or was it that she did, and she was just in denial? I sighed and would have raked my hands back through my hair but I didn't want to move for fear of waking her. Instead I tried to settle myself more comfortably on the bed and pulled her carefully until she was settled firmly against my chest and my arm was wrapped around her waist.

As much as I hated to admit it, it felt nice holding her so close to me. I felt protective of her for reasons I still couldn't wrap my brain around. Maybe because she'd taken care of me?

"You know, it's pretty much impossible for me to get any sleep at all with you doing that." I blinked, staring at the wall on the other side of the room for a moment before it sank in that Ava had spoken. I hadn't even noticed that she'd woken up. Or, had she ever truly been asleep?

"I'm not doing anything but breathing," I blurted out, slightly confused and more than a little offended as well. What, I couldn't even go to sleep correctly to her?

"Quit jabbing me," she grumbled and shifted her weight on the bed, grinding her ass back against me and the raging hard on that I hadn't even noticed, so distracted had I been with my thoughts. A low groan slipped from my throat before I was able to clamp down on it and I turned it into a low growl.

"If you want me to quit jabbing you, then you need to quit rubbing that hot little ass of yours against my dick."

There was a moment of silence before she moved again; grinding herself back against me even harder and I could hear the grin in her voice when she spoke. "But it's so much fun, seeing the cracks in that hard assed exterior of yours," she whispered.

My arm tightened around her waist and I purposely shifted forward, my dick sliding into the cleft of her cheeks, nothing but two thin layers of clothing between us, as far as I could tell. I couldn't feel any sign that she was wearing any panties under her tactical pants but I resisted the urge to slide my hand to her hips to check. She could still decide to kill me for touching her; I was pretty sure I was fast enough to prevent any *serious* bodily harm, but she was smart and had gotten the drop on me before. Calculated and patient, I liked that about her. It was another thing that called to me on a more basic level.

Whatever game she was playing, tease the wolf-kind, or something, I could play along until it looked like she was done. Besides, it wasn't much of a hardship on my end. Murderous bitch she may be, but I had come to learn that Ava was a woman of integrity as well, and wouldn't likely start something she wasn't willing to finish. If she had just ignored my erection we both would've fallen asleep eventually and that would've been the end of it. Still, by acknowledging it, and even pressing herself against me... the implications spoke volumes.

I held still. As still as if I were out hunting and the prey suddenly looked in my direction. I didn't want to spook her, I didn't want to derail the uneasy truce and trust that we had been building.

Seriously, when did sex become so damned difficult? It used to be if you liked someone you made a pass at them and if they responded we moved on. Nowadays a woman could seem completely willing to jump into the sack with you then suddenly they're turning around and accusing a man of rape.

With a woman like Ava I was pretty sure more bullets or perhaps sharp objects would accompany any accusations of dissatisfaction over my behavior.

"Seriously?" she muttered a minute later and turned onto her back so she could more easily look at me.

"What?"

"I'm laying here rubbing my ass against your dick and you're not going to do anything?" she demanded. "I'm basically telling you to shove that pipe you call a cock inside me and you're not picking up the clues?"

When I didn't say anything I could almost hear her roll her eyes, "I don't understand how you ever manage to get laid. Seriously, I'm trying to make what is probably going to be a monumentally poor life decision here, now would you get on board? I thought you men were all about that."

"Hey, in my defense most of the women that I find myself in such close proximity to haven't *shot me*," I protested. "Excuse the fuck out of me for being a little leery." I moved my hand to her hip and pulled. She moved easily, throwing her leg over my body and I rolled with her until a moment later she was straddling me as I lay flat on my back on the bed, the blankets shoved to the side as we moved. I could feel the heat between her legs hovering just above my straining cock even through our clothes.

She paused with the hem of her shirt in her hands and looked down at me.

"You understand this doesn't mean that I like you or anything, right? I'm just tired of fighting the attraction and it's been a minute since I've been laid. This is just convenience."

I gave her an incredulous look and almost laughed but I bit it back and simply drawled sarcastically, "Duh."

"You might be a long time enemy," she pointed out. "But you're hot, and I really need to blow off some steam."

"Understood," I muttered impatiently, "Lose the clothes already." She grinned and her hands came up, taking the shirt with them until she pulled it over her head and tossed the garment aside. My hands slid up her body, silken skin beneath my fingers until I was able to cup her breasts in my hands. As big as my hands were, her tits were still big enough that they spilled out of my palms, nipples already hard and wanting so I pulled her down with one hand on the back of her neck and brought my mouth to her left nipple.

A quiet sigh escaped her as my lips and tongue slid over her skin and I sucked at the hardened nub of flesh, tugging gently with my teeth causing her to jump slightly; a strained moan slipping from her mouth.

"It's been too damned long since someone did that," she muttered as I shifted my attention to her other breast, kneading both carefully in my hands. "I'm not here for the foreplay, big boy," she moaned a minute later and I couldn't help but grin against the soft skin of her tits. Gun oil and jasmine swirled around me like a cloud and the scent of her just turned me on even more.

"Well if you don't want foreplay you'd better lose the pants, and that means you gotta lose the boots. You're gonna have to be on top since my leg's still fucked up."

"Yeah, yeah, whatever," she drawled as she got off me, sitting on the edge of the bed, she pulled off her boots and let them fall. She stood and unzipped her pants. "Just an excuse to make me do all the work."

She shimmied her way out of her pants in that way that only a woman can manage and kicked them aside, revealing that she hadn't been wearing any panties underneath, just as I'd suspected. I used my good leg to push my hips off the bed and pulled my sweats down as best I could. The bloodlust of earlier switched to just plain lust as her pheromones perfumed the air along with the jasmine and gun oil I associated with her.

She grabbed the waist of the sweats and pulled, helping me get them off and tossed them on the floor by the rest of her clothes.

I have never felt more exposed in my life, save back in that crazy bitch's lab of terror, as I did when Ava turned to look at me, her jade green eyes sweeping over the length of my body. I know I'm a decent looking guy and that's without being vain or bragging. I'm aware that I don't have much to worry about in regards to my appearance, but somehow, under her scrutiny, I felt as if I wasn't measuring up somehow. It was a new sensation and wasn't helped by her slow walk to the foot of the bed. Fuck, it was hot watching her. I was already hard to the point of pain, and now we could add throbbing to the mix.

She stopped at the foot of the bed and eyed me for what felt like forever, I almost couldn't stand it when she lowered herself and started crawling up the length of the bed, her breasts hanging heavy as they brushed along my good leg, sending shivers through my entire body.

Eventually she reached even with my cock, giving me a sly grin before her lips parted and she took me into her mouth, sinking almost entirely down my length in one smooth stroke. My hips jerked of their own accord and shoved the last inch or so down her throat. She swallowed me whole, throat muscles contracting around my head and I groaned, my head falling back against the pillow at the sensation. Her tongue slid against my skin, soft lips wrapped tightly around me in a hot, wet, embrace.

She pulled her head back, sliding slowly back up my length until just the head was left in her mouth and one hand closed around me, stroking slowly up and down. Her tongue teased at the tip and my hands fisted themselves in the sheets beneath me as I resisted the urge to shove her head back down.

"I thought you weren't looking for any foreplay," I groaned. "Not that I'm complaining, mind you."

She chuckled quietly, my head still between her lips and another shiver ran through my body at the vibration. I groaned inwardly as she pulled her mouth from me to speak, "You do have a point," she admitted. She kissed the tip of my dick once and slid further up the bed. She leaned over, reaching for the bedside table and I cupped one heavy breast in my hand, kneading it gently. Her skin was incredibly soft and warm under my fingers, surprisingly so.

When she leaned back, moving her breast from my hand, she held a foil wrapped condom and I couldn't help but arch a questioning brow at her. "You were expecting to need one of those?" I asked, amused.

She flushed slightly but glared at me and slapped my chest once. "No, I wasn't expecting to need a condom when I brought you here. But this *was* my brother's place. I found the box in the drawer the other day when I was getting you settled in here," she huffed and tore the wrapper open. In just a moment she expertly rolled the condom down over my cock, threw a leg over my hips and positioned my head at her entrance. I could tell she was more than wet enough, I could smell how aroused she was and it was driving me a little nuts that she had all the control.

When she slid down my cock, her body spreading to accept me, my eyes slipped closed and I moaned quietly in unison with her. The heat of her body, the pressure of her pressing down on me. The smell of her; arousal, jasmine, and gun oil, all coalesced together in a heady cloud that I wished I could live on forever. Her skin was like silk beneath my fingers as my hands found her hips.

I couldn't force myself to keep quiet when she started to move. She didn't lift up off of me like some women would. No, instead she rolled her hips, a gentle motion that electrified my senses and had me jerking my hips against her, driving my cock deeper inside her.

"Oh ffffuck," she moaned. "That is exactly wh-what I need." She rested her hands on my chest, using me for purchase, nails digging into my skin as she rose above me finally, sliding almost completely off of me before slamming herself back down. Our bodies met with a loud slap and I felt every muscle slowly tense as the seconds wore into minutes. Over and over she rode me like an expert. I growled and sat up, bringing my mouth to her breasts. With her right nipple between my teeth I bit down gently and one hand slid between us. I placed my palm flat against her belly and my thumb searched through the slick folds of her pussy until I found that taught little nub of nerve endings.

I flicked it gently, once then twice. The third time finally sent her over the edge. When she came it was a quiet thing. Tightly controlled, just like she was. She didn't scream and moan and shriek like a banshee. She stiffened above me, muscles coiling like steel springs beneath silken flesh. Her pussy gripped me like a vice as she trembled and shook and I groaned quietly, emptying myself into the condom. *Too soon, way too soon...*

It took me a few minutes to catch my breath and when I did, I realized that she had slid off of me and was lying on the bed next to me, sweat gleaming on her skin. I pulled off the condom and tossed it in a small waste basket under the nightstand before I rolled back, pulled her naked body against me and pulled the blankets back over us.

"Bout fuckin' time," I muttered against her neck.

"Been waiting a while to fuck me?" she muttered dryly.

"No, happy you finally lost those fuckin' boots," I growled and after a moment of silence she started laughing quietly.

No other words were said or needed for a while after that. And eventually we dropped off to dreamland. I still needed to talk to her about going to see my brother, but that could wait until after we'd had a good night's sleep.

Chapter 16

Ava

I'd never slept with someone before, let alone nude. It was a new thing for me, and I couldn't explain why Remus, of all people, would be the one I would finally do it with. Let me explain; I'd hooked up, fucked, had plenty of sex in the nude, with plenty of dudes in the past, but when the deed was done? I'd always gotten up, gotten dressed and gotten the hell out. I didn't stick around and I sure as fuck didn't *sleep* with them.

When I'd stripped down and gone to fuck him, I seriously had only meant to do just that, get on, get off and get on with things, but the look in his eyes and on his face as I'd taken his length inside me had given me pause.

I'd really only meant to get rid of this hormone induced state of horny but something happened, something I couldn't explain and not going to lie, had me thoroughly freaked out. The way he'd touched me... His hands, so gentle where they'd cupped my breasts, where they'd caressed my skin, I couldn't explain it. I didn't understand it, but something had made me return it in kind.

I'd meant to fuck Remus Reese, but instead, I'd been intimate with him, and then I'd gone and really let my guard down and I had slept with him and now I didn't know what to do. I felt like I was wound tighter than a Timex and anxiety gnawed at me. Shit. *What did I fucking do? Who was that?* Because it sure as hell wasn't the Ava Martine that I knew.

He pressed his lips to the bare skin on the back of my shoulder and it stole my breath. He hummed and the vibration made me shiver.

"Feel like a second round?" he asked.

Yes.

"I don't know."

He chuckled, "Don't tell me I'm too much for you, Babycakes."

I turned to look at him, expecting to see a smile, expecting to see that glint of ornery in his eyes that said he was just trying to get my goat. Instead, what I found was a careful consideration. The hunter stalking its prey, except not… he wanted me again. He really, *really* wanted me again, and I was surprised to find that I wanted him too.

I wanted him with an absolute fierce ache between my thighs, the like I had never experienced before. I rolled and he rolled with me until I was straddling his lean hips once more.

"A man could get used to waking up like this," he commented dryly and his hands were back, smoothing across my skin, along the tops of my thighs, cupping my hips, tickling up my ribs to cup my breasts. I closed my eyes and enjoyed the sensation of his touch, a little afraid. What if it was still there? What if I felt the same way I had last night, last time we'd…

"Hmm, we doing this bareback or you going to grab another rain coat? I don't think I can wait to be inside you," his voice was rough with need and I smirked, an act of sheer bravado on my part.

"What if I like the view from up here?" I asked, arching a brow.

"You can admire it all you want, once I'm inside you," he said and I couldn't argue his logic. I leaned way over and jerked open the drawer while his hands smoothed over every inch of me he could reach. I straightened and tore open the condom wrapper with my teeth.

Remus' eyes lit up, a dark and hungry light that had nothing to do with food and everything to do with lust and sex. I was okay with that. I wanted him, too. I wanted to know if what I'd felt last night was a one off thing.

"God you smell phenomenal," he uttered when I raised myself up to roll the condom down his length. I paused, and he smiled up at me, that wicked grin that I'd found made me just that much more wet, firmly in place on his lips.

"What do I smell like?" I asked, and fitted him at my entrance, I glided down his length and his eyes slipped shut, his back arching slightly, fingers digging lightly into my hips.

"Like jasmine and gun oil," he grunted, quietly.

"Oh?"

"If grace had a scent, it would smell like you, Ava."

The compliment completely caught me off guard. I froze, and he sat up, pulling me to him and before I knew what was happening his lips were on mine and we were kissing. I stiffened, but he remained patient, brushing his lips lightly against mine, his cock rubbing against the inside of my walls, suffusing me with that golden glow, until I yielded in his grasp and kissed him back.

What was happening to me? Was I seriously falling for one of them? How could this happen?

"Shh, I got you, Baby," he whispered into my mouth and drove his hips up into mine ever so slightly. I cried out, an impassioned plea for him to do it again, and he smiled and obliged and I wondered just when I had ceded control to him.

Fuck. Remus Reese had seriously knocked me off my game. More so when he rolled us suddenly, so that I lay on my back in the cage of his gigantic arms. He pressed his cock deeper inside of me and I moaned, eyes slipping shut. *He felt so, phenomenally, good.*

"Look at me, Ava. I want to see those gorgeous fucking eyes of yours looking at me, while I do this," he practically growled, but it was still a human kind of sound.

I opened my eyes and stared into his as he moved inside me and there wasn't any denying it. I was fucked and it had nothing to do with his cock, and everything to do with the care he was taking with moving inside and over my body.

"Hey, no, fuck! What the hell is this?" His hands went to either side of my face his thumbs gently grazing through the wet at my temples. He stopped moving altogether and stared at me intently, and I knew he wasn't going to let me go until he had his answer.

"I don't know," I said and his lip curled in derision.

"Lying is a bad idea, Princess. Especially since I have you at a slight disadvantage." He thrust his hips gently between mine to illustrate his point.

"I didn't expect this," I said and was surprised that I *was* being honest with him.

"Expect what?" he arched a brow and the demand for clarification was crystal clear.

"I expected to fuck, I didn't expect you to be gentle about it, or that we'd be…" I swallowed hard; I didn't exactly want to say it out loud. It was real, but somehow, saying it out loud was going to make it more real.

"Be what? Good together?"

"Yeah." Sure, okay, we'd go with that.

"Is that a bad thing though?" he asked simply.

"I… I don't know."

He rested his forehead against mine and breathed out, a frustrated sigh, "Why you fighting it? I'll never understand that instinct some people have to fight something that should be simple. It feels good, right?"

"Yeah."

"Then that's all this needs to be for right now, right? Just something that feels good." He rocked his hips and I gasped, shivering with delight beneath him. "If it isn't anything more than it isn't anything more, it's that simple."

"Sure, yeah, okay…" I whispered.

"Can I kiss you some more?" he asked and my breath caught, I found it both strange and wonderful that he would ask.

"Yeah," I said evenly and then we were kissing again and *god* that added to it, deepening the pleasure, adding another dimension to his touch. People weren't kidding when they said kissing was intimate. For some reason it felt more personal to be kissing him than just a quick fuck would have been. He moved slow and deliberate, until I think we were both floating on that euphoric cloud of pleasure with no telling how much time passed. To be honest, I didn't care. I kind of wanted to stay this way forever.

We took our time this time, and when he finally slipped his fingers between us to tease my clit, to shove me off of that edge into a shining free fall, it didn't surprise me in the slightest when he was at the bottom of the cliff waiting to catch me *from* that fall. It didn't surprise me, but it did unnerve me.

We stared into each other's souls from inches away, breaths

mingling as we struggled to catch them, hands on each other, holding one another close and I was speechless. Remus dipped his head forward and pressed his lips to mine and I kissed him back, because I wanted to, because it felt right, and I wondered where the fuck along the line I'd lost myself, but then that ever present niggling voice of doubt entered the picture and, of course, shook me up even further by asking me: *Are you sure that you don't have that backwards? What if you aren't lost? What if you've been found?*

Well fuck, wasn't that an interesting question?

Chapter 17
Remus

The problem, I've always found, with using a fucking condom is there's always a delay from finishing sex, to relaxing in the post euphoria. There's a cleanup period of removing the damn thing and disposing of it that is just annoying, but in the end, she slid off of me and I was able to quickly take care of the raincoat and then pull her against me again. She lay along my left side and I was stretched out on my back so I wrapped my arm around her and pulled her, unprotestingly, until she was half sprawled across my chest, one slim leg thrown over mine.

We didn't say anything, neither of us could really think of anything *to* say, I guess. But after a few moments I felt her tapping on my chest with her fingers.

Tap-tap.

Tap-tap.

Tap-tap.

It took me a minute, but I finally figured it out.

"Are you following my heartbeat?" I asked and the tapping stopped for a moment, her fingers freezing in the air before resuming their motion.

Tap-tap.

Tap-tap.

"Maybe," she muttered and I held back a quiet chuckle. When did the bad ass bitch, Ava become... cute? I kept my observation to myself; she would probably have grabbed my balls and twisted them into a knot for me if I'd mentioned it. Instead I just pulled her a little closer, settling her across my chest and let my hand trail lazily up and down her back.

The sensitive tips of my fingers found numerous imperfections in her skin. Scars. And I traced each one that I could reach, mentally mapping them out as a history of Ava Martine. Each scar told a story about the path she'd led in life and they were as much a part of her as her jade green eyes or her dark hair.

"How long do you intend to stay here?" I asked.

"Until you're healed enough to travel. Then we should get moving," came the immediate response. She didn't even have to think about it so this was a plan that she had already considered. I imagine there were also back up plans and contingency plans mapped out in her ever active mind as well, but I decided not to ask and instead focused on the first plan.

"And where do you think we should go?"

"I want Mathias. Whatever he's doing, whatever he's done, he needs to be stopped. And he lied about my brother. He sent him to his death, or he had him killed, either way he lied and James died for it."

"Romulus too," I muttered before I could stop myself and she turned her head to look at me, a question reflected in her eyes. I sighed and settled myself more into the thick mattress. "Romulus would never have been put into the situation that he was in if it hadn't been for Mathias. We might have made our own choices, our own decisions; but the path was set before us by that manipulative son of a bitch. He wanted William to die. He wanted his own daughter to die. And instead, because of his half-baked schemes my twin died and I was banished from my pack."

I didn't realize that my voice had been rising until the end when I almost barked out the last couple of words and I took a deep breath to settle myself and let some of the tension ease out of my shoulders.

"Mathias has a lot to answer for. Whatever he's done to us is nothing in comparison to what he's done over the years, I can promise you that much. If ever there's a person that just needed to die, it's Mathias Young."

"You're preaching to the choir here, Fido." I arched an eyebrow at her at that but she simply gave me an entirely unapologetic smirk and continued blithely on. "But how are we going to do that?"

"I thought you had a plan."

"My plan stopped at getting us here so you could heal up. We need to keep moving after that because I honestly have no idea if they have other ways to track us and we've been sitting here for more than a minute. When you're on the run it doesn't do to sit still."

"So you don't have any idea where we should go when we leave?"

"Not in the slightest. I was just going to get us as far away from here as I could and then try to see if I can get ahold of any of my contacts in the Order. I'm pretty sure there are at least a couple that might still be loyal to me and we need all the information we can get."

I considered that for a moment, mulling it over and over. "Not entirely a bad idea. But there are a few flaws."

"Such as?"

"So you get the information you need. Like when and where Mathias is going to be so we can try to take him down, for example. How do you intend to do it?"

"..."

I nodded at the silence and let my hand continue sliding along her skin for a moment before I gave her bare ass a tiny slap and started to sit up.

"Come on, let's get dressed and head downstairs."

She seemed startled by the sudden shift in position and gave me a wary look. "Why?"

"Because I'm starved and we have planning to do, we can do that while I cook and we can eat while we hammer out the details."

I threw aside the blankets and swung my legs out over the edge of the bed, pushing myself to my feet before it even occurred to me to worry about my wound. I froze but the pain and weakness wasn't there. Well, it was, but not nearly as bad as I had expected. I was healing, *finally!*

"You're looking better for a guy that kinda seemed like death warmed over the other day," I heard her say behind me and I could almost hear the smirk in her voice.

"You're staring at my ass, aren't you?" I muttered and she laughed quietly but made no further comment. "I'm finally starting to feel a bit more like myself. Looks like the silver is totally out of my system. The wound itself is still gonna take a while to heal, but I'll be able to really move in a day or so."

"Thank god, I hate sitting still."

"You've mentioned." I pulled on my sweats and turned to face her. She was sitting up in the bed, blankets pooled in her lap with her breasts bare to the world, or to me, at least. And she seemed either unaware or just supremely uncaring that she wasn't bothering to cover up at all. I couldn't decide if that meant she was finally getting comfortable around me or not, but I didn't want to push things so I let it go and started toward the stairs. I briefly considered the broom handle I had been using as a crutch but decided against it. I could limp around just fine on my own.

"Come on, breakfast awaits us, Babycakes," I called over my shoulder and I grinned as an irritated growl floated from her lips after me.

In the small kitchenette I pulled out pots and pans, pulling open every drawer and cupboard in the place to find the essential tools I would need to complete the breakfast I had in mind. The food stores she had bought were relatively simple, so breakfast wasn't going to be anything fancy as I turned on the oven and cranked up the heat a bit.

While the oven was heating she came down the stairs behind me and seated herself on the couch, dressed once again in her black pants and shirt, watching as I busied myself with cooking.

"If we're going to get back at Mathias then we're going to need help, agreed?" I asked as I placed bacon and sausage on a cookie sheet covered with foil and shoved it all in the oven.

"Agreed," she said, a somewhat bemused tone to her voice as she watched me. I ignored it and grabbed a carton of eggs quickly cracking three into one bowl and six into another.

I started hunting around for a whisk. "You think you might have one, *maybe* two contacts still on your side within the hunters, right again?"

"Right again," she said and I let out a quick cheer as I finally found a whisk and started mixing the eggs together in their separate bowls. A bit of milk poured into each bowl later and I whisked them again until they were smooth.

Two frying pans made their way onto the stove and I turned on the burners, butter melting slowly as the metal warmed. I bounced on the ball of my left foot, keeping a great deal of weight off of my still injured right leg while I waited impatiently and checked on the sausage and bacon in the oven. Coming along nicely but nowhere near ready to pull out, so I turned everything over on the sheet and by the time I finished it was time to pour the eggs into the pans.

I noticed her watching me intently out of the corner of my eye but I ignored her scrutiny, choosing to focus on cooking so I didn't burn anything. The eggs were cooked carefully, I sprinkled some cheese in the middle and folded them both over into a pair of omelets. More cheese was sprinkled on the outside and within ten minutes I had two plates of omelets, and two plates piled with sausage and bacon dished up and set on the small table in the corner of the room.

I sat with a sigh and a slight groan and stretched my leg out in front of me. It really had started hurting more as time went on but I hadn't really noticed, so focused was I on the task at hand. On the plus side, it was almost completely healed. A few more days and it would only be a minor annoyance at best. A few weeks and it would be gone.

"Interesting." I glanced up, surprised at the sound of Ava's voice.

"Huh? What's interesting?"

"You."

I blinked, even more confused by the simple answer.

"You're gonna have to vague that up a bit for me there, Darlin'. Not sure it's obscure enough for me to latch onto your meaning."

She threw a balled up napkin at me, something I didn't remember grabbing but I guess she must have at some point and laughed quietly.

"I mean... I've always had this image of you." I arched an eyebrow at her and she dipped her head, changing tracts pretty quickly. "Not you, specifically, but wolf-kind. We're always taught that your people as a whole are... broken, I guess you could say.

Lacking in social skills outside their own kind, lacking in normal skills that regular humans regularly use to care for themselves, such as cooking."

She gestured to the three egg cheese omelet on her plate. "I don't know how many times I've tried but I have never been able to make a proper omelet before. I always over cook it or it falls apart, I've never been able to figure it out."

"So, in general you guys seem to have a lot of information about my kind that we lack, but the most basic information you have completely wrong? Is that what you're saying?"

"More than that, I think. It's not that the information is *wrong*. I mean ignorance isn't an excuse but at least it's an explanation. This isn't about the hunters not knowing how your kind aren't really that different from us. I think it's more willfully lying to us about your people. Trying to make sure that we see you as nothing but animals and not as, well, as human as you are."

I nodded. "It's easier to put down an animal than it is to kill another person. That makes sense. It's a kind of brainwashing, or desensitizing."

We ate in silence for a few more minutes. By the time we finished I was feeling a lot stronger and decided that I could weather the potential storm.

"So if you don't have a specific plan of attack from this point, I might have a suggestion," I ventured. I tried to sound casual about it, but I think the very reason I sounded casual set off alarm bells in her tactically inclined mind because she gave me a sharp look and slowly set her hands on the table in front of her.

"And what might that be?" she asked, deceptively calm.

"We need to go to Washington and see my brother."

She blinked, probably a bit confused. "But, your brother is dead?" It was more a question than a statement. I think I threw her off with my wording.

"Not my twin; he *is* dead," I said, ignoring the painful stab in my chest at the words. "My *other* brother. William. The current Alpha of the Pacific Northwest Pack."

"Are you out of your fucking mind?"

I pursed my lips and gave a thoughtful sort of nod. "Possibly," I admitted.

"I'm serious!" she snapped at me. "Did that silver fuck up your head or something? You've been banished from your pack if I remember the file correctly. That means you're on a hit list if you go back into the state and I'm a Hunter. Do you really think we'll get anywhere near William without getting our faces chewed off?"

"I think we've got better odds than I did a week ago, to be honest."

"Why? Are you suddenly not banished anymore for some reason?"

"Nope, still an Omega," I said, jerking a thumb to the brand on my chest. It still hurt, even months later it burned. That might have just been my imagination but it always felt like it was still burning. "Still banished from my pack."

"Then why do you think that we won't get killed just for setting foot in the state? On top of the fact, that doesn't Mathias have people watching the routes in? You really think he's not going to know that we went there?"

"Who gives a shit if he knows?" I countered. "You think he's ready to launch a full out offensive against the entire pack? And if we get someone to send out the blast and call in the rest of the pack from out of state? It's possible they're being watched anyway, we might want to bring them in to be on the safe side."

"So your pack might be ready to deal with the Hunters showing up, but you still haven't explained to me how you intend to get to William without getting killed just for stepping foot inside the state borders. How do you plan on not getting caught?"

I couldn't help the smug smirk that stretched my lips. "I don't."

She blinked and waited for a moment while I grinned at her. After several seconds passed where I didn't say anything she finally sighed in exasperation and glared at me. "I'm not going to ask," she growled.

"Then you're not going to know." I kept grinning and stood to clean up the dishes.

I'll give her credit where and when credit is due, she lasted a lot longer than I thought she would. Almost five full minutes before she finally growled angrily and burst out, "Ok, fine!" she snapped. "What do you mean you don't plan on not getting caught?"

"The entire goal is to get caught. If they catch me they have to take me to William to face judgement. I can't make my case to William unless I get in front of him, and there's no way I'm going to do that peacefully unless I'm dragged in front of him pending an execution order."

The look on her face was priceless. Her jaw dropped open, and she just stared at me, completely shocked. "So your whole plan hinges on them pausing to talk before they execute you for violating your banishment?" she asked and I nodded.

"It's not entirely as stupid as it sounds. They can't actually execute me without a direct order from the Alpha."

"And who is to say that he doesn't give that order over the phone before you can talk to him?"

I shook my head. "Not how it works. I have to be brought before the Alpha so I can explain myself. Yes, violating banishment is a huge deal, but there is no wolf-kind that would do it without a serious reason. My reason is the information that I can bring to him about the packs vulnerability and information on the Hunters themselves." I put the last of the dishes away after drying them and turned to face her, arms crossed over my chest. "I'm pretty sure he'll let me live for that."

She watched me for several long minutes, studying my face for any sign that I might be lying. Luckily I wasn't. Not completely. So it was easy for me to keep a straight face.

Unfortunately, she didn't buy it, even for a second. "Yeah, you're shooting in the dark and probably going to get yourself killed, so why would I let you drag me down with you?"

I sighed and pinched the bridge of my nose between a thumb and forefinger. "Look, there aren't a whole lot of other options. Your one or two contacts that *might* still be loyal to you isn't going to get us in to kill Mathias. But a whole pack of wolf-kind attacking the facility might just give us a chance."

"I'm not saying you're wrong," she said. "I'm just saying that it won't work and you'll just get us both killed."

I snorted a laugh. "That is saying that I'm wrong." She gave me a mock surprised look and put one hand dramatically to her chest.

"Really?" she mocked me. "Why I had no idea that pointing out that you're going to get us killed is the same as saying you're wrong."

"Yeah, yeah, cut it out. Look, the long and short of it is we need help and there's no one that has more of a vested interest in helping us than my brother. And he needs to know that Mathias has his hooks in the pack. They might need to move territory over this."

While we were talking a noise had been bugging me. Something in the distance so I hadn't given it much thought other than the fact that it was irritating, to say the least. But as the conversation had worn on it had been getting louder and just a moment before it had cut off, suddenly.

"Are you expecting anyone?" I asked suddenly as a set of car doors opened in the distance.

Ava leaned forward in her seat, suddenly wary at my change in direction. "No," she said. "Why do you ask?" Her voice was, once again, deceptively calm. I could practically feel her pulse quickening and her body reacting to the instinctive fight or flight response. She didn't even know if there was anything to worry about, her standard paranoia was working overtime.

"I just heard a car stop some distance from here still and the doors opened." I closed my eyes and tilted my head slightly, focusing on the sounds even I could just barely make out. Ava would have no way of hearing them.

"Three... maybe four people, I can't be certain. They're walking too close together." I opened my eyes only to find that Ava was no longer in her chair, instead she was standing by the couch, peering through the curtains out the window. When the hell did she get up? I didn't even hear her move and she was only a few feet away from me. Jeez the woman moved like a damned ghost.

"There shouldn't be anyone at all coming out this direction," she muttered. She turned her head, looking at a large black duffle bag on the far side of the room. In two strides I snatched up the handle and tossed the bag through the air in her direction. It landed heavily on the couch right next to her and she grunted a thanks, unzipping it quickly and began pulling things from the bag.

"Fuck," she hissed a minute later and I slid up next to her, ignoring the dull throb in my leg to peek through the curtains over her head. Tubby and some chick were standing outside. I'd never caught the girls name but they had both been in the truck when they were transporting me to that damned holding facility. I really didn't like that guy and without thinking my nostrils flared as I breathed in deeply.

It was that animal instinct that I couldn't get away from and in that moment it might have saved our lives.

"Those two shouldn't be here," she muttered.

"Who's the girl?"

"Her name's Harper; fucking bitch." The last was added with an impressive amount of disgust for just two simple words. Outside Harper sneered suddenly and that was all the proof I needed for the suspicion I had been forming.

"Ava, we need to get out of here," I hissed quietly into her ear, so quietly she probably only barely heard me. "Those two aren't human anymore."

She turned, her head whipping around toward me so fast I thought she was going to give herself whiplash for a second there and her eyebrows shot up toward her hairline in record time.

"Say what?" she asked, slowly and deliberately.

"I'm telling you, they're not human. They're wolf-kind."

Chapter 18

Ava

I didn't know how to feel, knowing that Donnell and Harper had apparently given up their humanity. I didn't honestly know whether I believed it, but as I assembled the assault rifle with mechanical precision, the look on Remus' face told me it was true.

Shit.

I did *not* want to kill one of my team, let alone two, but if it were me or them, I would do what I needed to do to stay alive. *Fucking Mathias.*

"What makes you say they aren't human?" I asked, ramming the magazine home and pulling back the slide on the side of my weapon.

"Silver in there?" he asked, by way of answer.

"Works on humans or were…" I stopped myself, "Wolf-kind," I amended.

Remus flashed a feral grin in my direction, "The way they're moving, fuck, a lot of little things. But mostly, I can smell them. Their scent has changed and it matches up with wolf-kind. You got that ready? They know you have it. They could hear you cock it."

"They know I have it because they're my team. They know almost all my secrets."

I wasn't happy about that, the good news is, my brother taught me to be paranoid as fuck before he'd died, so even though they knew *most* of my secrets, they didn't know *all* of them. Or the depths of paranoia that James had gone into before he'd been sent out on his suicide run.

"Almost?" he murmured.

I went nearer to Remus and said to him, "Good catch, Fido. Where they at?"

He growled low in his throat and instead of scaring me, the sound just thrilled me. I smiled in spite of myself and ditched maintaining my badassitude in front of him. Kind of hard to maintain after writhing on his dick last night and this morning.

"You going to use that, or do you just think you look pretty holding it?" he asked of the gun in my hands, I raised the stock to my shoulder and sighted down the scope out the window, choosing to ignore the jab. Harper and Donnell had gone low to the ground and were moving fast, faster than human, but I'd been trained for that. We all were. I sighted just ahead of where Harper was, gauging where she would be and pulled the trigger.

The gun went off, the explosion loud in the cabin with the smallest footprint ever and Remus clapped his hands over his ears. I breathed out and wasn't disappointed… Harper's head exploded in a cloud of pink vapor but Donnell had disappeared.

Shit.

Remus growled and I held very still, waiting, breath held, checking the area for movement. Finally, Remus gripped my elbow lightly and I slung my weapon over my shoulder. He placed a finger to his lips and I nodded carefully. We stepped back cautiously into the center of the room and waited, the seconds ticking by into minutes. They were waiting us out, but we had the benefit of cover and I wasn't giving it up.

Remus and I ended up back to back. I cleared my handgun out of its holster and held it, at the ready, waiting for something – anything to aim at.

"They're waiting us out. It's a siege."

"Yeah, it's what I would do." I murmured back.

I went to the bag and held up a flash-bang grenade and Remus' eyes widened. I gave him an evil little smirk and he rolled his eyes. He looked uncertain, and I could see the wheels turning, the calculations being made… finally, he nodded and covered his ears with his hands. I smirked and handed him the headphones I had in the bag; the ones I used out at the firing range. He smirked and shook his head and put them on, they would afford a hell of a lot more protection than his hands.

Me, I was used to loud noises and gunfire and they wouldn't affect me nearly as badly so I put up my gun long enough to pull the pin and get the party started; hurling the flashbang at the window – the glass crashed, Remus grabbed me and pulled my face into his chest to protect me from flying glass which was sweet but unnecessary, and I let him do it, focusing instead on having my guns out.

The flashbang went off, there was a muffled curse from outside, and we were moving. Remus kicked out the door and I followed his breech, a blur of motion off to my right. I aimed and fired without really looking, trusting that Remus was behind me. Besides that, I knew it wasn't him because the blur was colored similar to the woods around us. Logan's eyes widened as at least one slug caught him in the gut and he crashed into me. Hunter's camo explained the blend into the trees, but this was a bad place for me to be.

I went down and rolled, his fingers scrabbling at my jacket, the nails growing longer. I sucked in a breath, but just as suddenly as he was on me, he was gone. The sickening crunch of bone and he was dropped in a heap. A meaty hand closed around my upper arm and hauled me up to my feet.

I expelled the breath I'd drawn in and shouted, "Remus look out!" But it was too late. Donnell, or what used to be him, leapt from the small cabin's roof onto Remus' back and down we both went, Remus on top of me this time.

The breath was knocked out of me. I caught a smoldering flash of fury in Remus' eyes, followed by a quick dash of apology, before the hands to either side of my head started shifting, the bones sliding beneath muscle, popping and clicking like a demented bowl of Rice Krispies.

Remus reared up with a roar and threw Donnell off of him. Deep furrows bled freely along Remus' flank but his flesh began to knit back together almost immediately. I guess his healing superpower was back online. I didn't have time to think about it, I aimed and tried to ignore my body's need to breathe while I sighted down on Donnell. It was useless though. Remus and Donnell were as engaged as two wolf-men fighting could be, and it was clear that

Remus had this. Even with training, Donnell had become fat and lazy and I guess against another wolf-kind who was fit, it really showed.

They swiped and clawed at each other, hands the size of hubcaps swinging through the air. Each one with five fingers tipped with claws that could rip through bone as easily as they sliced through skin and muscle. And Remus proved it with a quick series of slashes. One, two, three. His left hand swiped across Donnell's face, drawing deep furrows all the way down to his skull. Right hand punched him in the left kidney as Remus side-stepped smoothly to give himself access. When Donnell reared back because of the pain Remus' left hand flashed out again and with a disgusting, wet sound, tore open his abdomen in one smooth strike. There was a squelch as a pile of ropey intestines poured out of the new opening in Donnell's stomach and splattered on the ground.

In the next second, Remus had gotten behind my former team member and with a triumphant, almost bark, tore out Donnell's throat. Donnell dropped to the leaf litter, writhing but he was healing. His throat was closing even as he attempted to push his guts back inside his own body. Damn it. I went over before Remus could break his neck and put two slugs into Donnell's skull.

I stood across from Remus who slowly shifted back to human, both of us panting. He eyed me cautiously, looking me up and down as if to gauge my reaction or mood. I raised an eyebrow at him and he pursed his lips into a grim line.

"We should go, in case there are more on the way."

"This way," I jerked my head in the direction where I'd left my brother's FJ Cruiser parked and Remus nodded. He made to walk past me but I stepped in front of him, holstering my gun.

"We should move." He went to go around me and I side stepped into his path again, only this time I stepped into his space.

"Ava…" he sounded impatient but I didn't care. This was important. I went up on my toes because he was just that fucking tall, and pressed my lips to his in a quick, chaste kiss. I went flat footed and looked at him pointedly. He regarded me; expression hooded and finally gave me a curt nod.

"We've gotta go, Babycakes."

"I've got you," I murmured and still went back inside to grab my bag of goodies. I threw it in the back of the truck and went around to the driver's side of the vehicle. Remus was already in the passenger seat.

He asked me, as I started up the truck, "What was that for?"

"Because you're right. We need some help, and your brother might be the only place we've got left to turn to. If that's the case, we're pretty much as good as dead."

"A last kiss then?" he asked with a smirk.

"I hope not," I murmured and turned on the truck and put it into gear. I was surprised to find that I meant it. I really hoped it wasn't. Remus Reese was starting to grow on me.

Who would have thought?

Chapter 19

Remus

Three members of her team were down and out. Three people that she'd worked with, fought with, and bled with. And here she was, with me, the enemy.

I cast another sidelong glance in her direction out of the corner of my eye. I wasn't entirely certain how I felt about her throwing in her lot so solidly with me. Before that point she could have gone back to her organization with a story about trying to get information out of me. She could have made up something at least. Now, however? There was no doubt that she had turned her back on them completely. Nothing sealed the deal more completely than killing some of their number, and helping me to kill them too.

There was no way that this wasn't going to get worse before it got better and I really didn't like the way things were going. I wasn't nearly as confident that William wouldn't just kill me outright as I made myself seem. But I had to fake it to get Ava to go along with the plan. Despite some misgivings, going to William really was the best possible solution to our situation.

Well... not even a solution really. More like step one of... who the fuck knew how many it would take? I bit back on a sigh, and turned my attention back to staring out the window before she caught me looking at her.

"You know," she said. "When you sit there staring at me, even out of the corner of your eye like that, it makes me feel like there's ants crawling all over my skin. That whole being watched thing."

Oops.

"Sorry, I didn't realize."

"What? That you were watching me? Or that I knew about it?"

"Both?"

"Well cut it out. If you've got something to say Fido, just spit it the fuck out already. This staring and looking away is driving me up the damn wall."

I hesitated for a second and she growled again, that growl I was really starting to enjoy hearing from her, and I bit back a laugh, gauging that laughing at her would probably not go over very well. "I just wanted to admit that this is a risky move. Going to William."

"You were faking the confidence. I know."

I blinked, turning my head to stare straight at her this time. "You knew?" She nodded, a small smirk turning up the corners of her lips. Lips that had earlier been wrapped around my- I shook my head roughly, trying to dispel the thought before it really formed and forced myself to focus. "And you just let me go on with the BS?"

"So your brother doesn't have to see you before you're executed?"

"No, he does. Pack law dictates it."

"But..." she said, sensing the unspoken sentences that should have followed.

"But that doesn't mean that he has to give me a chance to speak, or even that he'll listen if he does. It's a risk, but a calculated one."

"How so?"

"William isn't the type to shoot first and ask questions later, so to speak. He always wants all the possible information before making an informed decision. It's part of what will make him such a good leader for the pack. He doesn't fly off halfcocked, but at the same time..."

"This is a serious breach of protocol."

I nodded, "To say the least."

"We'll deal with it when we need to."

I considered her for another moment while she kept her eyes firmly glued to the road. "It's strange," I said a minute later and she glanced at me for a brief second.

"What is?"

"You. You've got a very blasé attitude about this whole thing right now. I find that to be somewhat strange behavior for you in the short time we've known each other."

"I do not have a blasé attitude," she insisted. "I've just come to understand that our options really are limited. It's either run for the rest of our lives from my people and yours, or take a chance that we can get out of this in one piece and take Mathias down in the process. If an option includes taking down Mathias, then that's the one I'm picking."

Revenge, I realized and nodded silently as I considered it. That was a motivation I could get behind. I was feeling a similar desire to want to kill Mathias Young. He had masterfully manipulated Romulus and I, and I really wanted to see him pay for all the misery he'd caused, and used us to do it in the first place.

I didn't like being fooled, especially not by someone like Mathias fucking Young. Fucking bastard needed to die. I really wanted to do it myself, and I'm sure Ava did too. Honestly though? I didn't give a shit who killed him anymore, as long as he ended up six feet under, I would be happy.

We didn't talk much for the next few hours. Only when it came time to stop for food or gas. At the first of those stops she pulled off of the road and into a truck stop's gas station. Turning off the SUV she tucked the keys into her pocket and then reached into the inside pocket of her jacket. That was when she paused, a frown marring her features and she pulled out a folded rectangle of dark brown leather, staring at it as if she had no idea what it was.

"Is that my wallet?" I asked.

She flipped it open and there, behind its clear plastic window, was my driver's license. "Apparently. I completely forgot I shoved it in my jacket when I went to get you back at the facility."

I shrugged and reached for it. Digging around for a moment I came up with my gold card and smiled. "Works in our favor. Gas and food's on me."

Without a word, but with a small smirk on her lips, she plucked the card from my hand and jumped out of the truck, telling me to stay when I started to follow after her. Before I could get annoyed she gave me a pointed look up and down and I glanced down, realizing that I was still wearing nothing but a pair of sweat pants. She had been fully dressed when we'd left the cabin. I think mostly as a byproduct of her childhood and training.

I settled in and sighed, exasperated with the whole situation but in ten minutes she was back with a pair of jeans, t-shirt, and another hoodie. Not my usual fair but it'd do, for now.

While she got the gas going I stripped out of my sweats, ignoring her low wolf-whistling at me through the window, and pulled on the jeans. I stuffed my feet into a pair of generic boots that she'd picked up and was as dressed as I needed to be for the moment. The boots were a little smaller than I liked, only a single size too large for my feet as opposed to the two sizes or bigger that I liked, but I could deal with that. The hoodie she had picked up however was a different story.

It was a solid white number that zipped up in the front and while it would fit overall, the sleeves were just too small. They wouldn't fit properly around my arms. I thought about it for a second before I shrugged and just ripped them off at the shoulders. I shoved my arms in the openings I had torn, pulled the garment on and zipped it up part way. The t-shirt I ignored.

"Not bad at all," she admitted a moment later when I got out of the fancy FJ Cruiser and stood before her; I flashed her a grin. Wasn't long before we piled back into the truck and hit a fast food joint before getting back on the freeway.

That was basically how the day went. Stopping for gas, or food, or restroom breaks, but otherwise heading steadily west toward Washington. It was weird how familiar the situation was, too. Seven months earlier I had made a similar trip. That trip had been on the back of my Harley, with Rom riding beside me. And we were the ones doing the chasing back then, not being chased. William, with Chloe who he'd recently kidnapped, had been able to keep ahead of us and got inside of the Washington borders before we were able to catch up to him more than just the one time.

It left me with a feeling I couldn't quite place. It wasn't nostalgia, but it felt similar to it. Maybe just wanting for a simpler time? Back then, even such a short time ago, the world seemed simpler. It was cut and dried. We do this to avoid that or to escape something else.

Now though... everything just seemed like the nastiest snarled mess of a knot that you could possibly imagine. In my hands I held many threads. William, Chloe, Ava, Mathias, the Pack... All of these different threads and I wasn't entirely positive where one started and any of the others ended anymore.

It took a little over a day, but eventually we rolled into Washington. I directed her to stop at a hotel in Spokane. We'd traded off back and forth on driving while the other slept and we'd made good time, but more than anything I wanted a shower and a good night's sleep.

And, to be honest, I really wanted a bed available to bury myself to the hilt inside the beautiful woman riding with me. Guess I was starting to learn how William could have so easily fallen for the daughter of a hunter. Ava was really starting to grow on me.

An impressive cloud of steam followed Ava out of the bathroom when she finished her shower. I glanced up from the TV where I hadn't really been paying attention to a news report on wildfires, and my finger jerked on the power button as I took in the sight of her.

She'd obviously dried off in the bathroom and had already pulled on her black pants again. The same ones she'd been wearing, I thought, that was all though. As she came out into the room her arms were raised, a towel in hand as she ran it over her hair, her breasts shaking slightly as she moved.

She dropped the towel and moved over to the room's single table where we'd piled some supplies from the truck; drinks and some food. Sitting in a chair she grabbed a bottle of water and leaned back as she twisted the cap off and wrapped her lips around the neck, drinking deeply.

I realized a moment later that my mouth was hanging open and I hadn't stopped staring at her since she'd entered the room. By the knowing look in her eyes I figured that was exactly the reaction she'd been looking for too.

"Having fun?" I asked her and she lowered the bottle, that same sexy smirk twisting her lips.

"Maybe a little," she admitted and I laughed quietly.

"Are you going to come over here, or am I going to have to drag you, kicking and screaming?" I growled and she shivered. With a quiet sigh she cupped one breast in her hand, kneading it gently and tugging at her already hard nipple.

"No dragging or kicking required," she sighed. "There *will*, most likely, be screaming." She stood and made her way over to the bed, hips swaying hypnotically for the few steps required to reach me. I was sitting up with my back against the headboard, still in my jeans but divested of the rest of my clothing and she quickly climbed on, straddling me once again. It really was beginning to become one of my favorite places to be.

Without a word she grabbed my head, taking a double fistful of hair and pulled my mouth against her breasts. My hands slid up her back, pulling her tighter against me and she moaned quietly when I flicked one hard nipple with my tongue. I'd noticed her nipples were sensitive before so I paid rather careful attention to them, and each time my tongue flicked over that hardened nub she would moan quietly and grind herself down against me.

I'd been with a fair number of women in my life; I am over two centuries old, but honestly, there wasn't a woman I could ever remember that got me as hard as Ava did without even trying. The feel of her skin and the scent of her, surrounding me. It was absolutely intoxicating.

I don't know when I raised my head to kiss her but our mouths were locked together, tongues dancing around each other, her breasts crushed against my chest. Reaching between us I undid the button on her pants and she yelped, surprised when I suddenly pushed her back and off to the side so that she fell onto the bed beside me.

Before she had a chance to react I slid down the bed and grabbed the cuffs of her pant legs and tugged, yanking her pants off in one pull. With her completely naked I tossed the pants aside and laid back down, rolling so I was on top of her.

We both paused and I could feel the nervous energy in her. The fighter, the *hunter* in Ava, didn't like someone covering her like that. She wasn't immediately thrilled about being pinned to the bed, helpless against my weight and superior strength. I held myself up on my elbows, keeping as much of my weight off of her as possible, but still. She knew the potential threat this position represented to her.

After a few moments where neither of us moved I started to move aside, to lay down next to her, but her arms came up and wrapped around my neck, pulling urgently at me. There was no way she could have made me meet her kiss but I didn't see any reason not to, so I went with it.

Her kiss was urgent, desperate almost, a low moan coming up from deep in her throat. I supported my weight on one arm, letting my other hand come up to cup a breast. A tweak of her nipple and another moan escaped her. I loved that. Every sound I could force out of her was just further evidence that her rock solid control could be shaken. To hear her cries of pleasure was damn near making me drunk with the power I could hold over her.

I grinned and started kissing my way down her body, letting my lips glide along her skin until I had settled between her thighs. "Fucking shit," she gasped when I first let my tongue flick across her clit. If her nipples were sensitive, they were nothing compared to that tight little bundle of nerves.

Her moans came longer and louder as I sealed my mouth over her, sucking gently and flicking my tongue while I slowly worked two fingers inside her. Her legs tensed and flexed, thighs alternately clamping down on my head and spreading wider to give me better access.

"God dammit." She grabbed a fist full of my hair and pulled my head up and away from her. "You're going to fucking kill me if you keep doing that," she groaned and I grinned and twisted my fingers inside her.

"You mean, that?" I asked and she squeaked, her eyes widening slightly.

"No, not that. Get your pants off and get your cock inside me, now." She really *was* demanding, but who was I to disappoint? I had my pants off in record time, and without tearing them; something I was inordinately proud of. By the time I turned back to her she was sitting up, a condom in hand and reached for my cock.

And of course, as things will go, it was at that moment that there came a loud pounding at the door to our hotel room.

Fuck. They seriously couldn't have waited till morning?

"Go away," I yelled, biting back a groan as she took me in hand and stroked the condom down over me. I prayed that it was someone from the hotel and they would just leave.

"Remus Reese, open the fucking door before I'm forced to break it down and kick your damn ass, Pup. I ain't playing with you."

"Fuck me," I groaned and flopped down on the bed next to Ava. Even through a door I would recognize that voice anywhere. The Arbiter, Markus.

"Who the fuck is that?" Ava hissed. Calm and collected as she was, she had already dived for her pants and was wriggling her way into them, an action that did some very enjoyable things to her anatomy from my view. When she saw I was just staring at her she reached out and slapped my shoulder. "What the fuck is going on Remus?" she snapped, eyes flashing angrily and I winced, sure that I wasn't going to hear the end of this one for a while.

"Remember back at the cabin when I said some of the pack would have to take us to see William?" I whispered and she nodded silently.

"Yeah, I wanted to talk to you about that. I don't agree with giving up the tactical advantage by letting them drag us in. Who knows what could go wrong?"

"Well that's them outside the door right now." The look on her face is one I'll never forget. Somewhere between dumbfounded shock and monumental anger. She was pissed at me, no doubt.

"How the fuck did they find us so damn fast?" she hissed as she jumped out of the bed and grabbed for her shirt. Forgoing a bra she pulled the black shirt over her head and yanked it down, eyes flashing dangerously at me.

"This hotel is run by a couple of members of the pack. I knew word would get back to them but I figured they would have waited until morning."

"I can hear you two, you know that right?" Markus called through the door.

I sighed and pulled the condom off, tossing it into a waste bin before I went over and opened the door. Behind me I heard a strange noise from Ava, probably in reaction to my answering the door completely naked, but I didn't really care. Nothing the old man hadn't already seen before anyway. Nudity wasn't as frowned upon amongst wolf-kind, as it was among humans.

When the door swung open Markus simply glared at me, steely gaze locked onto my eyes for a moment before dropping to take in the brand burned into my chest. Despite my insistence that it still burned, it had healed well over the months and was nothing but a scar. A scar that would probably never truly fade, but a scar all the same. It matched the new scar on the side of my face, a pale white line caused by the silver bullet that had first fired from Ava's gun the night her team caught me. Silver always left a scar, even when it healed up. Scars that took ages to vanish, if they ever did.

"You've got a huge hairy pair, coming back here like this Remus," Markus growled. It was strange to me, that in that moment, I realized I had kind of missed the old man's voice. He had one of those deep, gruff voices that you hear described all the time as belonging to those strong, upstanding types, salt of the earth and all that; he looked the part, too. His hair was a little grayer than it'd been the last time I'd seen him but he still appeared to be a man in his mid to late forties. Military style haircut and in good physical shape, the sort of muscular that his jeans and loose flannel shirt did little to hide. His stern expression was almost permanently etched onto his face as if it had been carved from marble. Yeah, I'd missed Markus. *Imagine that.*

He stepped forward and I stepped back so he wouldn't walk into me. He kept walking, so I kept backing up until he was all the way in the room and was able to close the door behind him.

As soon as it was closed, he growled.

Not like how Ava would growl at me, not even how I had growled at Ava in the past, that throaty kind of growl people do when they're pissed off. No, this growl came from somewhere deep, seeming to bypass his throat entirely. His entire torso vibrated with the bass tones of it and it was a sound no human vocal cords would *ever* be able to make. This was a growl that would send all lesser creatures scurrying for their dens in terror and it had the effect of sending an immediate shiver of fear up and down my spine.

Behind me Ava grunted again and I heard a slapping sound. I was reasonably sure she had just tried to pull her guns from her thigh holsters. The very holsters that she wasn't currently wearing, so her hands must have just slapped against her thighs instead. Markus didn't even glance her way, his focus centered entirely on me.

"Well?" he barked, suddenly. "You got a good explanation for this, Pup?"

"Mind if I get dressed?" I made a point of keeping my voice calm and even. No sense getting him worked up when he was already pissed. As Arbiter of the pack, Markus handled a lot of the ins and outs involved in maintaining a pack and a territory of the size that we had. *They* had, I corrected myself. The entire state of Washington belonged to the Pacific Northwest Pack, and that was by no means a small parcel of land. So issues were always dealt with swiftly and decisively whenever Markus could manage it.

"Make it quick."

I did. I practically jumped into my jeans, careful not to catch myself on the zipper and threw on the sleeveless hoodie. I ignored my boots for the moment and turned, sitting down on the end of the bed, keeping my hands in plain view and remaining as still as I possibly could.

"Markus, this is Ava Martine. Ava, this is Markus, the Arbiter of the Pacific Northwest Pack of wolf-kind. He's sort of William's right-hand man in dealing with pack issues."

"It's nice to meet you," Ava said as calmly as she could manage. I could hear her heart pounding and smell the fear rolling off of her, but she didn't let any of it show in her face or in her tone. Gotta say I was pretty damn impressed.

Markus nodded but still never took his eyes away from me. "You're an Omega, Remus," he snapped. "You were never supposed to return to your former pack's territory."

"Unless I had a very compelling reason to do so," I said. "I think those were the words that William used when he made me an Omega in the first place." I'd been thinking about it for a while now. William had to have had a reason for not ordering my death, as pack law dictated. He had to have had a reason, other than making me suffer with the knowledge of what I did; what I lost. He's not a vindictive kind of person. He wouldn't torture me without good reason, and I think I finally figured out what that reason was.

"And you have a reason that you think will stop William from ordering your death this time?" he asked, one grey brow arched questioningly at me. I nodded.

"We need William's help. We need the pack's help. And I needed to warn you, warn *William*…" I took a deep breath. "Salt the earth protocol needs to go into effect, immediately."

Both steely brows rose at that one but his face didn't change in the slightest otherwise. "Why in the hell do you think William would ever help you? After what you did?" he asked, ignoring my statement for the moment.

I took a deep breath and stood slowly, looking Markus directly in the eye as I sensed him subtly tensing in case I attacked. Without looking away for even a moment I spoke calmly and clearly. "We need the pack's help to kill Mathias Young."

Chapter 20

Ava

I was pissed, but I didn't let it show. Instead I schooled my face into a calm, neutral blank and waited to see how things would play out.

The older man looked Remus up and down, eyes narrowed in calculation, chewing his bottom lip. Finally, he nodded.

"Get her weapons and get down to the trucks. You two are coming with me."

"I'm not leaving my brother's rig behind; we'll follow you." I said curtly and he looked me over, raising an eyebrow.

"And who might you be to Remus?"

I gave him a nasty little smile and Remus sighed out, "Ava…" he intoned, pinching the bridge of his nose.

"Remus…" I imitated him and hoped it was fucking irritating. Yeah, petty, but I was seriously annoyed. The old guy, Markus looks like he was waiting for my answer so I gave him one.

"I'm the chick that shot him. I'm also the chick he's currently fucking; does that satisfy your curiosity?"

The older man's eyebrows shot up the same time mine crushed down. I had weapons at my disposal, the only trick was getting to them – I was *so* going to kick Remus' ass for this later down the line.

"Right then, you can stay with Remus – I'll ride with you two. Craig!" He called back over his shoulder.

"Yeah?" A voice called up from outside.

"You ride with us, have Grayson and Rory take my truck and follow us up."

"You got it, Markus!"

"You might want to get dressed and leave them guns right where they're at."

"I've got 'em," Remus grumbled when I set to pop off. He

collected my guns and handed them over to Markus, holding out my empty holsters to me. I pressed my lips flat and shook my head at him, taking the holsters and strapping them on. I would need a place to put my guns when I got them back, or a new pair later. At this point, I would be hard pressed not to shoot his ass again.

"Ava, just get dressed and let's finish this drive."

"Eager to die?" I asked.

"Tired is more like it, and eager to get the Pack on the move, to safety."

"Uh huh." Well it looked like those cross roads of cross purposes had come up much faster than I would have liked. Damn. Oh well, nothing lasted forever. I was surprised to find that it hurt more than I'd expected it to.

Remus caught my arm as I bent to grab my boots, "Chill out, Babycakes, it ain't over yet. Not by a long shot."

"Take your hand off me before I take it off at the wrist," I growled and he did, jerking back as if he'd been burned.

Markus scoffed a laugh and I sat on the edge of the bed, pulling on first one boot then the other, glaring at each man in the room in turn. I was vastly outnumbered with no real way of evening the odds against me.

I caught the solemn look on Remus' face and it gave me pause. I laced my boots to the knee and sighed out; maybe it wasn't just me and I was jumping the gun here. I picked up my bra and went into the bathroom.

"Hey, I would prefer if you stayed in sight, Sweetheart." Markus said after me.

"Deal with it," I grated and shut the door in all their faces. I pulled off my shirt and got my bra on, pulling the shirt back on over it. I caught my makeup free face in the mirror and frowned.

In the words of Elizabeth Taylor it was time for me to *"pour myself a drink, put on some lipstick, and pull myself together."* So I did just that. I turned on the bathroom sink, drank some water to clear the bitter taste out of my mouth and smirked when I heard the boys out in the room muttering.

"You can fucking hear me, you know I haven't gone anywhere,

you can just fucking wait." I told my reflection in a normal, controlled tone of voice. Then I picked up my toiletry bag, slipped the small Ruger LCP 380 ultra-compact pistol out of it quietly and into the cargo pocket of my pants on the left side.

I rattled through my makeup as I did it just to cover any small noises I made doing it and then I set about actually *doing* my makeup. Black liner, and fuck it, I went with a crimson lip. I'm pretty sure at one point I heard one of the guys outside the bathroom door ask, "Is she actually doing her makeup?"

I heard Remus' dark chuckle, "She doesn't give a fuck, it's one of the reasons I like her."

I threw all my makeup back into the bag, zipped it up and opened the door with it and hairbrush in hand. I'd used a generous amount of my jasmine perfume oil to hopefully hide the gun's smell and moved to my bag on the table. Shit. They'd been through it and gotten the other guns, Markus had most of my arsenal slung over his shoulder and tucked into his waistband.

I picked up my Joe Rocket and put it on, satisfied with the distribution of weight that let me know he may have gotten the guns, but he didn't get any of the other hidden treasures.

"Why you packing this much heat, Sweetheart?" Markus asked and I smiled, it wasn't nice.

"I'm a firm believer in the second amendment," I answered dispassionately.

"Ava's a Hunter," Remus disclosed, and once more I wanted to hoof him in his front butt. Motherfucker wasn't keeping anything back or to our advantage!

"I'm driving," I grated, shouldering my bag and leading the way out the open motel room door. I had the keys anyways. They were still in my jacket pocket. I went downstairs, the boys right on my heels and tossed my bag in the seemingly empty cargo area of the truck. I got into the driver's seat and Markus got in on the passenger side, handing weapons back to the guy riding behind me who passed it into the cargo area.

Remus got in on the passenger side behind Markus and I glared at him. He gave me a look that practically begged me to trust him but fuck that, he should know how this went by now. I started up the Cruiser and put it in gear.

"I-90 West, Sweetheart. Don't get any ideas."

"Can't police my thoughts, Grandpa."

We drove for a good long ways and even got onto a boat across the water. Remus made a surprised noise when Markus told me to pull off to the left and down a driveway. I glanced at him in the rearview and his face closed down into a neutral look that was pretty much unreadable.

I had no idea what he was up to, but I could only assume it wasn't good for me. *Fuck, fuck, fuckity, fuck!* I'd played right into this, right into his hands. My need for revenge all consuming.

Son. Of. A. Bitch.

There were two peo- wolf-kind, waiting at the end of the driveway in front of an impressive log cabin that would have made James give a low whistle and when I stopped the truck, Remus clued me in.

"William and Chloe, try to not be you, Babycakes."

"Fuck you," I uttered and he laughed quietly for a second.

We got out of the truck and the guy behind me, got out on Remus' side and shoved him forward. I hid behind the door while they drew out Remus, distracted and got out my Ruger. I came around the truck and leveled it, not really pointing at anyone in particular but I was enough of a distance that I would take at least one of the wolf-kind royal couple out before anyone got to me.

I gave a sharp piercing whistle to get some attention, and growls emanated from all five throats. I shook my head.

"Careful, my trigger finger gets twitchy when I'm nervous. You should ask Remus about that, I've already shot him once and I'm a might tempted to do it again seeing as he hasn't really filled me in on his plan all the way here."

"Ava…" Remus started in a low warning tone.

"Shut it!" I barked, "You had plenty of fucking opportunity, now before I go any further along with your tenant relocation program I want a few assurances."

The redhead and only other woman smirked a bit at me and

touched William's arm, "Let's hear what she has to say," she said levelly and I quirked an eyebrow.

"Practical like daddy, I see."

"Something like that. More like I can smell the fear rolling off you all the way from over here."

"Be stupid not to be afraid, five on one. Pretty sure I'm going to die here tonight and you know what? I'm okay with that. It's a much better option than being held captive, especially after what we did to him."

I didn't glance in Remus' direction, but I saw him frown out of the corner of my eye.

"Speaking of which, you should really listen to him, he's got some important shit to say and he's not lying."

There, I did what I could for him. I swallowed hard.

"Cause we're just supposed to believe a hunter bitch 'cause she says an Omega isn't lying to us?" the meathead growled, but we all ignored him.

"Why are you here with him?" William asked and he was sharp, once he got past his initial anger and started thinking.

"I don't know, why am I here Fido?" I asked Remus.

"Ava's the Hunter that captured me; she's got intel on Mathias, and these... facilities. Mathias had a deal with our father, William. He had a deal with Declan. In exchange for neutralizing threats to the territory, Declan was letting Mathias and the Hunters take pack members from the fringes."

"Why would he do that?" William demanded and looked startled.

"Experimentation, trying to figure out how you fuckers tick," I said.

"Put down your gun," William said and rubbed his forehead.

"You told me not to come back without a compelling reason, Little Brother, if ever there was one, this is it. You need to start the salt-the-earth protocol, now. The Hunters know where we are; they've been herding us, keeping us contained and *Dad knew it*. He fucking *helped* them, but Mathias got fuckin' greedy. Their deal wasn't providing him enough of our people. So he played Rom and me, and this whole thing is going to fall the fuck apart unless something happens. That's why I'm here, that's why I brought Ava here. I guess I wasn't clear enough on what needed to happen," Remus shot me an apologetic look and I scowled.

"Right, fine, what will it take for you to put up that gun?" William asked.

I chewed my bottom lip, "We're here for the mutual benefaction of each other's interests. We're not prisoners. You give me back my toys as a show of good faith, and you give me your word that you won't hurt him or kill him. That's the deal, then we parlay." William and Chloe exchanged a look.

"Damn, you must be giving her some really good dick for a *Hunter* to protect a wolf-kind," the meathead muttered.

"Craig," Markus said and hung his head.

"And I get to shoot *him*, first round in this gun is non-silver, a warning shot. What do you say?"

"I say you aren't shooting *any* of my people, silver or not, and I say yes to the rest until a time we find you're lying."

"She's not lying," Chloe said and I frowned.

"Not like you'd know anything about it, we were under the strictest protocols to keep you out of it. Mathias' orders."

"I know that, and you know that, and these guys know that, hell *everybody* knows that... I'm not saying you're not lying based on anything that happened before. I'm saying it because I know you're telling the truth. I see it on your face and in your eyes and I know that if my father trained you, that it wouldn't come out of your mouth if it weren't true. You may have been trained by that monster but I was *raised* by him... Put down the gun, let's go in and eat. Remus you look half starved."

Just like that, Chloe Young turned on her heel and headed back into the cabin, William looked after his wife, a smile on his lips that made me ache to see it before I shoved that lost little girl who had wanted things like that for herself, way back down inside.

"Ava..." Remus said softly and I glanced in his direction, his dark eyes raw and crackling with suppressed energy in the night, "Put it down, Babycakes, you got us in the door. Time to use words instead of bullets."

I put up the gun, "As long as I get to use bullets in the very near future…"

"Yeah, well, we'll see about that," Markus said darkly and he didn't sound at all happy about any of the information that'd been revealed.

That made a whole fuck of a lot of us. I put the small Ruger back in my cargo pocket and held out my hands.

Markus hesitated but William changed his mind, "Give them to her," the Alpha ordered, and just like that, I had my guns back and holstered where they belonged.

Remus shot me a look that screamed we would be talking about this later and I couldn't disagree, we really would be talking about this later and I couldn't guarantee it wouldn't get nasty.

Chapter 21
Remus

I followed William and Chloe as they walked up the river stone path to the front door and stepped inside. Ava was behind me, Markus walked next to me and Craig followed along behind Ava. Just over the threshold I heard her growl angrily and turned to see that Craig was practically stepping on her heels, so close was he following her.

"Scooby, you really want to back the fuck up before I'm forced to shove a gun barrel up your ass and empty the clip." Craig blinked and I snorted at the mental picture.

"I'd back up if I were you, Pup," Markus snapped. Craig was mid snarl, his lips curling in disgust at Ava when the sound of the Arbiter's voice cut through his anger. He seemed to shrink in on himself for a moment before he stepped back, giving Ava some space.

When all of us finally got inside the house I could see it hadn't changed much from the last time I'd been there. The bottom floor was still one large room with metal tables laid out in an orderly fashion. Tools and parts of various projects were scattered about, but it always looked like even that was done with an almost obsessive precision.

"I see you're still as anal about your workshop as ever," I muttered and William chuckled quietly. Chloe laughed outright and I stopped, startled for a moment, turning wide eyes to her. She must have sensed my reaction because she paused, one foot on the bottom riser leading up to the living portion of the home and turned to face me.

"What?" she asked, confusion written clearly across her face and I gave myself a firm mental shake.

"It's nothing, It's just... the last time we spent any time around each other, I don't think I once heard you laugh, at least not really."

The realization, or the memory, of what Romulus had put her through when last we'd encountered each other bubbled to the forefront of my mind and I couldn't help but frown. Pissed at my brother, and at myself for what had happened. This state was my home. This was where my family, for I would always consider this pack my family, lived. And it was also the place where I'd made the biggest mistakes of my life.

Romulus and I were caught up in the spider's web and made to dance to his tune before we were consumed by our own hubris. What had made us think that we could possibly have gotten away with our actions? Good intentions being what they were, I had more than paved my own road to hell with the bodies of my father, my brother, and even that psychotic bitch Lucinda, may *she* rot in Hell.

I blinked when I suddenly felt a gentle touch on my cheek and came back to the present as my eyes focused on the air above Chloe's head. She was such a tiny thing that I had to look down to meet her eyes and I could tell, instantly, that she had really grown from the scared, weak woman I had first met. Even then, she'd had had a core of iron inside her. That core had tempered into something stronger, wilder, and far more powerful than she had been in the beginning. And it wasn't just her status as Alpha Bitch of the pack that'd caused the change.

One glance and I could tell that it was her bond with William that had truly molded her into a powerful and beautiful young woman.

"Stop it, right now Remy," she whispered and her thumb stroked across my cheek, wiping away a tear I hadn't even realized had fallen. "Mistakes were made, lapses in judgement. You have, and *will*, continue to pay for your actions, but for now, you're coming to us as family… and you'll be treated as such by me and everyone here, *isn't that right?*" Her voice was calm and quiet until the end when she raised her voice slightly, a commanding edge to her words. Even though she didn't look away from me, I knew she was talking to the other wolf-kind in the room. There was a smattering of murmurs from the others including a quiet, 'yes, dear' from William and I almost snorted, amused by his cowed tone.

William may well be the Alpha, but he knew better than to cross his mate without a damn good reason.

"So come on upstairs," she said and turned from me again, a small smile on her lips. "William started cooking an hour ago when Markus called us, so food should be up soon."

We followed them up the stairs, Chloe leading the way with William behind her, his hands on her trim waist as he murmured something quietly into her ear.

The stairs opened up next to a small, but ample kitchen. It looked like some modifications had been made to the living quarters from the last time I was here. The left hand wall appeared to have been knocked down, and the room behind it, a guest bathroom, appeared to have been redone to expand the kitchen and to allow for more space. A *much* larger table occupied the area than the one William had near the kitchen before, back when he was still single. It had a distinctly feminine touch to it too; a crystal vase sat in the center with fresh cut flowers resting in it. The scent of the flowers, roses and lavender, were all but overpowered by the intoxicating aromas coming from the oven and from several pots that simmered quietly on the stove.

Ava sidled up beside me and reached up to hook a finger in my collar. Obligingly, I bent down to bring my ear closer to her lips and she muttered so quietly only I would have been able to hear, "Are all you wolf-kind males so homey and domesticated?"

I laughed. I couldn't help it, thinking of the omelets I had made just a day or so before. It was a deep laugh, one that I couldn't have stopped even if I'd wanted to, but it felt good to do it. It felt amazing, really, to find something amusing in the storm that surrounded us. The rest of the pack gave me a strange look, probably wondering if I was losing my mind but I just shook my head and waved them off.

Craig, the lunk, walked toward the hall and leaned against the wall directly across from the open kitchen, his arms crossed comically across his chest. I say comically because his arms and chest were so heavily muscled that he physically couldn't cross his arms completely, giving him an awkward look to what he must have thought was an intimidating pose.

I couldn't really say much, I was similarly unable to really cross my arms that way, my own muscles got in the way of it, but I had lost some weight in the last few months, not keeping up with my workouts while on the move as I would have liked. With wolf-kind strength it was difficult to really find some place to work out that didn't have specially crafted equipment. I couldn't walk into any public gym and hit the machines since the highest weight they could reach would barely serve as a warm-up for someone with my strength.

While William busied himself around the kitchen, Chloe led Ava to the table and offered her a seat. My girl gave a wary look at the layout of the room and chose the chair at the end of the table, closest to the hall. Grabbing the high backed wooden chair, she turned it so the back was to the wall and sat, still eyeing each person in the room with the wariness of a cat in a room full of starved, wild dogs. Can't say I could blame her, but her paranoia might just be perceived as insulting. Luckily William and Chloe had better sense than that and took it in stride. Markus frowned at her and Craig actually growled until Chloe shot him a sharp look and the sound died in his throat, choked off as suddenly as it had started.

"Sorry," he muttered and ducked his head a little.

Ava gave Chloe an appraising look, and I could see her opinion of the small woman had just gone up a bit. Even *I* was shocked. Chloe really had grown considerably, and I felt a little bit of pride in that. My brother had chosen exceptionally well in going with it when his wolf had told him that Chloe should be his mate.

"Alright, that's enough out of all of you," William said. "Everyone sit down and we're going to eat and talk this out. Remus you had better have some good information to part out here or I'll have an easy decision to make, which will make it twice as hard to carry out. You realize the position you've put me in by coming back here, right?"

I nodded. At least I'd be getting a last meal.

"I have one condition, if I may," I said after we had all sat down and William and Markus had covered the table with dishes piled with food. Chloe and William both gave me a look and even Ava shot a glance my way. I had taken the chair on the corner, what would have been to her right if she didn't still have her chair turned with the back to the wall. William sat at the opposite end with Chloe on his left, Markus between Chloe and I; Craig had taken the spot in the middle between Ava and William.

"You're in no place to be demanding any further conditions, Pup," Markus snapped. A vein was pulsing in the old man's forehead and I wasn't sure what would happen for a moment before William reached out and set a calming hand on the Arbiter's arm.

"I can't make any promises, Remus. You know that," William said, slowly. "What's the condition?"

I sighed and closed my eyes, taking a deep breath before I opened them and met William's gaze. "Whatever you decide to do with me, I don't care. Follow pack law and order my execution if you need to, I accepted that possibility before we started on our way here. But whatever you decide; Ava leaves here in one piece."

I should have seen it coming, honestly, I really should have, and part of me probably did. Maybe I had decided I deserved it, somehow. Maybe as another piece to add to my punishment?

There was a loud sound, an echoing noise that faded into insignificance over the ringing in my ear. I'll give one thing to the girl, for a straight up human, she had a wicked left. The slap that Ava threw was so hard that it literally tossed me sideways out of my chair; no mean feat when you're talking about a dude my size. I pitched to the ground, glad that I had seated myself so close to the hall so instead of landing on the hardwood flooring in the kitchen, I landed on the plush carpet of the hall.

"...you, Remus!" she was screaming when I could hear again. "Seriously, *fuck you*! You don't get to pretend to protect me, you arrogant piece of shit! Who was it that dragged your naked ass out of that fucking freak show lab? Who carted your heavy carcass out to the middle of nowhere just to save your sorry goddamn life? Get the fuck off! Let go of me!"

It descended into a chaos of voices after that. I heard a pained grunt from Craig and Markus' deep growl rolled together with

Chloe and William both trying to calm everything down.

"**Stop!**" I bellowed. Silence fell, like I'd found the mute button on the universe, and I slowly pushed myself to my feet. Craig was standing behind Ava, his arms wrapped around her and a nice shiner was already blooming on his face where she'd most likely caught him with an elbow. Markus had somehow moved around me, more likely over, and had her by the wrists, his hips turned so she couldn't easily kick or knee him in the balls. Chloe and William were both standing but hadn't moved from their spots at the table otherwise.

"She's entitled to be pissed at me, don't hold any of that against her. Markus, Craig, please let her go." I worked my jaw up and down for a moment, pretty sure she'd loosened a tooth with that hit but I was already healing, still slower than I'd like, but healing. My leg gave a twinge of pain and I sighed at the reminder that I still wasn't at a hundred percent.

Reluctantly, after a glance at William for permission, they let her go and returned to their seats. Markus even clapped a hand on my shoulder as he passed. A gesture of support? Maybe. An acknowledgement of my actions? Who knew? Who even gave a fuck anymore? I was reasonably certain I was going to end up dead after all of this, but I couldn't worry about it at that precise moment.

I looked to Ava and she just stood there, eyes practically blazing with rage, face flushed; chest heaving up and down with every breath. Her fingers flexed and relaxed rhythmically, as if she wanted to wrap her hands around my throat or one of her guns, and she couldn't decide which.

"I never would have agreed to come here if you were so certain it was a suicide mission. I didn't go to all the fucking trouble of saving your ass just to see you throw it all the fuck away."

"Thanks for just clocking me and not shooting me this time."

I sighed, when my attempt at humor got me nothing but a raised eyebrow like I should seriously not test her right that moment. I pressed on… "And I'm not throwing anything away, Ava," I said that last bit quietly; resigned. I felt like I was facing a wild animal, staying still and speaking in calm tones as much as possible seemed to be the way to go, and wasn't *that* ironic? I'm sure she would have hated the comparison but at the moment that's what it felt like.

"I'm not," I insisted when she gave me a disbelieving look. "My life doesn't matter; it's not worth shit in comparison to the hundreds of wolf-kind that make up this pack. In comparison to who knows how many that Mathias has already taken," She flinched at that, but I kept going, "If this information helps save them at the cost of my life, it'll be worth it."

"Nobody likes a fucking martyr, Remus," she snapped but she didn't say anything else and dropped back into her seat, arms crossed sullenly across her chest as she glared daggers at me. I rubbed my jaw for a moment and noticed William giving me a wry smile as I picked up my chair from where it had fallen and sat back down.

"Without causing any more outbursts," he started, "You have my word, Remus, that Ava will leave here unharmed, as long as she doesn't try to shoot or otherwise harm any of us then we have no reason to harm *her*." Chloe nodded and, with that settled, started dishing out the food that William had prepared. Ava looked over each person at the table, her brow crushing into a frown and her jade green eyes calculating but no less tempestuous.

For a few minutes the only sounds were of cutlery scrapping on plates and of people chewing. William had created four large casseroles. A dish containing pasta sauce, ground beef, peppers, and wide noodles all covered in about a pound of shredded cheese. It was a specialty of his that he was constantly tweaking and adjusting every time he made it. It was relatively simple to make and filling so it worked for a table full of wolf-kind.

Ava poked at hers, barely eating. I wanted to remind her that she should eat something, but under the circumstances I figured it was the last thing I should probably do, not if I didn't want to get the shit slapped out of me again. So I left her alone and turned my attention back to my brother as I loaded a second helping onto my plate.

"Time to talk?" I asked and he nodded, swallowing the food still in his mouth.

"As good a time as any. Let's start with salt-the-earth. Why should we abandon the territory all of a sudden? Mathias has obviously known where we are for some time. That was clear when he approached you and Romulus about Father."

I blinked. "I wasn't aware that you knew it was Mathias that'd approached us, not the other way around."

He shrugged. "I didn't, at least not really, not until right now at least. It just seemed logical. We've never been able to figure out how to find Mathias. I mean we knew where his house was, obviously enough," he glanced at Chloe and she gathered his hand in hers atop the table smiling at him with such love and devotion it was sort of breathtaking... and heartbreaking at the same time. *You nearly fucked that up so hard*, I thought to myself, but it still didn't cause me to miss what my little brother was saying... "But it was always considered too dangerous to do anything to him directly."

"Until you kidnapped Chloe," I reminded him and he winced. Chloe's smile grew more, not less, and she squeezed his hand in a show of support. "Probably not my best move, but at the same time, the best I've ever made. We've been wondering about that for a while now. Why hasn't Mathias made any kind of move after losing his daughter?"

"He can't admit to the rest of the hunters that he knew where the pack was, or how long he's known." I glanced at Chloe and apologized silently for the next bit. "Mathias let me piece it together when he interrogated me after Ava's team caught me in Chicago. He planned the whole thing."

"How do you mean, Pup?"

"When Mathias approached Romulus, it had more than one purpose behind it. He wanted to galvanize the Hunters into an all-out war against us. The idea was; when a wolf-kind stole his daughter and then killed her, he could use that loss to his advantage. That he could play the sympathy card to his superiors and get them to sanction the experiments he's been secretly conducting on captured wolf-kind."

"Experiments?" Chloe was looking a little grim but her jaw was set, lips pressed into a firm line. That stubborn will of hers was showing through again. "What kind of experiments? To what end?"

I explained everything I could, leaving little out but what that bitch Helen was doing to me when Ava came to my rescue. Nobody pressed for details either. Ava remained stonily silent through it all.

"Mathias and Declan had an agreement. The Hunters were protecting our territory for us. They have been for a while now. Ever hear of the Nevada pack trying to push into our territory a few years ago?" I asked and Markus and William both shook their heads.

"Guy in Chicago told me about it. Apparently they tried, and were wiped out. The community at large believes the pack was responsible, and our reputation has preceded us. Fewer and fewer wolf-kind try to come anywhere near Washington these days, and that became a problem for Mathias.

"The arrangement that he'd had with Declan was that he would protect our borders for us, and Declan would turn a blind eye to the wolf-kind being taken from our area, maybe he even gave Mathias a few of our own now and then as payment. But with how the others in the country view us as unbeatable, they've stopped trying to come up this way. Mathias' need for subjects was outweighing the number he could get his hands on without tipping people off anymore.

"That's why he wanted Romulus in charge. He knew Rom wouldn't care and would just give our people over to him. Mathias is gearing up to attack the pack in its entirety. You need to get the email blasts and the phone tree going to the rest of our people out of state. We have no idea how much Mathias knows. If Declan told him where the other members were, they could be in danger. We definitely are."

Williams face was grave, his third helping lying forgotten on his plate as he listened to me. Even Markus was starting to look a little gobsmacked and Craig's mouth was hanging open, a forkful of food forgotten half way between his mouth and his plate.

"Chloe?" William asked a moment later and, without a word, she got up from the table and disappeared down the hall. Ava craned her neck around the corner to watch her go.

"She's going to start up the messages to the out of state members of the pack, and to get local members to gather here," I muttered when she turned back to give me a questioning look. She nodded but the angry glare quickly settled back onto her face a moment later. She hadn't forgotten that she was royally pissed at me.

"What else do you have for me?" William asked.

"That's not enough for you?" Ava snapped, cutting me off just as I opened my mouth. "He's bringing you information to try and save your entire damn pack and you're looking for more?" she scoffed a disgusted noise.

"Ava," I said in a warning tone but she ignored me and just glared at William who met her angry stare with a calm one of his own.

"You're worried about him, aren't you?" he asked and Ava blinked, obviously startled at the odd question.

"W-what?" she stammered for a half a second before she clamped her teeth together and glared at him some more. "What are you talking about?"

William just smiled. "Absolutely nothing at all," he assured her, which only served to piss her off even more. "No, the information he's brought, with you backing him up, I have to say is compelling enough, especially in conjunction with the research we've been doing over the last few months. We've been piecing together for a little while that Mathias knew way more than he should have and the fact that Declan was the one giving him the information doesn't entirely surprise me, and fits the picture I've been building. "All of that means you more than get a reprieve from pack law, Remus. I knew you would come through." The last he added with a wide smile and all of us present just stared at him as if he'd suddenly sprouted a second head.

"You manipulative little bastard," I whispered. I couldn't stop the words as they slipped out even if I'd wanted to. "You did it *on purpose*. I was starting to think so but... for you to just confirm it like that," I shook my head. "You know, you're starting to act a little bit like Mathias yourself."

"I'll take that as a compliment, under the circumstances. But, yes; when I branded you an Omega, I did have the hope that something like this would happen. Maybe not exactly this, but I'd hoped you would look for a way to right your wrongs and bring us something we could use. It wasn't like I could go looking for answers as Alpha, am I right?"

"So you just used and manipulated your own brother to save your own fucking hide?" Ava snapped. "God, I don't know who's more fucked up at this point, you or Mathias."

"The difference between Mathias and I is that he threw his daughter to the wolves, literally, for no reason other than to further his own goals," William snapped, all levity gone from his expression and his tone. "I didn't want to have to order my brother's death when by all rights *I should have*. Remus is no saint; I did what I could to keep him alive in the only way that I *could*, that the pack would *accept*. Was it a shit thing to do, planting the idea that he might find some redemption? Sure, but I could only hope that he would survive and figure it out on his own. I did the best I could to give him a chance to *live*, and to forge something new for himself." He looked Ava up and down for a moment and I felt the low growl erupt from my throat before I heard it as his eyes swept over her.

I choked the noise off as soon as I realized what I was doing and everyone's eyes snapped to me. Markus, Craig, and even Ava's gazes all held shocked surprise. Only William gave me a smug, knowing smile. "Looks like he's done better than I'd hoped, I'm glad for that."

He turned his attention back to Ava. "Back to what you originally said though; no, I don't expect more for his safety. I think Remus has done admirably and that's more than enough for me, but Markus said something about you two needing the packs help, and that hasn't yet been addressed, so if I'm not mistaken, you have more for me?" He said the last to me as a question and I nodded.

My little brother had pretty much masterfully put Ava in her place and she looked like it was leaving one hell of a bitter taste in her mouth. Still, I could see the wheels in her head turning and I had to wonder if that were a good or bad thing. I couldn't spend too much time speculating, not with William and Markus staring at me expectantly.

"We know where Mathias is. Or where he *was* at least. He might have moved on, but either way, there's a large facility where a chapter of the Hunters lives and operates from. Ava might be able to help get us in, but the two of us won't stand a chance against the entire place on our own. We need help. Especially since Mathias has started making wolf-kind out of some of the Hunters."

Williams's eyes narrowed dangerously and Markus actually flinched at that one. "He's doing what?" the old man asked, aghast.

I stabbed a finger in Ava's direction. "When she broke me out of that place, we were attacked by two wolf-kind in the parking garage. After that we went on the run and eventually had to hide out in a cabin that used to belong to her brother. I was in rough shape and we needed to lay low so I could heal. We were forced to go back on the move when three members of her team showed up and they'd all been moon forged into wolf-kind just like the fuckers back at the facility."

"And you're sure they weren't wolf-kind when they captured you?" William asked curiously.

I scoffed and Ava scoffed with me. I waved a hand dismissively at him. "Not a chance. I'm not so stupid that I wouldn't have noticed. The smell alone would have tipped me off."

"No offense, but I am what I am and after hunting you fuckers for as long as I have been, I would have known if one of my own damn team had turned." Markus gave Ava a dirty look and Craig growled again.

"Knock it the fuck off, Scooby, before I find a newspaper."

Craig went to stand up and William barked, "Enough!" He fixed his eyes on Ava and asked her, "Could you please refrain from threatening my people while you're in our territory? There is no guarantee that I could keep them all from going off the deep end and tearing chunks out of you."

"I can take care of myself," she said defensively but I could see her visibly cool. She wasn't normally so out of control. What was her deal?

William nodded, and made a humming noise in the back of his throat. I'd heard him do something similar hundreds, if not thousands, of times in the past. It was William's way of acknowledging what you'd just said without having to actively agree or disagree with it.

He suddenly stood, hands placed flat on the table in front of him. "Look," he said. "Long and short of it is, this isn't something we're going to hash out right now, not without a full exploration of our options. It's three in the morning by my watch so why don't we all get some sleep? Markus, Craig, we'll see you both tomorrow morning. Come by around ten and bring the Betas with you. We'll need to go over how salt-the-earth is going and fill them in on some of the details of what's going on."

"Yes, Alpha," Craig said and snapped to attention before he made his way around the table and took Ava by the arm. He paused when I turned and glared at him.

"If you don't want me to shove that hand so far up your ass you'll be able to scratch your nose with it, then I suggest you take it off her right this fucking second," I snarled.

"Down boy, I can take care of myself," Ava cocked her head to the side and I saw the small pistol in her hand, which, she had pretty friendly with Craig's balls.

"You may rip my arm off, and I may die, but I'll do it with the satisfaction that I took everything that counts to you with me."

"Craig..." William's tone had a hint of warning to it and Craig slowly released his grip on Ava's arm. A glint of light told me when she slipped that little mini pistol of hers back into her pocket. William's shoulders relaxed and he hung his head, pinching the bridge of his nose. Craig backed off.

"Your people stop threatening me; I'll stop threatening them, deal?" Ava leveled William with a steady gaze.

"Deal," William said wearily.

"Still stands, you two need to come with us. We'll take you to a hotel and guards will be placed outside the door," Markus said unhappy.

"Oh stow it, Markus," Chloe snapped, returning from where she'd gone. "I do believe I said that while here, Remus would be treated as family and you don't make family go to a freaking hotel."

I was impressed. William had held onto his temper longer than I remember him usually managing but there it was, bubbling to the surface with his next words, "You know as well as I do that Remus poses absolutely zero threat to me, and if he vouches for Ava then that's good enough. Craig's been nothing but a shit," he put up his hand staving off Craig's rebuttal, "Not without reason, *she is a hunter*, but…"

"But he's an Omega!" Craig sputtered indignantly. The way he said Omega was like he'd suddenly caught a whiff of something foul smelling, his lip curling into a disgusted snarl.

"And he's my *brother*, who's brought us valuable information that could help us land a solid blow to the Hunters and a Hunter who appears willing to give us inside information. That alone means you need to *cool it!* He's gone above and beyond to help the Pack after we branded him Omega and deserves some fucking leniency." He turned to me and Ava, "You and Ava are welcome to stay in the guest room, Remus," he added the last to me directly. "You know where everything is so I'm just going to show these two out," he finished in a hard tone and with an added glare to make his point clear to the other two wolf-kind.

"Thanks, g'night, William; same to you Chloe." I didn't say anything else or stick around to watch the aftermath; I just made my way down the hall and motioned for Ava to follow me.

The guest room was down the hall, twenty feet from where we stood and I opened the door, ushering her inside before I followed her and closed the door quietly, but firmly, behind me. The room was relatively simple. Queen sized bed with two nightstands, a closet and a dresser and a small door on the back wall that I didn't remember seeing before. A quick glance revealed the room to be a bathroom. Another obvious addition to the house since I had last been there. Fresh towels hung on a rod bolted to the wall and the shower was stocked with soap and shampoo. Everything one might need.

When I walked back into the bedroom I didn't see Ava. Senses immediately on alert I spun as a small sound reached my ears from behind me only to find the sole of her boot planted firmly in my chest as she gave a hard shove. I stumbled backward, more from surprise than from actually being shoved by the force of her kick. It was enough though for the backs of my knees to catch the bed and I fell, flopping onto my back. I winced as my leg gave a sharp twinge again, but a moment later it was the least of my concerns as Ava landed on top of me, straddling my chest.

"What the fuck do you think you're playing at?" she hissed at me. "Trying to protect me from the big bad wolf?"

"Something like that."

"You don't get to protect me," she snarled. "I'm not some delicate fucking flower you need to put in a glass house safe from the world. I know it's a fucked up place with dangerous people in it. I was prepared for that when we came here."

"William and Chloe aren't fucked up people, Ava. They're family. And aside from that, I don't think you were really in any danger to begin with. Me, yes, it was possible, but not you."

"Are you serious!? Setting aside why you think they wouldn't kill a hunter that's responsible for they don't know *how many* deaths of their kind, if you knew it was a suicide mission for you, why would you come back here at all?"

"Because they needed the information."

"You could have called him. You didn't have to drag us half way across the country for this shit."

I arched an eyebrow at her, ignoring just how damn sexy she was to me when she was legit angry. "You honestly think that's a conversation that we could have over the phone?" I mimed dialing a phone and held my hand against my ear. "Hello? William?" I said. "Yeah, it's your brother, you know, the one that got our dad killed and helped force you into a situation where you had to murder my twin in order to save your mate and secure yourself the position of Alpha? Yeah, there's a problem we need to talk about–"

Before I could finish she sat up and her arm swung back. When her hand flew at me again I didn't let it land this time. I reached out and snatched her wrist in one hand. "The first one was for free. I deserved it for not telling you the whole situation and surprising you like that. But just because you got to hit me once doesn't mean we're going to make a regular thing out of it."

"Fuck you, Remus," she spat and tried to pull her wrist out of my grip. I held on tight enough that she couldn't pull free but tried not to squeeze too hard, I didn't want to hurt her.

"In a minute, Babycakes," I muttered and she growled angrily at me. Probably not my best move but damn she was hot when she was pissed. "Seriously, I'm not going to apologize for wanting to keep you safe. You slithered your way into my life so you're just going to have to deal with a little protectiveness now and then, get it?"

"No!" she snapped and started tugging harder. Her free hand came around and her nails raked down my chest before I could stop her. Four lines of heat bloomed across my skin in the path left by her nails. Heat that grew rapidly into pain. Pretty sure she broke the skin with those and the wolf inside growled.

My throat vibrated as I answered the mental growl with a verbal one of my own and I rolled, pushing her off of me until I was covering her again. Her wrists were held to the bed above her head and she kicked and fought, twisting and squirming in my grip. Her lips pulled back, baring her teeth and her head started to dart forward to bite me.

"You *really* don't want to do that," I warned her and something in my tone made her pause. Her head jerked back, pressing hard against the mattress for a moment before she suddenly smirked and jerked forward again. I leaned as far back as I could, my hands coming off of her wrist and she reached up to shove me. I fell right off the end of the bed, the collar of my hooded sweatshirt hooked by her fingers. A loud tearing sound filled the room for a moment as the front of my shirt tore away at the zipper.

I stood and pulled the tattered remains of the garment away, tossing them aside before I dove back on the bed. Ava turned into a hellcat, all teeth and claws and nearly impossible to hold on to through her squirming and fighting. Her hair tossed back and forth and her eyes glinted in the light from the single lamp by the bed. She tried to punch me but I caught her fist. Somehow we had both ended up on our sides, facing each other, with our legs tangled together.

"You don't get to try to protect me," she snapped again and

pulled back to punch me. I caught her fist again with a loud smack as her knuckles struck my palm. "You don't protect me, *no one* protects me." She pulled back again and paused for a moment, her eyes locked on mine from only a few inches away.

A moment later her hand darted forward and I almost flinched, but instead of trying to punch me her hand went to the back of my head and she pulled herself forward until her lips crashed into mine. There was a hunger to her kiss. A passion different from lust or simply wanting to get laid. It was almost desperate. She was still angry; her nails digging into the back of my scalp as her other hand gripped my shoulder. She shivered and trembled, almost as if she were afraid.

"Ava," I pushed her back slightly. "Ava what's going–" she cut me off by pressing her lips to mine again.

"I don't want to talk about it," she growled a minute later. "Just shut up and deal with it."

I gave myself a mental shrug and pulled her shirt up and over her head. She lifted her arms obligingly and I grabbed the front of her bra, tearing it down the middle rather than try to fight with those stupid little hooks on the back of the damn thing. She grunted quietly as her breasts spilled free into my hands and a low moan worked its way up her throat when I gently rolled her nipples with my thumbs.

She rolled, coming up on top of me again and I went with it until I was on my back. When I went to sit up though she planted her hand on my throat and shoved hard until my back slammed back into the mattress. I let out a low hiss a second later as she raked her nails down my chest, definitely drawing a bit of blood that time, but I *really* didn't care.

I don't remember entirely when she managed to tug my pants down but suddenly they were bunched around my knees and she was tugging at the button on *her* pants. When I noticed she was having some trouble with them I decided enough was enough. I was hard as a rock and I wanted to be inside her more than just about anything right at that moment.

I shoved her off of me and she let out a surprised shriek as she fell, landing with her back to me. Reaching out I grabbed the waist of her cargo pants with both hands and pulled, tearing them right down the middle so I could easily pull them and her panties down, it took me a minute to get her out of her damn boots, to get to the *and off* portion of things.

"Come here," I growled and laid down on my side, pulling her back until her back was pressed against my chest. She lifted her left leg slightly and reached down between her legs to grab ahold of me, stroking my length a couple of times before positioning me at her entrance. I don't think either of us even realized at the time that we'd completely forgotten to grab a condom but I know neither of us cared at that particular moment.

When I sank slowly into her, it was while fighting off the urge to just slam my cock into her. I wanted to, I wanted to so bad, but she was only human and I didn't want to hurt her.

"More, dammit," she panted and pushed her ass back against me.

"Be careful what you wish for," I muttered and let my hand find her hip, holding her still as I pulled halfway out of her and suddenly shoved myself back inside, sinking all the way to the hilt in one hard thrust. She grunted and her body shook, fingers clenching in the comforter on the bed.

"Son-of-a-bitch," she groaned as I pulled almost entirely out and slammed back in again. I set a heavy pace. Our bodies slapping together. One arm snaked under her to wrap around her body, my hand tightly gripping her breast as my free hand slid down her stomach to find her clit. I flicked it gently with one finger as my dick slid easily in and out of her. With each thrust in she groaned in a rhythm broken by the sound of her ass slapping against my stomach. When I ran the tip of my finger over her clit she bucked against me, muscles clamping down on my dick like a fist, almost making it difficult to move inside her.

I growled and opened eyes that I hadn't realized I had even closed. I was taller than Ava, by a fair amount, but it was mostly in the legs. With her positioned as she was, my chin was even with her shoulder and the first thing I saw on opening my eyes was that gentle curve just where her neck sloped into her shoulder. I leaned forward and pressed my lips to her skin, savoring the taste of her and the scent of jasmine and gun-oil that would forever cling to her body.

Her moans had grown louder with every thrust and she squeezed me harder, really making me work to fuck her. I let my finger gently slide across her clit again and her hands found mine, pressing them hard between her legs as she let out a frustrated groan.

"God fucking dammit, Remus," she growled. "Don't fucking tease me; I'm so fucking *close...*" she trailed off into another low moan and I grinned, finally attacking her clit with a firm, steady stroke.

I think it only took a half a dozen times rubbing my finger across that incredibly sensitive bundle of nerves. When it happened, she almost seemed to explode; she let out the loudest shriek I had heard anyone make in a long time and I slapped a hand over her mouth to muffle the sound. At the same time I could feel her pussy spasm around me, squeezing my dick in a rhythmic measure as she came and I forced myself into her one last time through the tightly grasping muscles and, buried as deep as I could get, waiting as she came around my dick.

I kicked my pants and boots loose, somehow, without pulling out of her and pushed, rolling us until she was lying flat on her stomach, my knees on the bed between her legs. As she came down from her high I started stroking in and out of her again, that pressure slowly building up that told me I was going to find my own finish soon. She grunted every time I shoved forward and took a deep breath when I pulled back, as if my dick slamming into her was actually pushing the air out of her lungs. Her fingers clutched at the bed spread, twisting and knotting the material in her fists.

I grabbed a fist full of her hair and she let out a choked shriek as I pulled her back, up onto her arms. Holding my weight on one hand I wrapped my free arm around her waist and held her tightly as I slammed myself into her one last time and buried my face against that intoxicating curve of her neck.

The world disappeared around me, my eyes sliding closed as all my senses centered on the woman in my arms, the feel of her body against me and surrounding me. She clamped down on me again as I emptied myself inside her and I shuddered violently at the sensation.

When I was finally able to get my breath back, I carefully slid back and away from her, both of us letting out a shuddering gasp as I slid out of her and stood, heading quickly for the bathroom to grab a glass and a washcloth. The cloth I soaked in some warm water and wrung it out after filling the glass with cold water. Back in the bedroom I handed her the glass and she took it, looking bemused as I gently cleaned her off with the washcloth.

"Done?" I asked a minute later and she nodded, handing me the empty glass. I tossed the washcloth into a clothes hamper in the bathroom, drank a glass of water myself and returned to the bed to find that Ava had already pulled back the blankets and climbed under them so I turned the light off and slid in behind her, wrapping my arm around her and pulling her back against me again. "Come here," I muttered against her smooth skin, still warm with the flush of good sex.

She wasn't nearly as stiff and rigid in my arms as she had first been the other night at the cabin. But she definitely didn't relax immediately against me, either. "What is it?" I asked after a minute. The tension in her back and shoulders was pronounced to someone with my senses. A regular person might not have even noticed it.

"I'm sorry," she muttered so quietly that even I almost didn't hear her.

For a half a second I wanted to tease her and pretend I hadn't heard but I decided caution was the better part of valor and simply asked, "For what?"

"For slapping you at dinner. And for trying to punch you."

I shrugged one shoulder. "Pretty sure I deserved the one at dinner. A bit at least. You've got a hell of a left, by the way."

"So I've been told." I could almost hear the smile in her tone. It wasn't a bright, happy smile, but there was a distinctive lightening in the set of her shoulders, as if some weight had just fallen away.

"And don't worry about the others either. I'm fairly sure you had your reasons. But I'm not looking to pry. I figure if you wanted to talk to me about whatever it is you would," I muttered. "Some people would say I should ask you about it, try to get you to open up, but I figure if and when you want to, you will. You know now that I'll be here when you do, so why don't we leave it at that and get some sleep?"

There was a tense silence that stretched out to nearly a full minute before the last of that tension in her body suddenly melted away. She turned in my arms until she was facing me and the single window let in enough moonlight to make out the pensive expression on her face as she looked at me, studying my face in the dark. She leaned up and pressed her lips to mine again, and I had to say I was finding myself more and more pleased to find that the kiss she gave me before we left the cabin really hadn't been our last.

Her body formed easily to mine, all soft skin and gentle curves, breasts heavy against my chest as she draped herself across me. Her tongue dueled with mine for a moment, fighting for dominance until she finally bit gently at my bottom lip and pulled away. She opened her mouth as if to say something but a moment later her lips closed again and she laid down, her head on my chest and one arm wrapped around me. One leg came up to lay across mine as I settled onto my back and I wrapped my arms securely around her, holding her within the cage of bone and muscle.

"Sleep, Babycakes," I muttered and she snorted a small laugh, slapping my stomach lightly.

"Jack-ass."

Within minutes we were both sound asleep, and I can't remember the last time I slept so deeply.

Chapter 22

Ava

I slept, *hard* and when I opened my eyes in the morning it was to a deep, dark set peering back at me. Remus' fingertips ghosted along my exposed skin, trailing along my body in a pleasing touch that didn't fit at all with his physique.

"Good morning," he murmured and I felt my guard go up.

"Morning," I murmured back, unsure.

He sighed out and his face became resigned, "Want to talk about it now?" he asked and I didn't. I really didn't, but I guess I kind of owed him *something* for my weird assed behavior of the night before.

I wasn't used to feeling things for people. I didn't know how to quantify it, or know what to do with it.

"I don't want you to protect me," I blurted.

"I got that already, Babycakes. You want to tell me why?"

Because James protected me with everything he had and look where it got him...

"You don't have to tell me," he sighed and I could hear the disappointment. His fingertips stopped their soothing idle travel and he splayed the hand on my hip.

I closed my eyes so I wouldn't have to look at him, and spilled my truth, "Because protecting me gets a whole lot of people – people I *care* about, dead. I don't want anyone else to die. I don't want *you* to die."

He exhaled and his hand moved away, I opened my eyes and expected him to get out of the bed when it shifted, but that wasn't what he was doing. He reached for me, and wrapped those tree trunks he called arms around my body, pulling me tightly against him. He rolled me beneath him and looked down into my face, dark eyes carefully searching.

"Care about you too, Baby," he uttered and pressed himself between my thighs and inside of me. I shuddered in his grasp; eyes locked to his as he slipped his length inside of me, so slowly, so carefully, I thought he would never find the end. He wouldn't let my gaze go, not to kiss me, not for anything, and I found it to be crazy intimate.

"What are you doing?" I gasped and he smiled, his coal black eyes warming as much as they were capable of.

"I'm making love to you, I think it's time you learned what that felt like." He dipped his head and silenced anything I would say with a kiss. Probably the gentlest kiss I'd ever received.

I brought my hands up and let myself have this, wrapping my arms around his shoulders as he slowly moved in and out of me, his lips finding that sweet, sweet, spot on the side of my neck that left me gasping. The entire side of my body his lips were on became awash in tingles and I twined my legs around his lean hips and let out a gasping moan that sounded suspiciously like a plea. A plea for this warm, soft place I was in to never end.

Remus pulled his lips from the side of my neck and one of my arms from around his neck. He placed a gentle kiss in the center of my palm and guided my hand between us. He watched me, a subtle heat and silent command in his dark eyes to touch myself and for once, I wasn't difficult and simply did what he asked.

I found my clit with my fingertips and played with myself, letting that energy spiral and coil between us, winding us up and tighter together. Remus smiled and his eyes slipped shut, head bowing as I tightened around him. He kept the slow steady rhythm of his thrusting up, and I think it was the expression on his face that pushed me over the edge more than anything else.

Pleasure and joy, appreciation and desire, he looked at me and I saw devotion and I lost myself. To my orgasm, to his touch deep inside of me, but mostly, I lost myself to Remus; the important part anyways. The part of me that I had always held in reserve no matter what.

Fuck... How could I let this happen?

I shuddered beneath him as he slipped free of my body and

sighed. He immediately gathered me against his chest like some kind of porcelain doll and as much as I wanted to be pissy about it, I couldn't. It felt too good.

"Make you a deal," he said, voice low; the timbre of it soothing... which automatically made me suspicious.

"Depends on what it is," I said carefully.

"We protect each other. I'll protect you, you protect me... partners, from here on in. As far as I see it, Ava, we're there already. What do you say?"

I turned it over in my mind and nodded slowly, carefully against his chest.

"Okay, we can try that," I agreed, and he squeezed me a little tighter.

"Okay, it's a deal," he murmured and sounded, dare I say, at peace? I turned it over and over in my mind and I couldn't for the life of me say that I felt any different. It felt right, it felt strong and we needed to be strong.

"Partners," I whispered once again, tasting the word like candy.

"Equals," he murmured back and I really liked the sound of it.

"If we're that, then we need to talk. No more keeping information back, no more not telling the other important things."

"I agree."

"So who goes first?"

"I believe I've told you a hell of a lot more than you've told me, Baby," he followed this up with a hasty, "Not that I blame you."

"Okay, what do you want to know?"

It was a long conversation, mostly carried out in whispers. One that was interrupted by first Remus holding out his hand and pressing it down twice in the classic sign for a request for quiet. There was a tapping at the door, ending our back and forth, though thankfully, as we were both winding down, the talk nearing completion.

"Yeah?" Remus called out, pulling the sheet over my body to shield it.

The door popped open and Markus dropped my bag of clothes

onto the carpet from the truck, which I hadn't bothered to lock the night before.

"Quite the armory you got out there," he commented dryly.

"We're going to need it," I said levelly.

He raised an eyebrow, "Get dressed and get out here, the both of you. The food's on." He backed out the door and shut it, and Remus tossed back the sheets for me. I stood up and stretched but good.

"You really think there could be?" he asked, and I eyed him before heading to the bathroom.

"I'm a hunter, and I wouldn't put it past him."

Remus frowned and I went in to shower, when I stepped out, he was rinsing the last of the residual shaving cream off his face.

"I like this look much better," I smiled.

"Noted. If it *is* a problem, what do we do about it?"

"Kill them," I said lifting a shoulder into a shrug.

He didn't look surprised by my answer, and I smiled thinly without humor, letting him have the shower. I got dressed, and just as I was tying the laces on my boots the door opened, the lady of the house leaning a shoulder against the frame.

"Doing okay?"

"Jim Dandy, fucking wonderful." I performed weapons check and she raised her eyebrows.

"Didn't sound like it last night," she mused.

"None of your fucking business, Princess."

"Oh I'm not a princess, Sweetie," she smiled a thousand watt smile, "In case you haven't noticed, I'm the motherfucking queen, and you're in my husband's – that would be the King's, house. So you might want to show a little respect."

I gave her an appraising look, "Sorry, old habits die hard."

"Old habits?"

"You've been called 'The Little Princess' behind your back since the day you were born. I know, I was thirteen and already into my training by about six years."

She crossed her arms and leaned a little harder into the doorframe, "Why are you doing this?" she asked.

"Doing what?"

"Helping Remus, helping the pack."

I shrugged, "Because Daddy's a dick."

"Your father or mine?" she asked frowning.

"No, Chloe, you've got it all wrong... *Our daddy*. At least he was in the way that Declan was William's father. Mathias pulled me and James out of the system when we were six."

She stared at me, blue eyes wide beneath her copper hair. I could tell she was mulling it over, I could also tell it was hitting her hard, even though she was trying to hide that part. Remus came out of the bathroom rubbing a towel over his hair.

"Brought these," Chloe murmured and reached down to the floor outside the bedroom door, tossing in some clothes and boots.

"They're William's, so on you they'll fit. Sorry, it's the best we could do."

I gave her a nod and she inclined her head in return and walked stiffly up the hall. I stared after her and asked, "You get all that?"

"You hear me asking what you girls were talking about?"

"Nope."

"Then there's your answer."

He tugged lightly on my waistband and I turned, letting him tow me up against his body.

"Curb your attitude with her just a little?" he asked gently.

"Working on it," I promised.

"Thank you."

I nodded and let him kiss me, even though it was awkward for me, knowing the door stood open at my back. He let me go and smiled a knowing smile.

"Thank you for that, too."

"No problem," I lied and he gave me that rakish grin that set my panties on fire, or maybe that was just my little white lie.

He dressed and we went out to the dining room where several of what had to be the pack were milling around.

I took a deep breath and stopped, pulling my right gun, sighting and firing. The shot landed true, the dude's head snapping back; a Goth girl next to him screaming and I gritted my teeth. I guess it was time to see if Remus and I were partners for real.

Markus snarled and lunged but Remus shoved me behind him as I pushed it out of my mouth in a bellow I hoped would carry over the din, "He was a Crusader, I mean a Hunter! He was a plant and I can prove it!"

Remus held Markus who was half shifted off of me and I put up my gun, holstering it in a show of good faith. I put up my hands, using one and sweeping my hair away from the back of my right ear, exposing the tattoo behind it.

"Check behind his ear, if it's not there, try the arch of his foot."

"Nothing behind the ear," Craig said and started working on the boots. He pulled off the guy's sock and there it was.

"How did you know?" the Goth girl asked. "How did you know Eamon was one of…?"

"Because we trained together and occasionally fucked when I was sixteen, until James beat his ass."

"Who's James?" Markus demanded, scowling. At least he'd backed the fuck off Remus and was more human than not.

"My brother. Mathias had him killed in revenge for questioning his authority; now I want Mathias seven different kinds of dead for hamstringing my twin and letting y'all use him as a chew toy. It's a whole different kind of crusade I've got going on over here, but the enemy of my enemy is my friend and all that jazz."

The wolf-kind in the room all stopped and stared, even Remus. I looked at him and he nodded once. It suffused me with an emotion I had no name for. Not pride, not exactly, it was foreign but it felt good so I mentally shrugged it off and looked at all of the people left gathered in the room. There had to be twenty-five of them here.

"We work in teams, Kids. So if he was here, there are more and the Order is too big for me to know them all by looks. Your salt-the-earth protocol is pretty much a sham." I looked at William and Chloe who were standing at the kitchen island, "What are all of these people *doing* here anyways?"

"They wanted answers," Markus growled and I raised my eyebrows.

"I'm starting to see why it was so easy for the Romans to pick you off in the first place." His brows crushed down even further into a heavy scowl, and I jolted when I realized he seriously didn't know what I was talking about. *Hunters really* did *know more about their history than they did...*

"Oh for fuck's sake," I muttered, "You don't even know where you come from? Okay, I'll give you the 'too long; don't read' version of it. The first were–" I stopped myself and corrected, "Wolf-kind, were druids. The Romans and the Catholic Church were sent to wipe you guys out; it didn't exactly go according to plan, because whatever nature deity y'all's ancestors worshiped back then flipped some sort of primal switch and turned you guys into whatever you are to save your furry asses. It's been the mission of the Crusaders, that's what we call ourselves, to wipe you out ever since. Okay?"

Silence, Markus looked like he was going to have a fucking heart attack, his eyes met mine and his voice, gruff with emotion, said "Tell us more, tell us all of it," I shook my head.

"No time, you need to mobilize if you want to survive and we need to hit their central nervous system. Knock out their comm's and destroy their data storage. That's only if you want any hope of survival now."

"I suppose you know where all that is?" Chloe asked.

"Damn right I do," I answered giving her what could probably be described as a wolfish grin. "There's more than one facility like the one in Indiana. The center we need to go after is going to be more heavily guarded. They know I'm helping you now, in some capacity or other. This shit is going to be harder, not easier. The only thing we have going for us is the element of surprise."

I thought about it for a minute and drew breath, "We're going to have to hit more than one facility at once in a coordinated attack."

My idea was met with silence and grim looks and I looked at everyone present in turn. This wasn't going to be easy. Not by a long shot. It was like arming farmers with pitch forks and sending them in against the might of the U.S. Military, which, by the way, had nothing on the Crusade.

People were going to die... but that was the nature of war, now wasn't it? If these people wanted to survive the genocide Mathias

Young was bringing to their door, then they needed to get on board with that. I exchanged a grim look with Remus and he nodded. I guess it was time to impart some grim reality onto these people, as if the body of the Crusader cooling on the floor weren't reality enough.

Why did I always net myself the shitty jobs?

"Why are you doing this?" The Goth girl asked and I raised an eyebrow at her.

"I told you, Mathias had my twin brother killed. You have no idea what that's like. Having the other half of your being ripped away. Mathias wanted to make an extra special point, so he sent me and my team in to clean up the mess. I found James like that, after one of you…" I sucked in a shuddering breath, hands twitching. Remus' hand landed on my shoulder and I jumped. He immediately took it back.

I pursed my lips, "Mathias needs to die and if the other Crusader's want to get in my way, then I have no problem going through them."

"Why do you keep calling them Crusaders?" William asked.

"Because that's what we are," I swept my hair aside so he could see the red Templar cross tattoo behind my ear again, "The order has different splinter cells in each country. Our splinter cell is a descendant from the Knights Templar. The rest of the world at large thinks the Catholic Church tried to wipe us out for being corrupted; which is where they get their little Friday the Thirteenth legend. The *truth* is, wolf-kind actually managed to mobilize for once and you guys nearly succeeded in taking us down. We crawled out of the ashes though, and socked it right back to you."

"Holy shit, this is a lot to process," Chloe said and placed her hands flat against the countertop leaning into them.

"Sorry, Princess. It was a bitch and a half keeping it from you, but Mathias had an entire team dedicated to keeping you oblivious. All your nanny's, the butler, even plants in your school."

William gathered his wife to his chest and she leaned back into his support.

"How do we know where all these facilities are?" he asked.

"Ever see a Red Cross?" I asked and the wolf-kind all looked at one another startled.

"As in the American Red Cross?" Markus asked.

"That would be the one."

"Fucking-A," Craig muttered.

Wow these guys were clueless. I exchanged a look with Remus and he finally spoke up, "We can't talk about this here. We need to find neutral ground, but we need to ferret out any of their operatives first."

"Agreed," William nodded, "Time for plan C."

"What's plan C?" someone asked.

"Good question," Markus said and a lot of frightened looks were traded.

It was going to be a long day.

Chapter 23
Remus

"Seriously, why is the old cow coming with us on this? We need people that can move and we don't need to be held up because she broke a hip," Ava muttered, crossly as she glared out the back window of the FJ Cruiser.

"Sharon is a lot tougher than she seems. She might have been around the block a few times, but she's still wolf-kind," Markus growled from behind me.

"Doesn't make any sense. Aren't there any more like you and Remus back home?" she asked Craig where he sat in the seat behind her. He didn't say anything so I assume he shrugged or shook his head. Ava let out a frustrated sigh and turned back around in her seat. "That's just great. I wouldn't mind a little more muscle on this field trip yah know. They're going to realize we found their facilities eventually."

"And if we play our cards right, we'll be inside causing trouble before they do," I reminded her. "Now just settle down. We'll be there in ten minutes." She glared at me but huffed and crossed her arms.

A glance in the rearview mirror showed that both Craig and Markus were staring at Ava. Not with the wary distrust from the day before though. I hesitated to think it, but Markus actually looked in awe of her.

After her bombshell about our origins, and how we had Hunters that'd been turned wolf-kind planted in our own damn pack, we'd had to figure out how to ferret them out without tipping them off. In the end, it had been relatively simple, if slightly distasteful to some of us.

There were seventy-three members of the Pacific North-West Pack on the peninsula at the time. So we called them, five at a time to come to William's house. As each one arrived, Chloe would lead them into the downstairs workshop where we had moved all the tables to give us space and five of us stood around in Hybrid form. We told them to show us the bottoms of their feet and behind their ears or we would look for ourselves. Those that argued with us on it, we found out were more often than not, marked as a hunter.

We'd found three by the time the last batch had arrived. Two were in that last batch and it had gotten a little hairy in subduing them. The whole thing had been time consuming, but it worked and it had all been Ava's idea. That wasn't what had the boys in the back looking at her in such a different light though.

No, what really did it was how she went about getting the information that we'd needed to bring us to our present point. When securing a member of wolf-kind, extra efforts were needed. We had shackles, designed and made expressly to confine our kind. Extremely heavy and thick, the inside coated with silver. Even I would have been hard pressed to break free quickly and none of the plants had anywhere near my level of strength.

They'd been sitting on the floor against the back wall to William's shop, their buddy's body lying beside them, while most of us had been trying to figure out how to go about getting information out of them. While *we'd* been working on *that*, Ava had suddenly heaved herself a deep sigh, and fed up with the pack's arguing back and forth on the matter, had pushed away from the wall.

She marched right over to the first man in the line, pulled her pistol and chambered a non-silver round, pressed the barrel to the guy's left knee and pulled the trigger. With no one around for easily a mile in any direction, she'd let him howl in pain while the rest of us clapped our hands over our ears to try to blot out the mind numbing shriek.

"Now," she'd said, leaning down to the guy's eye level as his knee slowly started to heal. She pressed the gun to his left knee and gave him the most evil smile I had ever seen before and said in the sweetest tone of voice, "Are you going to give us any useful information, or am I going to have to ventilate all of your joints for you, one after another?"

The guy she'd shot had just glared at her but the only woman of the five of them immediately started spilling her guts. Mathias had moved from Indiana, a piece of information that had royally pissed me off at first. Luckily it turned out he'd moved *closer* to where we were. He was rumored to be traveling to another Red Cross facility, this one located near Denver, Colorado. We had two days before any of them were supposed to check in with their handlers so if we wanted to attack, it would have to be fast.

Worked for most of us.

Then came the arguing over who was going to be a part of the attack team hitting the facility in Colorado. Ava had given us the location of several other Red Cross facilities that were being used to hide Hunter activities. Apparently not every facility was an active Hunter front at all times. They tended to move around with only a small few being permanent installations.

We were sending teams to three different locations, the other two teams were made up of volunteers from amongst the local members of the pack and they had been given detailed instructions by Ava on what they were to do.

Attacking Mathias was a job I wanted, no matter what anyone said, and Ava was right there with me. There was no chance in hell that William was going to pass up the opportunity to go after the old bastard and if William was going, then Chloe wouldn't be left behind; no matter what anyone did or said. With both Alphas going, Markus was a sure thing; no fucking way was the Pack's Arbiter going to get left behind. As for Craig? He was just the kind of musclebound idiot that we needed on our team when things got rough. He had former military experience and a decent tactical head on his shoulders when his temper didn't get in the way. I wasn't terribly familiar with him myself, but Markus had vouched for him, so that was good enough for the Alphas.

Bringing Sharon along had been seen by Chloe as a chance to let the former Beta regain some of herself. Sharon had once been captured by Hunters, and was apparently subjected to some crazy experiments herself, but she had refused to ever speak of them no matter how many times Declan had asked her in the past. Of course, we'd always figured it as torture, not experimentation; now we knew different. Chloe had figured that the chance to really strike back at the hunters would be good for the old bitch. I wasn't sure I agreed, but nobody could talk her out of it, and when William caved to her demand the rest of them followed suit.

As the Alphas willed it.

I turned onto Sherman St, and parked the truck across the street and down the block from the entrance into the Red Cross.

"Ok, look chuckleheads," Ava said, turning once again in her seat. She paused for a moment and glanced at me. "Can they hear me?" she asked and pointed out the back window at William's grey sedan parked behind us. He tapped the horn once a moment later and I grinned at her.

"That answer your question?"

"Yeah, yeah, you guys are great eavesdroppers, don't act all smug. The upstairs is usually staffed with normal volunteers and employees. As it's after business hours, we won't need to worry about that. Keep in mind that the American Red Cross may be a front for the Hunters, but it also really is a legitimate enterprise at the same time. They do a lot of good for people that need it, so if we can avoid causing any damage upstairs it would be greatly appreciated."

We all nodded silently and William tapped the horn once again. Ava stared at him through the window for a moment before she just sighed and shook her head. "Seriously never going to get used to that," she muttered and William tapped the horn again, causing me to grin like an idiot as she growled and glared at him through the window. I didn't look back at him but I'm pretty sure he had an ear to ear shit eating grin on his face.

"You know, your brother's a really immature character," she added, turning to look at me and I grinned again, nodding.

"I've been telling him that for forty years now. He just doesn't seem to want to grow up. I think he's got a bit of a Peter Pan complex or something."

"That is our Alpha that you're insulting," Markus growled and I had an instinctive moment where I found myself wanting to apologize to the Arbiter when he spoke up again. "Just because he wants to act like a twelve year old doesn't mean we don't afford him some respect." Craig burst out laughing and my mouth dropped open. I don't think I'd honestly ever heard Markus make a joke about the Alpha before. Of course, the previous Alpha had been my father, so I guess it's doubtful that he would have made any kind of jokes where I could have heard him, anyway. Declan had never had much of a sense of humor.

"Yeah well, tell him to keep it up with the horn, might as well just let them know we're here. You don't think that won't be investigated?" We all sobered up quickly at the thought, the silence stretching.

Ava sighed, "Alright, kids," she said, finally. "Enough with the fun and games. It's important to keep things light but time to focus. I'm not used to working with you people." Craig started to open his mouth but she held up a hand to stall him. "And by 'you people', I don't mean wolf-kind, though that's true enough as it is. I mean you." She pointed at Craig. "And you." Markus. "And them," she finished, pointing through the window at William's car.

"I'm used to working with *my* team. People that I've known for a long time and fought and trained with. I know what they're going to do under different circumstances. I know how they'll react and I know what they're capable of." She frowned. "Or I thought I did, at least. Right now the only person in there I think I can count on is my man Mason. He's in the communications hub and he'll help keep the alarm muted for as long as possible."

"I still can't imagine how you managed that one." Markus muttered. It'd been bugging me for a while too. Before we'd started out she had borrowed Chloe's phone and made a call, but she'd walked far enough away that none of us had been able to hear her.

"And you'll just have to learn to live with that, Sweetheart." She shot him a smug little grin. "Girl's gotta have some secrets. Anyway, when we get in there just follow my lead, and please, try not to get yourselves killed."

We all nodded and as one piled out of the truck. Craig handed Ava her canvas armory and we quickly made our way across the street, stopping against the side of the building.

"That wasn't funny," William muttered to me as we made our way around the corner of the building.

"Are you kidding?" I shot back in a quiet undertone. "It was fuckin' hilarious. Only thing funnier is looking at the bunch of us right now. Good thing it's three in the morning, if there were any people out on the street right now, someone would've already called the cops.

Of the lot of us, only Ava looked remotely like a person that should even be out in public. The males were all wearing loose pants and jackets with no shoes, while Sharon and Chloe wore light sundresses, their bare feet padding silently across the ground. Ava in her boots, cargo pants, and shirt with her jacket over it looked downright formal next to us.

Around the side of the building was a small metal door with no knob but a deadbolt. Pulling a knife from her pocket Ava slid it into the small gap between the door and the frame and with a quick twist of her wrist the door popped open.

"You have got to be shitting me," Craig muttered, staring wide eyed at the door. "That kind of crap only ever works in movies."

"I wouldn't shit you," she muttered in a saccharine sweet tone of voice. "You're my favorite turd."

"The latch is taped open, genius," I scolded him. "Ava's inside man, helping us out." He shut his mouth, lips pressed into a thin line and I could tell I'd upset him. Oh well, suck it up buttercup, time to move on. We didn't have time to deal with Craig acting like a yokel when we needed speed and stealth.

The inside was dark, all the lights out and as soon as the door closed behind us, Ava pulled a small flashlight from somewhere inside that Joe Rocket jacket of hers and turned it on. The beam was plenty bright for such a small light, and even though the rest of us hadn't needed it, Ava still did.

The thought rose, unbidden for a moment, and I considered it, startled that it had even occurred to me as my body moved on autopilot, following behind the scent of jasmine and gun-oil. Wait; *still?* As in there was a possibility in my mind that Ava might one day join me as wolf-kind? I nearly scoffed at the very idea, but aware of our situation, I was able to keep myself silent and simply shove the idea to the back of my mind, focusing on the dangerous task ahead.

Ava stopped outside an elevator and turned to look at us. "I'm not positive we'll all fit," she muttered, eyeing us all. I looked at the elevator doors. It wasn't a small elevator. One human woman and six wolf-kind should fit just fine.

"How long does it take you guys to change into a more combat ready form?" she asked, and suddenly I understood her concern. If all six of us went hybrid we would seriously tax the amount of available space in the elevator.

"Only a few seconds, but of all of us I believe William is the fastest. Fucker always was quick."

"You're just slow," William muttered and I could hear the grin in his voice even though he was behind me. "And actually, you didn't get a chance to see her before, but Chloe is a natural Alpha. Her change is even faster than mine."

I had to admit, I was impressed by that. I had seen as much when she didn't change immediately on her first full moon, but I hadn't seen any more of her after that until I had been sentenced and branded, and we hadn't exactly been showing off transformations at the time.

"So what I'm hearing," Ava cut in. "Is that you four," she pointed at me, Markus, Craig, and Sharon. "Should get your game faces on and you two can change on the fly. Close enough?"

I grunted and nodded. "For government work." She shot me a grin.

"Alright, people. Get pretty." As one we all started shedding clothes, even William and Chloe. Once we were all naked, Ava watched with a kind of horrified fascination as four of us began to change. Her eyes were centered on me and somehow I felt a pang that she would see the monster underneath my skin that had always been here. The beast she'd spent most of her life fighting.

I was already tall to her but as I changed I grew and she seemed to shrink before my eyes, getting smaller until my head touched the ceiling and I was forced to hunch over slightly. There was a sickening sound of bones breaking and reforming, an almost liquid sloshing noise as my internal organs shifted and moved inside my body. My knees suddenly cracked loudly and bent backwards as my feet grew longer and I stood up on the balls, heels in the air. Lastly my arms lengthened as thick short fur sprouted along my body and my face pushed out into a short snout, mouth filled with two rows of wickedly curved teeth.

I knew my eyes had taken on an amber gleam and I growled as my senses grew even stronger, a low rumbling deep in my barrel sized chest. In hybrid form I was just over eight feet tall and just as massively muscled as in my human shape. Throughout it all I never once took my eyes from Ava's and I didn't see the fear or revulsion that I expected. I sniffed lightly at the air and all I could smell was jasmine and gun-oil. There was no fear in her scent as she stared at me and I resisted the urge to yip with pure joy at that realization.

"Come on little doggies," she said in a sing-song voice. "We've got damage to do." And with that she pressed the button to open the elevator doors.

I was in the far back in the corner as the largest of our group with Markus and Sharon next to and in front of me respectively. Craig stood closest to the doors with the still human William and Chloe standing with Ava by the bank of buttons. Beneath the buttons for the floors above us Ava used her knife to pry open a small, locked panel, to reveal another set of buttons that any of the regular staff and volunteers that frequented the building would likely never have found.

The line went down seven floors and Sharon whined slightly, her ears lying flat to her head as she saw the ascending row of numbers. I was sure she had her own memories of a place like this, and I couldn't say I wasn't feeling a bit of trepidation myself. Psycho Doc Helen was all too fresh in my mind at the moment but I pushed it down and growled quietly, a reassuring sound that seemed to calm her some. Ava glanced back at me once before she nodded and pressed **B7**.

"Alright. We've got a few goals here," she said, and we all gave her our undivided attention. "Goal one; destroy the communications hub in the server room. That'll be located on the bottom floor at the end of the hall directly opposite the elevator doors when they open. We want to take that out before we do anything else, because if they manage to get word out that something's happening then we're as good as fucked.

"Item two; we need to destroy any research data that they've collected. Tissue samples, blood samples, computer files and hard copies. Everything needs to be torched." There was a general rumble of agreement from all of us at that.

"Item three; rescue any wolf-kind being held hostage in the facility. Item's two and three will both be on level 6. So Craig, you and Sharon will take out the server room." She reached into her weapons bag and pulled out an oblong silver canister with a round metal loop at the top and a long strip of metal running down one side. I shifted my weight nervously. I knew a grenade when I saw one, and I didn't enjoy the idea of being in such a small room with one of those things.

"Get to the server room, pull the pin, toss it in and duck behind the wall. Try to get it as close to the computers on the far wall as you can, then hoof it up the stairs to meet us, got it?" Craig and Sharon both nodded and he reached out to take the grenade in his massive hand. The device looked almost comically small in comparison but that thought did little to ease my discomfort.

The doors opened and we all tensed, prepared for a battle before we even got out of the elevator but the hall was empty. It was a very long hall though, far more than I'd expected. I could see the door Ava had been talking about easily two hundred feet down a perfectly straight hall. There was absolutely nothing to provide cover in the corridor, in the event that someone came out of any of the doors lining it with a gun, before either Craig or Sharon could reach the end of the long, stark line of linoleum.

Still, without hesitation they both growled quietly and slipped out of the elevator, loping down the hall with long, ground eating strides. They were a quarter of the way down by the time the elevator doors closed. Ava hit the next button up and the elevator started carrying us up to level 6.

I felt it more than I heard it. Before the elevator doors had even opened one floor up there was a vibration that ran through the entire elevator. The grenade had just gone off.

"Someone probably noticed that," Ava muttered, holstering her 9's and bringing her automatic weapon around on its strap. She checked that it was loaded for bear and held it at the ready.

"Then we'll just have to move fast," Chloe said for all of our benefit. I grunted and nodded my head, bumping it against the low ceiling. I really didn't like this damned elevator.

Finally, after what seemed like an eternity of a wait, the doors slid open with a quiet chime and we surged out onto the floor. And I do mean floor. Where below there had been a single narrow hallway, up here the elevator opened out onto a wide open space. Work stations set up at regular intervals throughout the room marked it as a lab and while the Red Cross facility upstairs had been a ghost town, down here things were humming along.

Nearly a dozen people wearing lab coats, gloves, and surgical masks stood about, working on various samples and peering into microscopes. Not a one of them looked much like combatants but the five guards, each armed with semi-automatic assault rifles that wandered the floor certainly did. Ava took a low, tactical crouch and brought up her weapon.

"It's Martine!" one of them bellowed and the few that hadn't turned in our direction when we'd exited suddenly did, guns coming up as the scientists screamed and scattered for cover. It rapidly descended into chaos and bedlam after that. Guns fired, lab geeks screamed and dove for cover as we scattered, putting as much distance as we could between us.

Out of the corner of my eye I saw William changing, his transformation smoother and less disturbing than my own but still disgusting to watch or hear. Whereas directly to my right Chloe didn't so much change as blurred. Her form became hazy for a moment and when she was back in focus there was suddenly a six and a half foot razor clawed beast where my petite sister-in-law had been moments before.

Damn she is *fast*, I thought. Then I didn't have time for thought.

Ava had opened up a split second before and I couldn't hear shit over the rapid staccato of automatic weapons fire.

One of the heavily armed guards popped up in front of me, gun barrel leveled at my chest as I ran. Without thinking I dropped to the ground, sliding on my hip across the polished floor as the barrel suddenly spat fire and silver coated bullets into the empty space I had just occupied.

I slid far enough that I was able to kick out, the sharp claws on my toes opening his belly and a gout of blood erupted from his mouth, gun dropping from suddenly nerveless fingers as he hastened to wrap his arms around his middle, struggling to hold his guts inside.

He wouldn't last half a minute with those injuries so I ignored him after that, grabbed the gun that he dropped and leapt to my feet, throwing the weapon at the first enemy I saw. The gun spun end over end and hit the man in the side of the head so hard that his skull caved in. He was thrown violently to the side to skid on the floor, leaving a streak of red for several feet before he finally came to a stop.

Amidst the screams and yelling, interspersed with harsh breathing and gunfire a single shot rang out and a line of pain flared high across my upper arm. I jerked, stunned by the sudden pain and growled angrily; turning to find one of the guards had hung back a bit. He had a nine millimeter raised and pointed at me. A disgusted snarl twisted his lips and I could distinctly see the muscles in his forearm tensing as his finger applied pressure to the trigger. I watched him carefully, trying to determine which way I would need to dive to avoid the shot.

A loud report echoed in my ear a moment later and I flinched as the guard jerked, a spray of blood filling the air behind him and his gun arm suddenly fell limp beside him, blood spreading across the shoulder of his uniform. Several more shots rang out, Ava coming into view on my right, gun pointed directly at the Hunter as her finger pulled the trigger steadily, over and over, until no less than eight bullets had penetrated the man's body before he finally slumped, boneless, to the ground.

There was a pause in the chaos and I glanced over at Ava. William was on the far side of the room, chasing down the last of the hunters as the man attempted to escape with his life. Not honestly sure why William was chasing the man, he was missing his left arm at the elbow and was more than likely going to bleed out before he got very far, but to each their own.

"Don't make a big deal out of it," Ava muttered without looking at me. I grinned and turned my attention to the wound in my arm. It burned and itched like crazy, telling me more silver was involved. Not surprising since we were being shot at by Hunters. It was only a graze on the outside of my upper arm, and not even as bad as the one Ava had done to my face. I would survive.

"They weren't very good shots," I noted, changing back to my human form as most of the rest of us did to.

"They weren't an active team."

"Meaning?"

"They didn't go out and hunt wolf-kind down. They were just stationed here as guards. I'd be willing to bet this was the first time they'd ever actually had to fight wolf-kind before."

"Works in our favor."

"In a manner of speaking." She noticed the odd look I gave her and clarified. "That means that we're more likely to run into better trained and more experienced Hunters the longer this takes. Sooner we hump it the fuck out of here the better."

Nods happened all around and we set to work. Most of the floor was empty past the lab we first occupied. The lab geeks had all high tailed it out somewhere so Ava and I explored deeper into the facility while we left William, Chloe, and Markus, still in his hybrid form, to start destroying the research material and samples gathered in the lab.

At the far end of the room was a heavy door, the kind you'd seen in a bank vault or securing the entrance to a movie villain's secret lair or some shit. The outside had an electronic scanner of some kind.

"What the fuck is that?" I asked, pointing at the scanner.

"Fingerprint scanner." Ava grabbed the severed arm of the guard

William had been chasing and placed the hand flat on the scanner. Some blinking lights and electronic chirping noises happened and a second later there was a dull thud as restraining bolts slid away and the door popped open half an inch. Without being asked I reached out and grabbed the door, hauling it open all the way.

The stench was the first thing to strike me. Filth and waste, and below that, but more pungent somehow, was the scent of fear and pain. The feral scent of an animal mistreated and abused by humans.

The room beyond the vault door was bare of anything save a metal cage, much like the one I had been imprisoned inside of in Indiana. This one was stronger though, actually meant to contain the beast within as opposed to being just for show. The bars were easily thicker than my wrists, the whole thing bolted to a three inch thick steel plate, which was further bolted to the floor underneath. A low humming sound filled the room as well and I notice thick electrical cables hanging from the ceiling and attached to the steel frame at the top. The whole thing was electrified.

"William?" I called quietly, never taking my eyes from the contents. "You might want to come over here. I heard several sets of footsteps as all three of them made their way over to Ava and I. Chloe gasped quietly as she and William stepped into the room beside me.

Sitting in the center of the cage, covered in filth but still glaring defiantly, sat a young woman, maybe in her late twenties. Naked as most of us were, but equally uncaring. Lying on the ground beside her with his head in her lap was a man, equally filthy but unconscious despite all the noise and chaos that had occurred in the other room.

"She's wolf-kind," Chloe breathed, a slight hitch in her voice.

"Yeah," I said and nodded to the man. "And he will be too, if or when he wakes up." The girl frowned, her eyes softening a bit as she looked down at the young man, gently stroking his hair out of his eyes. On his naked left thigh, over a mass of scarring, there was a distinctive bite mark. The kind of bite mark that indelibly removed the man as a member of the human race… again, *if* he survived.

Chapter 24

Ava

Craig and Sharon nearly crashed into me, skidding to a halt on the blood-slicked linoleum. I frowned and put my hand over my nose and mouth, striding over to the power source and throwing the Frankenstein-esque handle into the downward position. The power shut down with a whine, the buzzing stopped and I looked to Remus and Craig.

"Get them the fuck out of there and let's *move!* I got business." I slid past them as they went for the cage, looking at it like they didn't know what to do. I rolled my eyes.

"You got a metric fuckton of dead Crusaders in the hall, tear off uniform pieces and wrap your hands to protect from the silver. Do I have to think of *everything* for you guys?"

Craig startled and Sharon went out the door first, a gunshot rang out and she pitched back into the room, stunned. She hit the floor and slid, eyes wide, blood blooming in the center of her chest and I hit my side and slid into the open door way firing out the open portal from down low.

I took out the three Crusaders out in the hall but they weren't just guards. They were tactical and as the last one hit the floor, the alarm system started with its grating rhythmic buzzing.

"Show's over! Let's fucking *move!*" I bellowed.

The boys ripped off vests and wrapped their hands and between Craig, Remus, Markus and William, they managed to put their backs into it and rip the door clean off the cage. The girl got up, and snarled.

"You want to live, Sweetheart, you better move your fucking ass!" I cried.

Markus slung the unconscious dude over his shoulder and the girl shifted, going low to the ground.

"Take fucking cover!" I barked, pulled a flashbang out of my pocket and the pin with my teeth, I slid it out into the hall. It went off; smoke filled the hall and there was cursing. I opened up and the cursing stopped, turning to cries. A couple of wolves flowed past me into the hall and finished the downed men off.

I waved us out, and hit the stairs, "Elevator's on lockdown, let's go!"

We started up to the sound of booted feet coming down. I wasn't having any of it, I charged up the stairs on point and as soon as I saw movement, took position and started firing to pin them down. Remus flowed past me, muscles coiling and bunching beneath his short black fur as he poured up the stairs, taking three at time with his unnaturally long gait.

I was careful with my fire, pinning them down while trying not to hit him became the trick, at least until he reached them and grabbed the bottom most dude close to him. He pulled him by the legs and swung him into the concrete wall, leaving a crimson smear behind before dropping the limp body past us down the center of the stairwell. He had several floors to go before he hit bottom and I was breathing a little easier that they were guards and not a unit up there. A contingent of our knights would have been very bad for my guy.

Remus made short work of the guards and waved us on. I slid past him, resuming point, and put us out onto floor four. Mason was just on the other side of the door, hands in the air. Craig snarled and I barked out, "Shut it Scooby! This is my inside man."

"Ava, I couldn't hold them off anymore, there's an inquisitor's contingent here, you've gotta go and you can't get out the way you came."

"Which way Mason, and what's happened to Jordan?"

"Right here," I brought my gun up and Jordan put his hands up.

"On your side, Baby Girl. Mason filled me in; this is some bullshit and not what I signed up for. Did some digging, and this goes way deep."

He was eyeing the wolf-kind behind us warily and I sucked in a deep breath, Remus' hand descended on my shoulder and I looked up into his foreign face, his eyes though, familiar and warm.

"He's right, we need to move, you guys coming?"

"No choice now, they know we've helped you." Jordan said and Mason was nodding readily. They fell in, the wolf-kind behind me shifting nervously. I couldn't say I blamed them. I didn't fully trust either Mason or Jordan, though I admit I trusted Mason more.

"The underground garage is our best bet," Jordan was saying, filling us in as we moved through this floor to the stairs leading up two floors and out into the base most level of the seven story, underground, parking structure.

Jordan made the breech and I followed through, calling back, "Clear!" in a harsh whisper-shout.

Remus followed, then Jordan then Mason and the rest. We moved around, heading up the ramp, we'd have to go three floors up before we hit a street level entrance/exit to the garage.

I swept in front of me, following procedure, Jordan flanking my left, and Remus on my right, one floor down, two to go and I rounded the corner. A shot rang out and I ducked down behind a cargo van, I eased over, and returned fire.

We went back and forth; I know I took out at least two, before my automatic weapon clicked empty.

"*Shit!*" I hissed, "I'm out." I unzipped my jacket to go for a magazine in the inner pocket and a shot rang out, much closer. I whirled to a course of growls. I had just enough time to register that Mason was down, Jordan standing over him with the proverbial smoking gun. He turned it on me and I was dead to rights a goner. Remus attacked, Jordan's arm jerked, the gun went off and I felt like I'd been punched in the gut.

Remus tore him apart, and I slapped a hand over my stomach, low and on the left of my body. And when I say tore him apart I mean it quite literally. He grabbed Jordan by both wrists and the muscles in his shoulders bunched powerfully as he pulled in opposite directions, ripping the man's arms off with a sickening squelching sound that I barely registered, so intent was I on the bleeding hole in my gut. He'd managed to stop Jordan from shooting me through the heart, but I was hit and it was bad. Real bad. I couldn't focus for a second. Hands were scrabbling at my guns in their holsters strapped to my thighs, it was Markus, he was human again and pulling my guns from their holsters like he knew how to use them.

I was sliding to the ground, and William and Chloe were over me, William pressing his hands over my stomach. I cried out and choked down the scream that was trying to come out.

Oh shit, this was bad. This was really bad.

"Remus!" I called. I wanted to say goodbye. I knew what this meant.

"Ava, hang on Babycakes," my vision swam in streamers of light and dark.

"Shut the fuck up, Fido," I coughed, from my prone position I could see it… I raised a hand and pointed. "Key, get the key." It was a magnetic key safe holder thing on the underside of the frame of the van. "Out, get us out."

It was the girl from the cage that reacted; she scrambled forward on all fours, and felt under the van and snatched the key holder open. She made a triumphant cry and went to the back of the van we were hiding behind while Markus laid cover fire. She got it open.

"Get us out, get us out; get us out!" I repeated over and over. I looked down my body at my shirt, soaking wet with blood and groaned, "Oh god!"

I panted, the pain unreal, and I made a solid mental note to never make fun of Remus for being a pussy after I'd shot him, again. If there would ever be an again for me… Christ there was a lot of blood.

I was lifted, a pair of arms sliding under my back and my legs, and I howled in agony. I was passed from one set of arms to another, the dim fluorescent lighting of the garage passed into shadowy dark. Doors slammed, an engine turned over and we lurched, and I passed right the fuck out.

Chapter 25
Remus

Fuck, fuck, fuck, fuck, fuck. That goddamn, piss ant, little fucknugget! I should've killed that waste of semen the second I'd laid eyes on him.

"Turn left, *left* I said, you idiot!"

Motherfucker had killed Mason; Whippy as I'd known him, and had tried to kill Ava. I wasn't too broken up about Mason but Ava... I looked down at her in my arms. Hardly aware of Chloe sitting next to me as Markus and Craig argued in the front. William was sitting behind us with the unconscious dude from the cage and the girl whose name we still didn't know.

There was a lot of blood; all of it Ava's.

I've never had a problem with blood. Not like I get woozy at the sight of it or anything; and it's not like I get turned on by it either. It just was. Blood kept the body operating. Remove too much of it and the body stops working. Like motor-oil in a car engine. But this wound. This gunshot in her gut...

There was a lot of blood.

"Remus!" My head jerked up, away from the blood still seeping slowly through my fingers where I had them pressed over the wound in her stomach. I snarled, baring my teeth.

Markus just gave me a calm stare, cell phone clutched in one hand. "We're gonna get her some help, Son," he said, quietly, as Craig fishtailed us around a right turn and then pressed the pedal to the floorboards. "Not so damned fast, Pup!" Markus growled. "I know we're in a hurry, but it won't help us if we get pulled over either."

"We can't take her to a hospital, they ask questions about gunshot wounds."

"We're not taking her to a hospital. We're going to take her to a Galen."

"She'll never make it back to Washington."

"Not *our* Galen. Now look, Son, calm down. I have an old friend, lives here in Colorado. He started his own pack. They're not that big, about twenty strong, but *they* have a Galen. I just got off the phone with the Alpha. They're already waking the Galen up and we're going to push it as best we can to get there. They're about twenty minutes out at this rate."

I nodded but didn't trust myself to say anything else and just focused on keeping pressure on her wound. Her complexion appeared paler to me, and was her skin really colder to the touch? Or was I just imagining it in my panic?

The next few minutes were a huge blur of motion and voices. Lights outside the van's windows slid by illuminating Ava's face in the harsh yellow glow of street lamps for just a moment before plunging the interior back into darkness as we moved through one pool of light and hurtled into the next.

It became a steady rhythm to me.

Light.

Dark.

Light.

Dark.

Light.

In those moments when I could see her fully illuminated I took every second to study her features, etching her face into my memory. *Just in case*, I thought and wanted to slap myself upside the head.

No just in case. She was going to make it. *She would!*

"She's going to make it," I growled angrily and Chloe suddenly reached over and placed her hand atop mine on Ava's belly. I flinched when her fingers touched the back of my hand but I refused to pull away. Doing so would mean letting even more of Ava's blood spill free of her body.

"She'll make it, Remus," Chloe assured me and I finally looked away from Ava to acknowledge my sister-in-law. "She'll make it. We're going to do everything we can to make sure she does."

"What's your name?" William asked and I craned my neck

slightly to see that he was talking to the girl we'd rescued from the facility. She stared at the man, lying with his head on her lap again, but said nothing for several minutes before, quietly, "Macy."

"How long were you in there, Macy?" William tried, but he got no further information from her no matter how many questions he asked or how he worded them. She simply sat there, staring at her unconscious friend, stroking his hair as if the rest of us didn't exist.

"Remus, we're here, Pup," I turned back to the front to find that Markus had directed Craig to pull into the parking lot in front of a warehouse looking building. Craig drove past a chain link gate that was pulled shut by a man in dark jeans and with a leather vest thrown over his bare chest. A line of motorcycles stood to our left, at least twenty of them, and I started to get a sinking feeling in my gut.

"Seriously?" I asked, staring out the window. Craig stopped the van and threw it into park before he pulled the key from the ignition and climbed out, coming around to pull open the door on my side "Seriously, Markus?" I asked again. "You think a dirty warehouse in the middle of the city is the place to go?"

"More to this place than it seems, Boy. Trust me and let Craig carry your girl inside."

"She's not my girl," I muttered, absently and Markus snorted and reached back, patting my shoulder once. When Craig tried to take Ava from my arms I snarled at him, teeth bared until he backed away. The bleeding had slowed considerably so I slid my arms under her and lifted her carefully.

"Sure, Kid. Whatever you say," Markus muttered behind me.

We all piled out of the van amidst a whirlwind of motion as people met us at the door, ushering us into the building. I could barely get half a second to gather in my surroundings as I felt a hand at my back, pushing me down a hall from what looked like a comfortably furnished rec room. A pool table, couches, and arcade games dotted the space, but before I could take much more than that in, I was being directed into the back. We walked past a large and well-appointed kitchen where half a dozen people moved and worked, spinning around each other as they made their way from one station to another, cooking up a veritable feast.

Then we were in a medical suite and I was being told to put Ava down.

"What tha fuck is this, Markus?" A voice growled. A high, nasally voice with a hint of an Irish accent. I could already tell I wasn't going to like this prick. "Ye told me ye had family tha' was hurt and asked fer me Galen. Now, tha only reason I'm lettin' so many o' the Washington Pack into me territory is because I owe ye fer that time in the Sudan. But I ain't lettin' ya bring no feckin hunter bitch inta—"

That was as far as the guy got before I lost my shit completely. I spun and lunged across the space, clearing five feet easily and slammed into the speaker. He was a lanky, gangly sort. Like Jack Skellington level skinny, but not nearly as cool.

"That 'hunter bitch' just helped us destroy three different hunter facilities where the fucking Hangman is doing experiments on wolf-kind. He's even turning some of his own men into wolf-kind to better hide them and to better fight us!" I roared, spitting in his face as I held him pressed against the wall. I jerked him toward me and then slammed him forward again and I heard a cracking sound as the wall splintered against his back.

"She's no more a Hunter any more than you are, you fucking twat-waffle. And if you're not going to help her then maybe I should just shove your head up your ass. Because if she dies right now I'm damned well going to punish someone and it looks like you're it." Someone was pulling at me, shouting at me, screaming in my ear but all I could see was blood, and all I could hear was the pounding of my heart and dimly, the weak beats of Ava's heart, struggling to pump blood through her body and instead just pumping it right out the hole in her gut.

"*Remus, fucking let him go right now!*" William roared and I finally turned, wide eyes staring at him but seeing nothing. The gangly little prick slid from my grip, collapsing to the ground as he coughed and wheezed, heaving in deep breaths of air into his battered lungs. William grabbed me by the shoulders and shook me, hard, until my eyes finally focused on him and not whatever images were playing across my memories.

"Go outside. Right now," William commanded in a low tone and I glared at him.

"You can't order an Omega, Little Brother," I snapped and he shook his head.

"I'm not ordering an Omega. I'm telling my *brother*, I'm telling *you*, go outside. Clean up and get some clothes. Play nice with the other wolf-kind and try not to get us into a full blown war. I promise you that Ava will get the best possible care. Markus and I will make sure of it. But you need to get out of here and get your shit together or you're going to end up executed under pack law, and exactly how will that help Ava out?"

It took a minute before all the words registered. It took longer for the blind panic and rage and madness working its way through my body to subside enough for me to see and understand reason. What the fuck was wrong with me? I was always the level headed one. When did I turn into such an emotional wreck that I couldn't see the big picture anymore.

I froze a second later as the thought came, unbidden to the front of my mind. It was probably somewhere around the time that I had started to realize that I was in love with Ava Martine.

"Ok," I sighed and took a slow step away from my brother. His arms slipped from my shoulders and I looked around at the half a dozen people still in the room. Stepping over the man on the floor I stopped by the hospital bed and leaned down to smooth the hair away from Ava's face and press a soft kiss to her forehead.

Then I made my way out of the room, aware that someone was following me but ignoring it entirely, instead making my way back toward the front room. Six people still worked in the kitchen, and based on the smell they'd be at it for a while longer before anything truly edible came out of that room.

By the soft sound of the footsteps behind me I could tell it was Chloe following on my heels as we finally got back out to the front room. Another even ten men and women lounged or stood around the room, all of them wearing the same black leather vest that I'd seen on the guy outside when he closed the gate behind us on our way in.

One of the women had her back to me, a tiny little thing with long black hair tied into a braid and under that I could just make out the patch in the center of her back. A wolfs head, tilted back as if it were howling up at the moon. Above the Head was the word 'Alpha' and below it 'Wolves' with a small MC in red stitching.

The Alpha Wolves MC. A motorcycle club made up entirely of wolf-kind? Not a bad idea at all. The girl turned and on her right side, was another small patch with the word 'nomad'. Brilliant idea, really.

"Heard you two had some trouble?" I looked away from the girl and turned to my right, finding that Chloe had come up beside me while I was staring and another woman had approached her. Almost as tall as me and blonde as anyone I had ever seen before in my long life. Her hair was similarly tied back in an intricate braid, huge set of tits pushing out the front of her leather vest like they were trying to escape.

In her hands she had a pile of clothes that she held out to Chloe and it was only then that it really registered that we were both still naked. We hadn't been in a position to grab our clothes from where we'd left them in the hall back at the Red Cross and I snorted slightly, amused by the thought of how confused the human workers were likely to be when they arrived tomorrow morning to find the clothes piled in the hall.

The lady gave me an odd look but I just shook my head and gave her a tired smile, remembering Williams's admonishment to play nice. "Just something funny I thought of," I said. "Sorry."

She pursed her lips as if she didn't entirely believe me but she shrugged it off and held a thin sun dress out to Chloe and the rest of the pile she handed to me. "Best we could do on short notice," she said looking me up and down. "And you're a big one, but I think the pants should fit you well enough." She turned and pointed down another hall on the left hand wall from where we came in. "There's showers down that way if you guys want to clean up and get changed. We'll have some food out here when you're ready and you guys can let us know why the Bloody Old Tool got us all up at four in the morning."

I arched an eyebrow at her and she grinned. "The Pres' name is O'Toole," she confided in a whisper and I snorted out another laugh. The appellation definitely seemed to fit. We accepted the clothes, Chloe offering a few quiet words of thanks and made our way down the indicated hall.

Cleaning up was quick. I didn't want to waste time so I showered off the blood and got out from under the scalding hot spray as quickly as I could. The pants did fit well enough. They hung a bit off my hips but not too bad and the included belt made sure to keep them from dropping any further. The boots were another story. Easily two sizes too small I set them aside and turned my attention to the last article of clothing that had been brought out.

It was a leather vest, identical to the others but new, obviously never been worn and without the patches and decoration that the other members of the pack wore on theirs. I shrugged and pulled it on. The leather felt good against my heated skin and it settled well, molding comfortably to my upper back and shoulders. A glance in the mirror told me that I really struck quite the intimidating figure in the jeans and black vest. The cut of the vest meant that the scarred omega symbol branded into my chest was completely visible, almost like it was on display. I'd been riding bikes long enough to know that the various clubs and bike gangs called the vest a cut, and losing your cut was tantamount to a mortal insult to you and to your club. The wheels in my brain started turning but I pushed the thoughts aside, letting them percolate on their own in the back of my mind as I went back out to the front, preferring to keep my focus on Ava and our new friends.

Out front I found the rest of them waiting. Already cleaned up and changed into new clothes. Of the lot of them I was the only male to be given a cut, and I wondered briefly about that before shrugging it off and finding a seat at a long table in the center of the room where the rest were sitting. A simple spread of food was laid out on the table along with two large metal tubs filled with ice and beer. I reached out and snagged one of the beers and a roast beef sandwich as William looked up from his food.

"They're working on her now," he said before I'd even settled fully into my seat. "The Galen says he's going to do his best but it's a bad wound, Man." His tone was somber and I nodded, appreciating the honesty as much as it seemed to twist a knife in my gut at the same time. I kept going over the events that had occurred in my mind, over and over, looking for somewhere where I had screwed up. What had I done wrong? What could I have done to stop her from getting shot in the first place?

"Worrying ain' gonna change nothin'," a nasally voice came from the far end of the table and I looked up at O'Toole, sitting at the head of the table directly across from me with his pack and my people between us. I hadn't even realized he was there. He looked none the worse for wear, not surprising as a wolf-kind. He would have recovered from the bruising that I gave him in record timing but I still felt a twinge at the fact that I'd attacked him at all so I stood, keeping eye contact with him the entire time.

"I would like to apologize for attacking you. Ask anyone that knows me and that kind of behavior isn't like me. I tend to keep a level head but that's no excuse. I'll take any punishment you may want to dish out but please also know, I am an Omega." I jerked my thumb at the brand on my chest, so well displayed by the vest I'd been given. "My actions shouldn't be held against the Washington Pack in any way as I have been banished from the pack. Any punishment should be directed to me, not to them."

Everyone remained silent, staring at the two of us. I'm pretty sure Chloe was holding her breath. After a long minute he stood, his chair scraping unnaturally loudly across the wooden floor and leaned forward, planting his hands on the table in front of him.

"I've known Markus fer a long time," he said. "And its cause o' that familiarity that yer even here in tha first place. I want that understood before anything else." I nodded. "Otherwise, don' think anything of it." That had me blinking in surprise, and a bit of confusion. "I get it. Ye were worried fer yer girl. Can't figure out why a man such as yerself got mixed up with a Hunter of all t'ings, but I get it. I apologize fer insulting her." He wiped his hands one over the other, like brushing dirt off his palms and spread his arms out. "Far as I'm concerned, we're square. Deal?"

"Deal," I blurted out, amazed that so little had come of my outburst.

"But," he continued, a glint in his eye. There was the other shoe. "If'n ye think yer gonna come inta my place again, and talk ta me like tha'? Think again. Get me?" There was a hard edge to his voice and as he spoke his eyes grew flat and cold. The eyes of a killer that I recognized all too well.

"Understood. Thank you, again, for your understanding and I promise you, it'll never happen again."

He suddenly blinked and his eyes shone with mirth, a broad grin splitting his face nearly in half. "Well," he said. "Then we ain't gonna have any problems now." With that he sat back down and resumed eating as if nothing at all had happened. I caught the tall blonde's eye as I sat; noting a patch on her cut that said her name was Valkyrie. She shot a glance in O'Toole's direction and then rolled her eyes.

Conversation flowed well enough between the rest of them while we waited, but I focused on eating. Mechanically so. I couldn't taste the food and worry continued to gnaw at my gut as Chloe and William filled O'Toole in on what had happened at the facility. They also explained the other two facilities that we attacked.

"We've all heard of tha Hangman, before. Obviously, he's like tha boogey-man for wolf-kind," O'Toole was saying some time later after the food had all been cleared and beers had been handed out. I had two empties sitting on the table in front of me and a third in my hand as I picked at the label on the dark bottle. "Most of us have never even seen a Hunter up close, to be honest. Only Valkyrie and I have ever fought them before. But the daughter of the Hangman became an Alpha Bitch, huh?" He gave Chloe an admiring look at that and raised a hand to his brow, as if tipping a non-existent hat in her direction.

"And ye went an' scored a blow to the Hunters tonight, eh?"

William nodded and set his beer on the table. "A pretty decent one. We've destroyed three labs worth of information, and samples, as well as rescued as many as forty test subjects from the other two labs. The one here in Colorado only had the two we brought in with us. I glanced around and realized that the girl and her friend weren't at the table. The chew toy was probably still unconscious and I imagined she was sticking close to him until he woke up. That was likely to be an interesting conversation. I wonder if he even knew anything about wolf-kind, or if the hunters just snatched the poor guy off the street.

I was the first to hear it, having been waiting for something, some sign from that end of the building. The door opened leading into the medical suite where I'd left Ava and I caught the tang of blood, that coppery scent drifted down the hall and into the room and as the footsteps started, heading our way, the rest of them suddenly caught the scent and heads swiveled in unison to face the hall.

I leaped to my feet, my chair bouncing and scraping away from me before it suddenly fell over with a loud clatter. Half the occupants at the table jumped; startled by the sound, while the rest just stared at the hall with me, waiting for whoever was walking out.

"It's Gale," somebody muttered.

"How's she doin', Doc?" O'Toole asked as a young looking woman stepped into view. She was wearing hospital scrubs with a large apron over it, blood staining her sleeves and down her front. With a heavy sounding sigh she reached up and pulled the scrub cap off her head revealing that her hair was as dark as mine but shaved close to her scalp, barely a quarter of an inch long. Piercing green eyes, lidded with exhaustion regarded us all before settling on me.

"She's asking for you," she said to me and I blinked.

"How do you know it's me?" I wondered aloud.

"Biggest dude in the room with an Omega branded on his chest, she said. You're the only one here that fits the bill." I motioned to William to follow me and started across the room in long, ground eating strides. William caught up to me just as we reached the Galen, Gale, I assumed, and she turned to accompany us down the hall.

"We've got to offer it," I muttered and William nodded, his face tight, unreadable, but I had the impression he wasn't thrilled by my suggestion.

"Did you get the bullet out completely?" William asked and Gale nodded.

"It wasn't easy, and I flushed the wound as carefully as I could. Luckily it was silver coated and not solid silver; it didn't break up much and didn't hit any bones either. But she's got some serious internal injuries. I really don't think she's got long but she's stable right now."

William sighed when we reached the door and he placed a hand on Gale's arm. She glanced down at his hand, one eyebrow raised slightly, but she didn't seem offended. "You go in," he told me, ignoring her for the moment. "Talk to her. *Tell her*, Remus." His gaze was intense, boring into mine. "Don't leave anything unsaid, trust me… Then make the offer. We'll be waiting here when you do."

I nodded, but didn't trust myself to say anything and opened the door, closing it quietly behind me.

The room was dark; lights dimmed to a low glow that gave me more than enough light to see by but didn't cast everything in harsh detail. Ava looked small in the center of the bed, hands laying to either side at her hips with a thin sheet and a blanket pulled up to her armpits. It scared me that she looked smaller than normal. Like the life, the presence that made her so big had dimmed to a barely noticeable level.

Machines beeped and pulsed steadily, measuring her heart beat and respiration and who knew what other things doctors measured in a patient just out of surgery. Her eyes were closed so I quietly grabbed a nearby chair and pulled it forward so I could sit at the side of the bed. Her eyes opened when the leather vest I was wearing creaked as I moved and she blinked at the ceiling for a moment before turning her head to focus on me. A small smile turned up her lips and I took one of her slender hands in mine, engulfing it in my grip.

"I love you," I blurted out before she had a chance to say anything or before I could lose my nerve. My stomach twisted and roiled, a whole flock of butterflies prancing their way about my insides and I pushed forward. "I don't know when the hell it happened but it did. I'm in love with you and I don't know what I'll do if I lose you. I already lost my pack and William was right. Banishing me gave me the chance to find something new, something I could build on for myself. And that's you. That's us..." I trailed off, uncertain what else to say as she just stared at me, expression unreadable.

"I'm glad you said it first," she whispered a moment later and I felt my eyes widen as the shock ran through me like a bolt of lightning, lighting up my nerve endings. "I wasn't sure how you felt, honestly. Or how *I* felt. It's been a long time thinking of your people as little more than animals, you know? And finding myself falling in love with one?" She shook her head at the very idea and I nodded, not sure I could trust my voice at that moment. "I realize, that there's a lot I was lied to about, and a lot I just plain got wrong. I've seen a lot in your pack that I respect in a human family, something I haven't had in a long time."

"You could," I muttered and she smiled wanly.

"Maybe. If I survive this. But I'm not sure I will. Gale wasn't exactly optimistic about my chances."

"Yeah, but she doesn't know how incredibly stubborn you are." She chuckled weakly for a second before it turned into a hacking coughing fit and the door opened behind me. The scent of pine needles and disinfectant rushed into the room accompanied by the sharp tang of burning metal as Gale and William both swept into the tiny room. William stopped at my side while Gale went and poured a small glass of water from a pitcher sitting on a table against the far wall. She helped Ava sit up slightly, adjusting the bed so she could drink and after a few minutes the coughing subsided.

"Tell her, Remus," William whispered and Ava turned her attention back to us.

"Tell me what?" she asked. "I thought we'd already gone over the big bombshell. Your idiot brother went and fell in love with a Hunter. Isn't that hilarious?" Her smile was small but mine damn near split my face in two. I was in love with a Hunter. I really didn't know how or when it'd happened but it was true and I didn't give two shits about what anyone else thought about it. I loved Ava, *who* she was, not *what* she'd been. She wasn't a Hunter anymore, hadn't been for a while.

"We might be able to save you," I said, taking a deep breath before continuing. "Turning you wolf-kind. It could repair the damage done by the bullet. You'd heal like we do and..." I hesitated, "And you'd live longer. We'd have longer with each other than if you stayed human."

"And a lot of people don't survive being turned even when they're in perfect health," Gale snapped. "She's weak and dying already, trying to turn her would just speed up the process and I'm not letting you kill the patient I just went through so much trouble trying to save."

"But you haven't saved her," I shot back. "You said yourself that she might not have long as it is."

"So you want to speed it up? Lose whatever time you *do* have with her on the off chance that this Hail Mary pass will work?"

"It's worth the risk," I growled and Ava grabbed my hand, squeezing weakly. All thoughts of the growing rage I felt for the Galen fled my mind and I focused on Ava.

"Let me see if I understand this correctly. If we do nothing, odds are good I'm going to die, right?" she asked and Gale nodded, somewhat reluctantly. "If we do this, then I'll still die, and even faster than I already am now?" I nodded. "But I *might* survive, and if I do I'll heal; I'll be strong, and fast, like you."

"You will," William cut in. "Not *exactly* like us, each person is different, but you'll be wolf-kind. Your life span will be measured in centuries and you'll be able to keep up the fight against Mathias and the Hunters, if that's what you want to do."

She considered the situation carefully. Eyes darting from me to William to Gale and back as her mind worked over the situation.

"James would be pissed," she whispered and I nodded.

"From what you've told me; I think James would understand. He went to his death, to protect you. He went to great measures to give you a fighting chance and I'm more than willing to fight beside you. We'll help each other through this mess and we'll take Mathias down with us for everything he's done."

"What do you think?" she asked me.

"I can't tell you. You already know what I would choose, but it's got to be your decision, Baby. I can't have you getting pissed at me later because we made the choice for you. And besides, you're not the type to let someone else decide your fate, are you? You never have been."

"This is fucking stupid; you idiots are going to kill–"

"Do it."

Even though Ava's voice was barely a whisper, her words cut through the air like a knife and Gale fell instantly silent. She lifted her arm, holding it out to me. "Do it," she said again. "I'll take the chance."

I shook my head but took her hand in mine, pressing a kiss to her palm. "I can't do it. William will."

"But I want you to," she whimpered, "No offense, William."

He smiled and waved her off. "None taken, but really, Remus can't bite you. To wolf-kind that'd be disgusting. If you two are going to remain in a romantic relationship he would be your father, in a sense. Serious squick factor going on there."

She still didn't look like she liked it but she nodded her understanding and turned her attention back to William as Gale threw her hands up into the air in surrender.

"I give up. You people are fucking morons. If she dies, I won't have you bitching to me. I've given you fair warning, I'm done with you."

With that she made her way around the bed and left the room, shutting the door a touch forcefully behind her, though it wasn't enough to crack the door itself or the frame.

"Give me a kiss goodbye?" she asked and I shook my head.

"I refuse to believe this is goodbye, you'll just have to wait till you recover for a kiss."

"Oh for fuck's sake, just kiss her Remus," William snapped at me. "If this doesn't work, you don't want to regret it."

He had a point there, and I knew just how miserable that regret would make the rest of my centuries on this earth. I couldn't even imagine trying to live through that weight on my shoulders.

I leaned in and pressed my lips to hers, being gentle out of fear for her injuries but I felt the fingers of one of her hands tangle in the hair at the back of my head as she pulled me insistently down, deepening the kiss. I did my best to pour my feelings into her through the kiss. Telling her without words just how much she meant to me, how much I needed her with me.

I have no idea if it worked, but when I leaned back her eyes were closed and a gentle smile curved her lips, her entire expression peaceful and content.

William quickly shed his jeans and jacket and shifted into his full wolf form. The cracking and snapping of his bones shifting didn't seem to register to Ava as she held my eyes with her own. Her jade green gaze still held mine as William took her arm gently between his teeth and I wondered how they'd look, spotted with the tiny flecks of amber so prevalent amongst wolf-kind.

Then he bit down, and Ava screamed.

Chapter 26

Ava

That ticking was driving me crazy.

Tick.

Tick.

Tick.

Tick.

Only marginally more than the fact that I felt like I was just, *boiling* to death. I mean, I was hot, and I know medical facilities, hospitals and such, had crappy pillows but Jesus, my head was on a rock and I felt clammy from sweating so hard.

I winced, and tried to move but I was stiff as a board from laying in the same position for so long…

I froze for two reasons; one, the thought struck me, *just how long had I been out?* And two, a gentle hand was tangled in my hair, the fingers smoothing it gently out of my face and behind my ear. I opened my eyes and looked up into the sparkling obsidian depths of Remus'. He smiled, a sublimely pleased, slow spreading of lips and I felt an answering one of my own.

"When you made it through the first night, we knew you were going to make it, but I was still worried."

The silence stretched between us, well, almost.

Tick.

Tick.

Tick.

"How long was I out?" I asked softly.

Tick.

Tick.

"It's been nearly five days," he answered and smoothed more of my hair behind my ear.

Tick.
Tick.
Tick.
Tick.
Tick.
Tick.

"What is that ticking!?" I demanded, growing upset.

His generous lips split into a wide grin and he laughed, "The clock at the end of the hall." I felt my brows crush down into a further frown and struggled to push myself into a sitting position.

"Easy, Baby. Don't try to do too much yet."

Voices overtook the ticking and it sounded like they were right outside the door, but it still took them time to get around to opening it. William was the first one through it and he had a plate of food in each hand. My stomach growled.

"Thought we heard you up." He passed the plate to me and I dug in.

"Thanks for cutting it up for me," I said between mouthfuls. I wasn't typically a fan of such rare meat but this was *good*.

"Easy, slow down, Pup." Markus remarked, he'd come through the door behind William, Chloe leaned against the door frame and I snarled at him.

"Shut it, Snoopy."

"Well, if I'm Snoopy that makes you Lassie, little girl." I stared at him, swallowed my food and started laughing.

Everyone smiled and I looked down into my lap, covering my face with shaking hands.

"Everyone out," William ordered quietly and Markus and Chloe slipped out the door. Remus made to slip out of the bed and I shot out a hand, wrapping fingers around his wrist. He looked to William who nodded. I stared at Remus, confused.

"William is basically your father now, for all intents and purposes, and you're considered a minor. A parent tells you to get away from their seven year old, you do it."

I blinked stupidly, and looked from one to the both of them, "I'm a grown ass adult," I started to argue.

"To a certain extent, but you're a newly Moon Forged wolf-kind now. We don't know what kind of level of control, or what kind of relationship you'll have with your wolf, not until after your first full moon. Until then, you're my child, and even after, you may still be considered my child. It all depends on your level of control and if your wolf and you can cooperate with each other."

"Is that what you're in here to talk to me about?" I asked, my plate of steak and potatoes nearly forgotten in my lap with the reality of the changes I'd blithely volunteered to undergo.

Remus slid a comforting hand up my back and I looked over at him. No, not *blithely* anything. I sighed out and closed my eyes.

With him is where I belonged. Partners, but there was more to it than that. I don't know. Maybe it was because we were both twinless twins. Maybe it was because we could be so intimately familiar with one another's pain. Or maybe it was that we both understood loneliness the way two people were never meant to, and in each other, we found we didn't have to. All I knew, was that somewhere down the line on the crazy train we'd been riding, I'd fallen more than a little in love with him and didn't want to imagine a life without his partnership.

"Eat," William said, "Get cleaned up, I'll leave you to take care of it." He told Remus and Remus nodded.

"Thanks, Little Brother."

"Just make sure she eats, you know how important that is. There's more in the kitchen if she needs it."

He left and I quietly, and a little less voraciously tucked into my food. Remus sat with the other plate in his lap and watched me.

"Aren't you going to eat?" I asked.

"Did already, this one is for you too."

"I don't think I could possibly eat any more than this." I scoffed, but before too long my first plate was clear, and with a shit eating grin, Remus passed me the second one.

"Asshole," I muttered and he laughed.

"Yeah, but I'm *your* asshole."

I froze and looked him in the eye, "I'm scared," I whispered and he nodded, hooking a hand around the back of my head and drawing me forward, he pressed a kiss to my forehead.

"You think you kicked a lot of ass before, wait until you get used to this new body," he reassured me. I swallowed hard and nodded silently.

"I both do and don't feel any different."

"Senses are heightened, but you feel like you?" I nodded, "That's the way I understand it goes."

"What, you don't know?"

"I was Blood Born, Baby. I've been this way since my mamma popped both me and Romulus out. I've never known any other way."

I nodded mutely, and tried to process through all these new and wild feelings while I dutifully cleaned the second plate. I had no idea where it was all going, but about two thirds of the way through it, I was finally full. Still, I finished it off anyways. Remus set the plates aside and I took in the room.

We weren't in the medical suite anymore. This room was pretty sparse when it came to furniture, a bed, two nightstands and a battered but serviceable dresser.

I looked down at myself, dressed in an oversized tee and pulled the sheet pooling in my lap away, raising the shirt so I could see.

A scar, shaped like a perfectly arcing comet graced my lower belly, off to one side. I touched it with my fingers, a pale, shiny, pink, flat scar but there were no straight cutting scars like from surgery.

"It's like nothing really happened." I twitched my feet and legs just to be sure, and everything moved and felt completely normal, except for being stiff from lack of motion for what? *Five days.*

"Take a shower with me."

I looked up at Remus and nodded. I felt gross, and probably looked like hell to match. A shower sounded divine.

"Easy," he reached out to steady me, having gotten out of the bed first and I grasped onto his forearms.

"Thought I was supposed to be better, stronger, faster, and all of that bullshit."

"Babycakes, you are, and you will be, but you got shot; with silver might I add, then turned within the span of like two hours. You shouldn't even *be* here." The raw emotion in his voice had me looking up, quickly. I blinked.

"You didn't think I would make it?"

The raw pain in his eyes was answer enough. I sighed out, and pulled myself in against his chest. I snorted a laugh and he asked me, "What's so funny?"

"Never pictured myself having to comfort the Big Bad Wolf," I murmured.

"Never thought the Big Bad Wolf would love the Hunter as much as I do. Not sure I was going to make it myself if I'd lost you, Ava."

"Well you didn't, I'm here, and I could really use that hot shower."

Remus chuckled slightly, "As my lady wishes."

I snorted, "Since when have I ever been a fucking lady?" He bent, and lifted me easily in his arms.

"Not *a* lady, Ava, *my* lady. My woman. You understand me?" I looked up into his deep, dark, and lovely gaze and nodded slowly.

"I... I think I do," I stammered. I wasn't used to these intense exchanges. I didn't do these mushy, deep, emotionally charged professing of feelings out in the light and open air. Where I'd come from, that was a good way to get yourself manipulated, and the ones you loved, killed. Where I'd come from the word 'love' was synonymous with the word 'slave' and I shook, deep down inside with fear, over how easily he spoke these things aloud.

It'd been one thing when I lay dying, if I'd gone, and there had never been another chance... well I didn't want to leave him with that, but now that I'd lived, I felt like these things needed to be put away. For our own safety.

"Talk to me, Baby," he murmured, carrying me out the bedroom door and down a rather unremarkable cement corridor to what looked like a small, tiled locker room with a bank of three open showers on one end.

"I don't know who might be listening."

"Doesn't matter, just talk to me."

I touched the side of his handsome face, trailing light fingertips along the line of white scar I'd left with a bullet graze, what seemed like forever ago in Chicago. His eyes closed and he lowered us both gently onto one of the benches in front of the shower area, situating me so I sat in his lap.

Despite how my muscles moaned about it in protestation, I pulled myself up so I could press my lips gently to his. He sighed out, his breath warm against my face, as he held me tightly against him. I couldn't speak the words, not knowing who might be listening, but I could show him.

"Ava..." he moaned out and I loved the sound of my name coming from his mouth.

"Let me get cleaned up," I whispered and he nodded. He helped me get stiffly to my feet and once there, lifted the tee over my head, letting it fall to the floor. He shoved the pair of basketball shorts he'd been wearing to the floor after them and led me into the broad shower enclosure.

He started the water on the far left one and turned me into the hot spray. I gasped, the warmth and heavily beating water wringing the tension from my muscles. I tipped my head back and let the water soak my long, dark hair; slicking it back from my face.

Remus didn't waste any time or opportunity; he covered my mouth with his own and pulled me in tightly to his chest, letting his hands slide over my wet skin in a tantalizing touch that left me damn near swooning. I'd like to blame the whole feeling weak thing, but what it really was, was relief. Relief that I had survived, that I could be here, kissing him, touching him back, that I hadn't left him alone like so many before him and that *I* wasn't alone either.

I didn't believe that when we died, we got to see our loved ones again. For me, it was just *it*. No more. We just blinked out of existence like the screen on a television set going dark after you'd switched it off.

There just was no more. Your life, your time on this rock was just *done*, and the ones you left behind, they were left in agony for it. Like I had been when Mathias had taken James, utilizing the wolf-kind as his method of disposal, for *my brother*. The only person in this world I had ever loved, until this man right here, in my arms, pressing my back against the cool tile of the locker room showers.

He bent, hands slipping along my hips and down the outside of my thighs. Despite my still-protesting muscles, I gave a little jump. He did the rest of the work, hauling me up his body, pinning me to the wall while I twined my legs around his lean hips. I let my arms go around his shoulders, pressing my mouth to his with an urgency that was only matched by the aching desperation I felt in my pussy, which throbbed with a want to have him inside of me.

I buried my fingers into the back of his hair and he groaned, sliding inside of me after a few gentle, seeking thrusts. He swallowed my cry and I quivered in his grasp, the angle, like this, sharper; deeper somehow.

We kissed languorously before he started to move, sliding his hips back before surging forward. There was nothing rushed, nothing frantic about how he took me, there against the shower wall.

He attacked the side of my neck with his lips and tongue and I tipped my head back against the wall, moaning as sparks fizzled down the entire side of my body, shimmering over my skin in a light dew of sensation.

"Oh, god, Remus," I half gasped, half moaned and he growled, deep in his chest, an impassioned and at once possessive sound that tripped my triggers in all the right ways.

He buried himself to the hilt inside of me and I felt like it opened me up, made me come alive, and I was just dying for more, but he was being so *careful* of me. I tightened my hands in his hair and used it to drag his head back. I met his eyes with mine and growled, "I'm not a delicate fucking flower, anymore. Fuck me."

He grinned, a wicked curve of lips, and lunged forward, biting my bottom lip and surging into me until I cried out. He drove into me, over and over again with powerful strokes, and I could swear I heard the tile crack at my back between the sharp impassioned moans that were spilling from my lips.

He did just what I'd asked. He fucked me, primal, sharp and

alive, teeth leaving perfect, neat little prints in my flesh, though he was careful not to break the skin. I loved it, I loved every minute of having Remus Reese inside of me and I couldn't get enough, as if there would ever *be* enough. I was drunk on him, on my desire and love for him, and it was a high I never, ever wanted to give up.

Chapter 27
Remus

I couldn't actually remember the last time I was with a woman that I didn't have to be careful with. I didn't try too hard to think of one either as I buried myself inside Ava. The tile at her back cracked under the pressure as our voices grew louder with each passing second. The feeling of her body writhing in my arms, legs wrapped around me as we came together over and over; after the fear of nearly losing her it was even more incredible than I could have possibly imagined.

I had come within a hairsbreadth of losing her forever. The enormity of that hit me as I pushed her over the edge and she clamped down on me so tightly that it very nearly hurt. I moaned loudly as she came around me and I joined her, both of us shaking violently and clinging to each other as the world fell away and then rose back up to meet us.

"I love you," I muttered against her neck as she held onto me.

She laughed, a quiet, throaty sound and wrapped her arms tightly around me. "I love you too, Fido."

"Hey!" I swatted her ass with one hand and she laughed again, a little louder. It was with a great deal of regret that I slowly slid out of her and we rinsed off under the cooling spray of water, quickly exiting the shower.

She winced occasionally still, but I could see that she was moving a little better than she had even half an hour before as she worked out the stiffness in her muscles. I dried her as gently as I could, but quickly since it was cold in the cement room, and got her into some fresh clothing before leading her back down the hall to her room.

"Where the fuck are we, anyway?" she demanded after I'd coaxed her back into her bed. In the end she'd only agreed to lay back down if I joined her, so I slid into the bed with her and pulled her against me so her head was lying on my chest, one leg thrown over mine. She started idly tapping on my chest with her fingers again in time to my heart beat.

"Neutral territory. After you got through the first day we figured you were going to make it and it would be safe to move you, so we loaded you and the whole bed up into the back of a truck and hit the road."

"So where'd we end up, and what's 'neutral territory,' what's that mean?"

"You mean you don't know?" I was honestly surprised by that. It was the kind of information I would have thought the Hunters would have had. "In most states; not all of them, but most, there are halfway houses. Places built and operated by the larger wolf-kind community for the loners."

She lifted her head, giving me a strange look. "I thought wolf-kind were pack animals by nature."

"We are, but there are occasions when someone loses their pack. Accident, death, Hunters, or even being branded Omega. A lone wolf-kind can't just wander into any territory they want, it'd be suicide soon enough. So places like this were set up, dotted all around the country. They're safe havens for wolves without a pack or without a territory of their own."

"Youth Hostels for wolf-kind," she muttered. "Huh, who'd have thought?"

"Close enough. So Craig's family apparently operates this one. We're in Wyoming right now, but we're ready to move at a moment's notice if need be."

"Why the rush to leave Colorado?"

"Our presence was a strain and a danger to the Alpha Wolves. O'Toole let us stay long enough to make sure that you were going to pull through, but then he started making some not so subtle hints suggesting that we get the hell out of their territory before he decided to just kill the lot of us and be done with it." She arched an eyebrow at me and I laughed quietly. "I told you he wasn't exactly subtle about it."

She chuckled again and settled against me. "So why Wyoming?"

"Closest neutral house we knew of. Again, Craig's family operates this one and it's sort of off season, fewer loners passing through the area than usual. That, and it's fortified to a certain extent. It basically originated as a bunker for American militiamen."

"So what else has been going on? I'm feeling out of the loop after sleeping for nearly a week."

"Well that couple we found at the facility are still hanging around. Though that's an ugly situation. The guy, Evan, woke up a day or so ago and he's been having a bit of trouble adjusting to things."

"He wasn't turned voluntarily, I imagine?"

"Not by a long shot," I scoffed. "Army vet, he's been homeless for a while now. His leg was messed up apparently while he was on duty so they gave him a medical discharge. He's got some serious burn and shrapnel scars and who knows what else. Apparently some of the Hunters scooped him up off the street and dragged him into that facility a few weeks ago. They had one of those electric collars on the girl, Macy, and it turned into a situation of bite the human and turn him or we'll see how long it takes for your head to explode from the current we run through your cranium." I was frowning. I had long hated the Hunters, and Mathias in particular. But these experiments... a large portion of the Hunters were misled, lied to, being manipulated and tricked into hating something they just didn't understand. Some of them were starting to remind me of that German doctor that supposedly did experiments on Jewish prisoners back in World War II. He was just plain evil, and he was gathering his own supporters, separate from the actual Hunters' organization.

"You think Mathias is trying to build his own little private army?" I asked suddenly and Ava's fingers stilled for a moment in their tapping on my chest before resuming the steady beat.

"I'm not certain," she admitted. "But it makes as much sense as almost any other theory we've thrown around in the last few weeks. Nothing about his actions really makes sense in the long run. I'm reasonably certain that only Mathias knows what the actual end-game is with these experiments of his."

I stared up at the ceiling while Ava continued tapping on my chest for a few minutes, when suddenly her stomach growled loudly and I chuckled, looking down to find a sheepish smile on her face.

"Come on, let's go see who else is up and around."

"I thought I was supposed to be resting."

"Pretty sure you've rested enough, Babycakes. We should probably get you moving. Work the kinks out and start teaching you what things are going to be like. The full moon is coming in about a week, so you'll need to be ready for that."

She nodded and pulled away, somewhat reluctantly, which made me smile like some kind of retard. To know that she didn't want to move away from me, gave me a sense of satisfaction like no other, gave me back a sort of missing piece of myself.

I pretty much immediately wanted to slap myself for acting like a sap, but I was really starting to understand what had driven William to fight so hard against Romulus. With his mate's fate in the balance, he would have moved mountains to save her. That desire to fight for the ones we love is built into us, and it has served our people well over the centuries. I'd never really felt it until her.

"What about the girl?" she asked as we dressed a little more completely. She pulled on her cargo pants and black shirt again but left the Joe Rocket jacket hanging in the closet where I'd put it, soon after we'd arrived at the house. Her clothes and equipment had all been cleaned and checked over, Markus even stripping and cleaning her guns for her. I had told him he didn't have to do that but it'd been a long time since the old soldier'd had a chance to play with some decent hardware like that so I'd left him to it.

"Which girl?"

"The one we grabbed from the facility. Macy?"

"What about her?"

"Well you told me about Evan. Veteran, wounded, homeless, so on and so forth; but what about her? All you gave me was a first name."

"Not even sure if that *is* her first name, could be her last, hell, it could be made up entirely to be honest. We don't know much about her. She keeps to herself when she's not around Evan. And he's been trying to avoid her as much as possible. He sticks pretty close to Markus, I think 'cause they both have a military background. The old wolf has sort of taken the kid under his wing. I get the feeling he's trying not to blame her for what happened but you know, it'd be hard, considering the circumstances. You at least got to choose, and from people that only meant you well. This guy was thrown into a nightmare from the beginning and he's just trying to find his footing."

"So you don't know where she's from or anything?"

I shrugged and pulled my new cut on over my bare chest. I'll admit, I kind of liked the dark leather vest. My brain was still turning over possibilities, ones I'd have to discuss with Ava in the near future, probably.

"We haven't really been able to get much out of her, not that I can really blame her. She's not an Omega, no brand, but she definitely doesn't have a pack of her own, either. She's been alone for some time from what I can tell."

Ava stretched, linking her fingers together and reaching as far over her head as she could until she actually came up on her toes. She wasn't wearing her boots, something I noted idly and figured had to be part of the wolf-kind mentality; that or she trusted I'd have her back. I liked that last one best of all.

Speaking of which, her back popped a couple of times and she suddenly relaxed and came over to hook her arm through mine.

"Food," she ordered and started dragging me from the room.

"Right turn," I said when we got out into the hall and she turned without a word, still dragging me along. We were on the second floor and at the end of the hall, next to the stairs leading down to the ground floor, was the clock she had heard when she woke up. A simple thing with a stainless steel finish and gold numbers on a black background. To a human's hearing the quiet tick of the second hand on its endless circuit around the face would have been nearly silent, but we could hear it clear as day with the enhanced senses that come with being wolf-kind.

She stared at the clock for a second, her face unreadable before the smell of the food still waiting downstairs urged her onward.

Downstairs, we turned left and headed back in the direction we'd come from to find the hall opened out into a large dining room. Almost like a cafeteria with a half a dozen long wooden tables arranged about the large space. At the far end was an industrial grade kitchen with three walk in coolers filled with food.

Most of the gang were sitting together at one of the tables. Actually, all of them, except for Macy but a quick look around found her sitting by herself at the far corner of the room, as far as she could get from everyone else while still staying in the same room. She looked a lot better, cleaned up and wearing some decent clothes. Her hair was long and dark, a lot like Ava's but had a bit more wave in it and her skin was a deep olive tan. Definitely some Italian ancestry somewhere in her blood.

I settled Ava at the table with the others, seating her next to Chloe who offered her a warm smile and went to grab us each a plate. Meat, potatoes, simple fare, but well-cooked and filling. It was the perfect kind of meal for a newly turned pup and old wolves alike.

"... to find a new place to settle the pack," Markus was saying in his deep growl when I returned to the room. I took a seat next to Ava and set one of the plates in front of her where she tucked in, barely even looking down at her food, so absorbed was she in the conversation.

"How exactly does this protocol work?" she asked. "I mean, you just send out messages and get the information to the pack members spread all over the country and they... what? Head to a safe house? Drop points or something?"

They all gave Ava a look, confusion on some of their faces, amusement on others. "We're not a military operation, Ava," he pointed out gently. "We don't have quite that level of organization, but you're not far off the mark."

"Arizona," I grunted. "There's a lot of empty land out there and it's always been sort of a neutral state just for this kind of thing. No packs set up territory in Arizona so whenever a pack needs to salt-the-earth, there's someplace to go." I glanced at her. "Is that something the Hunters know about?" I asked and she shrugged.

"Not familiar to me."

"We got that going for us at least." I moved my gaze over to William. "How's the protocol progressing, by the way?"

"Doing well enough. We got the entire state population out; they're all on their way. Most of the out-of-state members have gotten back to us on the protocol as well."

"Most?" Ava asked.

"Not all of them have responded yet."

"Are we worried about that?"

"Not especially. Maybe a bit for some of them, but a few are prone to working in areas where they have little access to messages and such, so it might just take them a little longer to get back to us." Chloe didn't really sound like she believed it, but nobody commented.

"How the hell have you people hidden for so long?"

Everyone looked at Evan, the new guy. His hands were balled into fists on the table in front of him, veins standing out in his forearms. He looked like a guy on the edge and that worried me. He would be hard pressed to survive his first full moon if he didn't make some headway on accepting his situation.

"A lot of practice," I muttered. "Wolf-kind have been hiding from the rest of the world for a very long time, Evan. And we've gotten really good at it. It really doesn't take much, to be honest. Regular people don't want to believe that there are real monsters in the world. They find ways to ignore, or explain away any of the weird shit they sometimes see. The human race's capacity to ignore things they don't want to understand is astounding."

"So there's werewolves–"

"Wolf-kind," Ava cut him off and I shot her a look out of the corner of my eye. She'd finished eating and was leaning back in her seat, arms crossed under her breasts, with her eyes firmly locked on Evan. I felt a warm little glow at that, her defending our preferred title for our people like that. I guess we were her people now too.

"Wolf-kind," he repeated. "So if wolf-kind are real, what about all the other stories you hear about? Vampires and ghosts and all that?"

I shrugged. He was asking me, not really sure why, but he'd looked directly at me while he spoke. "No idea, honestly. I've never met a Vampire, but I guess if we exist, it's possible they could exist too and be hiding from us just as much as we hide from humans."

The conversation bounced around a bit after that. It was agreed that we would be staying at the house until after the first full moon. We were about twenty miles from the Shoshone National Forest, so there'd be plenty of good land to run in that night, putting our new pups through their paces. I couldn't read Ava's expression during the conversation, couldn't tell if she was excited or terrified by the thought of her first change, but I didn't bring it up. If she wanted to talk to me about it, she would. When she was ready.

By the time the conversation wound down it was well into the night, and Ava was wilting in her seat. I wasn't exactly feeling bright eyed and bushy tailed myself either, so we said our goodnights and went back to the room.

We changed out of our clothes and slipped into bed, Ava molding herself against my side. Without a second thought I held her, smiling like a retard until we both drifted off to sleep.

Chapter 28

Ava

The dream was the first time I'd really felt any different. I knew in the front of my brain that I was dreaming, tucked into the furnace that was Remus but I wasn't awake. I wasn't really asleep either. I was in that place in between the two and staring at a black wolf with my eyes set into its face.

So this is what they all were talking about when they said 'their wolf' like it was almost a separate entity. I guess it was, but at the same time it wasn't. At least not really. I sank to the ground and held out my hands and it padded forward carefully, going to its belly in front of me and inching forward.

I held my breath and waited, hands out and finally, she lay her huge shaggy head in my palms and rolled, tongue lolling out of the side of her mouth. I laughed, and ruffled the thick, wiry fur around her ruff.

"Hi," I murmured and she yipped, excitedly.

"So how do we do this?" I asked in that same soft murmur, she rolled onto her belly and made a vocalization that wasn't a whine but wasn't a growl either. More ambivalent, than anything.

"Well that's helpful," another yip.

"I'm not sure how to share," I said truthfully and felt silly, to a certain extent, like I was talking to myself.

"It's supposed to be as easy as breathing, the change. At least that's what he tells me." I looked up sharply and scrambled to my feet.

"James!" beside him stood Remus, only... not. There was more of a glower to this man's face.

"Who are you?" I asked, and edged back, hands looking for weapons that weren't at my thighs.

"Chill, I can't hurt you here. Not that I'd want to." I blinked.

"How is any of this even possible?" I asked, frowning.

"The wolf is a spirit, isn't it? Kind of stands to reason it'd have a connection to the spirit world."

James smiled and held out his arms, I looked up into my much taller twin's face, into eyes that mirrored my own so closely in color, and looked at the proffered embrace.

"Can I really hug you?"

"You can do anything you put your mind and heart to here."

I hugged my twin, and his arms went around me, the dream so real I could smell his familiar cologne and the leather of his jacket. I closed my eyes and breathed him in, this one last time.

"What are you two even doing here?"

"Your wolf can't speak in this place; you're limited in communication except for in the real world. In the real world you can share thoughts and emotions but only if you're open to it." Romulus imparted.

"You gotta drop those walls, baby sister. The training might fuck with you; if it does, the natural path you're gonna take is to fight the change. You can't do that, Babe. Not at the first moon. It'll fuck you up. Maybe even kill you. I've seen it."

I pushed back from my brother, older by just nine minutes and stared up at him horrified, "The experiments?"

"Yeah, I knew, I saw, and I'm so fucking sorry but Av, you gotta listen to me. You have to, please!" He shook me and the dream started to dissolve, my wolf began to whine and I closed my eyes to shut the image of my brother, my brother who I knew deep down had done terrible things to protect me, and who had died trying.

"I got this," I told the three of them, "I'll figure it out, I promise." I looked at Romulus, "I love your brother too much to leave him now."

He nodded and the dream dissolved into the ether, my eyes opened to stare at the water stained false ceiling above the bed.

"Holy shit that was intense," I whispered into the dark.

Remus shifted, and I snuggled in closer to him, laying my head on his chest, my fingertips tapping out the steady thrum of his heart unbidden.

I thought hard, long and hard about the vision. I don't know that I should call it a dream. Finally, in need of some answers, but not wishing to wake my lover, I slipped from the bed and dressed, heading down to the kitchen to make some tea or something. I wanted to keep my hands busy.

I found Markus and Evan, sitting at one of the tables, steaming mugs parked between them.

"Well, what's got you up?" Markus asked.

"Sick of sleeping?" I hazarded, but the flippancy I meant to put behind it fell flat and echoed hollow in the large room.

"Want to talk about it?" he asked, leaning back in his seat. Evan eyed me with a mixture of respect and gave me a nod. A total soldierly thing to do. Guess the word had gotten around. I flung a leg over the bench and dropped onto it.

"I just had a very illuminating conversation with my dead brother, Remus' dead brother, and my wolf." I cleared my throat and felt seriously fucking crazy. I mean, I'd never believed in anything like this... There wasn't supposed to be anything after death.

"Did you now?" I looked up sharply, and searched Markus' face, and found not one ounce of disbelief there. Evan looked about as confused as I felt.

"Am I going crazy? This change flip my switch or something?"

Markus chuckled, "Nope, there are a few of us out there with the gift of sight. Something about being in tune with yourself. We call people like you the Median."

"Excuse me? Medium, like some kind of psychic?"

"No," Markus laughed, "Not to be pedantic, but it's *Median*, from the definition of literally being right smack dab in the middle. Not sure what makes a Median out of a wolf-kind. Maybe it was because you had one foot in the grave when you was turned. All I know, is that you're going to have those dreams and visions and you should probably listen to them."

I sat there and scrubbed my face with my hands, this was almost too weird. I'd never been one to buy into the whole mumbo jumbo of it. I'd never believed in an afterlife, or a spirit world, but at the same time, I couldn't refute what I'd just experienced.

"Ava? Babycakes, what's wrong?" Remus sat down behind me and pulled me back into his chest.

"Nothing, pretty much the opposite, Boy. She's a Median, just let her deal."

"Baby, why would he say that? What did you see?"

"I…" I didn't know what or how to tell him. I wasn't a chicken shit though, and I knew what I'd seen. I knew what I'd experienced and what I'd felt and smelled… I told him. Every bit of it and sat there biting my lips together, wondering why it was it was so *easy* to accept. Why it was I wasn't falling apart or freaking out.

Because you know it's true, and you've never really had the time to freak out over the truth.

True enough.

"So, are you going to listen?" Evan asked softly, meeting my eyes.

I met his stare with one of my own and found the spaces between Remus' fingers with my own, my palms to the backs of his hands. I gave them a squeeze, "As best I can. I'm not sure how to switch off a lifetime of training, but I'll do whatever it takes to stay right here." I leaned my head back and Remus kissed the side of my neck.

"That's my girl," he breathed and I hoped like hell it was enough. That just knowing what the problem was, identifying it, would help me avoid it when the time came because I had no idea what was coming. The mechanics of it.

They say that knowing is half the battle though, don't they? I wouldn't know until the full moon came, no matter what… so why worry about it until then? I cuddled back into Remus and felt my desire for him spike when he nipped the side of my neck again.

"Well, it's been swell boys, but the swelling's gone down. Remus, let's go back to bed."

"Anything you say, Babycakes."

"Call me that again, I'm going to cave your nuts in."

Markus laughed long and loud over our banter and even Evan

cracked a smile, after he recovered from blanching first. We went back to bed, and the sex, as always, was fucking amazing. God I loved his mouth on my tits as he drove up into me. It was enough to drive me fucking wild.

When we finally collapsed into a sweaty heap of blissed out goo, he smoothed my hair back from my face.

"A Median. Who'd have thunk it?" He said with a lazy smile.

"I'm still not sure I'm not going crazy," I muttered and he snorted.

"Bullshit, Ava. You're the surest person I've ever met, let alone stuck my cock in. You're fuckin' sure, you just can't help but question it to death. It's who you are."

I slapped a hand against his chest for being a Neanderthal, but he wasn't wrong.

"I think that might be what's bugging me more than anything," I admitted.

"What?"

"The fact that I'm *not* questioning it and poking at it to death."

"So, what do you want to do about it?"

"I want to talk about it."

He laughed good-naturedly, and I loved the sound, "That's a switch for you," he declared.

"I know, but it doesn't make it any less true."

"Okay, I'm game, what do you want to talk about?"

"What's it feel like? To change?"

He blew out an explosive breath, "Would you be cool with talking to Chloe about it? I'm probably not the best person to say, being Blood Born and all."

Shit. He had a point.

"You know what? Let me try Macy first instead."

"Macy? She won't talk to anybody."

"Gotta try all avenues before admitting defeat," I declared and got up.

"What, you're going to find her now?"

"No, I was going to take a shower, see if you wanted to fuck me from behind while I was in there, because that sounds really hot right about now, then I was going to find some clothes; *then* go talk to her."

"God I love that you're a planner and, might I add, a mighty fine plan it is." He slapped my ass, leaving a stinging hand print and I threw a half assed punch which he backed away from, letting it whizz past him.

"Oh so it's like that, huh?" he demanded grinning, and lunged.

We ended up fucking on the cement floor before we even made it out into the hallway. God I loved that we could play rough like that.

I showered, dressed and kissed my lover deeply before slipping off his lap and going off in search of Macy. I found her on this rampart looking part of the building, outside looking over the dirt road leading down to it. It was like some kind of modern day concrete castle in the middle of the woods. Not a half bad defensible position either.

"Hey," I greeted her, "Got a question for you."

"You can ask, but my answer will probably, most likely, be 'fuck off' if it's about Evan again. I'm getting kind of sick of the lectures about how I look at him." She made a face.

"Fuck 'em, I said with a shrug," and her eyebrows went up.

"What did you want to ask?" she asked gently.

"It might be a bit personal, for different reasons, but are you Moon Forged or whatever?"

She made another face, "What's that?" she asked.

"Did you start off as human only to be turned into what we are?"

She nodded, and pushed her hair back out of her face and behind her ears.

"Yeah, why? What's the alternative?"

"You know the big fucker?"

"The one you're constantly fucking since you woke up?"

I shrugged that off. One, it was true, and two; I'd been asking some pretty personal and rude questions pretty blithely at this point.

"Yeah, that guy," I said grinning.

"Kind of hard not to notice," she said dryly. I liked her sarcasm.

She and I would get along fine, probably after we whooped each other's asses at some point.

"Yeah, well he was born this way. Blood Born they call it."

"Good to know," she uttered and looked like she was actually processing the information.

"So, you're Moon Forged."

"Guess so."

"Great, next question," she rolled her cognac eyes.

"Sorry, only one per night," she said and turned back to the view into the trees.

"Yeah, well I'm asking anyways, and I kind of need to know the answer because I'm not particularly looking forward to dying."

She turned back around sharply, "What the fuck are you talking about? In case you haven't noticed, what we are, are pretty indestructible except for that allergy we all seem to share."

"What's it feel like to change?" I demanded, "We only get to live if we make it through the first one and I have some inside information that says I might be fucked when it comes to that. I kind of don't like to be told what to do."

"Me either," she grated and sighed.

We stared at each other for a long time and finally she sighed, "Okay, come here and stand. Close your eyes."

I arched an eyebrow and didn't move at first, a teasing smile curving my lips; she laughed and shook her head. She was a pretty girl when she smiled. She needed to do it more often.

"You want to know or not? I'm gonna try and show you, now c'mere."

I did as she asked and she stood with me, shoulder to shoulder looking out into the woods.

"Okay, now close your eyes."

I did.

"It's like an echo, of the woods, of the nature around you. That feeling you get when you're walking through the trees by yourself. Tranquil like. That's when the wolf shows up. You know? Like in real life, you look and it's just suddenly there and you freeze because you don't want to scare it off, but you don't want to run and have it chase you either." We stood there in the dark and quiet, and just as the feeling she'd described began to take hold, she spoke and it seemed, for lack of a better understanding of it, to scare off my wolf. I cursed silently in my head and tried to recapture the feeling in my dream as she went on.

"Before those assclown's caught me and dragged me off to that godforsaken place, I was almost happy to be what I am…"

"Watch it, Sister," I uttered, "I used to *be* one of those assclowns, as you so succinctly put it."

I had my eyes closed, questing for that feeling, concentrating so hard I didn't see it, feel it, or hear it coming. Her fist crashed into the side of my face and my ear started to ring as I went skidding across the deck.

My shoulders hit the low cement wall first, slowing me down, but once they met, my head whipped back and cracked painfully a split second later. White starbursts went off behind my eyes and I squeezed them shut, shaking my head and groping at the ground to push to my feet.

Macy snarled and my vision came back just in time to watch her hands shift into claws.

"You don't want to do this," I warned, my feet underneath me, even as my wolf rose inside me to meet the threat.

"You bitch!" she cried and lunged, untrained, uncoordinated; *shit* this wasn't going to be any kind of fight at all.

I sidestepped neatly and brought my knee up, kicking out and catching her right in the gut with a perfectly executed side snap kick. She reacted predictably, her arms going to her gut and doubling over, collapsing to her knees.

"Was, Macy, *was*. Operative word, Girl! Now fucking focus if you're going to come at me."

She got up and snarled, eyes bleeding to wolf, hands elongating. I stood my ground and felt my own wolf rise up to meet me.

I've got this. I told it, and I got the distinct impression that it agreed, though this wasn't the point of this exercise, was it?

I swore up and down I heard my twin in that moment, *"Let it happen, Ava."*

I closed my eyes and let Macy do her thing for a second as she dropped to all fours, bones sliding and popping pretty quickly, all things considered. I felt it in my face first, my front teeth and sinuses giving a throbbing ache as teeth elongated and began to change. She snarled and my eyes snapped open in time for her to make another lunge. I *moved* with super human speed and slashed out with fingers gone twice as long as they had been before.

She howled out in pain and dropped again as I gouged bloody furrows in her side. The door to the patio burst open and Evan, Chloe and Remus piled onto the balcony.

"Ava?" Remus growled.

"Stay out of it, Macy and I are having a difference of opinion. It's not my goal to hurt her." The words came out of my mouth accented and slurred around unfamiliar working mouth bits. I couldn't be sure any of them understood me.

Macy staggered to her misshapen feet, "Do you know what you monsters *did to me* in there!?" she screamed.

"Nothing good, but it wasn't me," I admitted.

She came at me again and I leapt up, and back, falling into a crouch onto the wide stone railing. I held my position, even as more bones slid beneath my skin. It was starting to hurt, and I got the impression my wolf was yelping in pain.

"Let it happen, Ava!" Remus cried, while Chloe was trying to talk Macy out of having another go at me. She swung and I took a chance, leaping back, off the porch to shouts as the rest of them rushed forward to see what'd become of me.

I landed on both feet and absorbed some of the shock of the jump by bending my knees before *going* to my knees and letting the wolf have free reign. It hurt a lot less the second I gave in and I thought real hard, *we have* got *to come to some kind of agreement on who's in the driver's seat during a fight.*

I stood, trembling on four legs instead of two and shook like a dog coming out of a bath. My paws… *holy fuck!* My *paws* were stuck in my shirt as Remus made a heavy landing beside me.

"Easy, Ava, let me get you out," he used his very human hands, complete with opposable thumbs, to untangle me from the remnants of my clothes. I whined, ears flat to my skull and he grinned.

"Fuck if you don't impress me more every day," he murmured sounding more shocked than I had ever heard him. He stood, and jerked his head for me to follow and broke into an easy lope away from the riotous voices, tangled on the balcony up behind us.

I was in agreement, and loped off into the woods behind him. Fuck the mess I'd caused for a minute. I needed to *run*.

Chapter 29
Remus

She changed without going through the full moon first. *She changed without going through the full moon first!*

I couldn't wrap my brain around it. It was impossible. It was *supposed* to be impossible. In a touch over two hundred years I had never once seen it or heard of it. I ran toward the woods, letting my mind spin as it would with Ava trotting along calmly beside me. Just inside the trees I stopped and shrugged off my cut. Hanging it from a tree branch I slipped out of my pants and tossed them over the branch as well, turning to find Ava sitting on her haunches nearby, staring at me intently.

"Here we go," I said with a smile and triggered the change into my wolf form.

I shrank as I changed, fur growing from my skin as my bones and organs shifted and rearranged themselves. My knees cracked and bent the wrong way as my hands and feet shrank into paws and my spine elongated into a tail. My face pushed out into a snout and my ears slid up my head, becoming pointed, to finish my transformation.

As soon I finished it happened. Like it always did. Every time. Every damned time I went full wolf it happened. A twitching, itching, burning somewhere between my fur and my skin; it wasn't really painful, more like the pins and needles you get when your foot falls asleep but over my entire body all at once. I yipped and dropped to the ground, rolling back and forth on my back, trying to satisfy the maddening itch.

When it finally faded I rolled onto my stomach, attempting to look as dignified as I possibly could despite the fact that I knew I had just been acting like a puppy. Pretty sure I failed entirely based on the huge canine grin Ava was flashing in my direction.

Yeah, yeah, keep laughing, I said in that strange non-verbal way of speaking that wolf-kind had. *Come on, I want to run.* I surged forward and nipped at her flanks, jumping back as she spun to try to catch me, and took off running as hard as I could.

She barely paused before she gave chase, paws drumming across the rich loam beneath us as we sped through the brush, leaping rocks and streams and chasing each other around the woods like a couple of juveniles. It was the most fun I'd had in a long time. We ran for nearly an hour, keeping to within the general area of the bunker, but taking the time to enjoy ourselves.

The thing that amazed me, again, was her discipline. New wolves, when they change for the first time are constantly distracted by scents, sights, and sounds that they'd never been able to detect when they were human. In the days that Ava had been recovering, after William bit her, my brother and I had taken some time to talk and catch up on what had been going on in each other's lives. He told me about the first time he went running with Chloe and how he'd had to keep getting her attention because she would constantly find herself distracted by every scent, game trail, and gopher den, that they came across.

Not Ava. She was trying to catch me and nothing would deter her from that. Her focus and ability to block out the sudden flood of new sensory information was astounding.

Eventually I shifted back to human, coming to a stop in a clearing a good minute ahead of her and turned to look back the way I'd come. I didn't see her. I waited a minute, figuring she was just following my scent when a twig snapped behind me and I turned, spinning fast on one foot, just in time to catch a glimpse of Ava in midair, flying at me. She was human once again and when she hit me she twisted strangely, some kind of maneuver I've never encountered.

Suddenly the ground was above my head and I had a momentary sensation of weightlessness before I slammed back into the earth with a punishing degree of force.

"Ha!" She bellowed and I gasped in a breath for a second before I looked up to find her standing next to me, hands on her hips and looking incredibly sexy.

"Don't think you've won already, Pup," I growled and my leg kicked out, knocking her feet out from under her. She yelped as she fell and I surged forward, colliding with her in midair with enough force that if she'd still been human I might have done some damage.

As it was, she shrugged off the hit and rolled with it. We hit the dirt and tumbled for a moment, rolling along the ground. I was on top, then she was, then me again. I came up above her again and the breath suddenly rushed out of my lungs as she planted her heel in my gut and kicked, *hard*. I had that flying feeling again as I was thrown back through the air and grunted when my back collided painfully with the trunk of a large evergreen.

Pine needles rained down around me and I looked up just in time to catch sight of Ava sprinting toward me, a broad grin on her lips and that sharp look in her eye. I sidestepped just in time, grabbed her arm and twisted it around behind her. I planted my left hand in the center of her back and pushed until she was pressed against the trunk, held there by my grip. She gasped and pulled, attempting to free her wrist but I had a solid grip on her. Even her new strength wouldn't break that hold.

"Quit fucking playing around," she growled. "You can do better than that."

"You mean like this?" I asked and pressed against her, pinning her to the tree with my body. The hard length of my dick slid along the crack of her ass for a second. I pulled back, letting go of her hand so she could reach down and grab ahold of me. With one hand stroking me she arched her back, lifting her ass and guiding me to her entrance.

I could smell how wet she was, a heavy, heady scent that mingled with the ever present jasmine and gun-oil, so I wasn't at all concerned that she was ready for me. As soon as I felt the head of my cock line properly with her I shoved forward, pressing her harder into the tree and burying myself inside her in one smooth motion. Without a pause I pulled back and shoved forward again and she pushed back against me, meeting me thrust for thrust.

This fuck was a frenzied, primal thing. Hard and fast, almost painful at times, all mingled with an insane pleasure that came from being with a woman that could not only handle my strength and the punishing tempo but urged me to fuck her faster, harder. The words spilled from her mouth between grunts and moans, her fingers clutching at the tree.

Eventually, I pulled out of her, ignoring a moaned protest from her and spun her around to face me. I reached down and cupped her ass, lifting her into the air and slamming her back against the tree as I slid into her again. Her legs came up to circle my waist and I dipped my head, licking and kissing at the small scratches left on her breasts by the rough bark of the tree.

Her nails dug into my shoulders as that pressure built up higher and higher within us both. She bit and scratched and clawed at my skin, drawing blood, driving herself down to meet me just as I thrust up into her, muscles clamped around me until that pressure finally became too much and I buried my face between her breasts. I exploded inside her, just barely having the presence of mind to slide a hand between us and gently rub her clit with my thumb. It took a few moments but just as I finished coming inside her she came apart in my arms.

It was like watching her completely implode then rebuild herself from the inside out. That moment when she came and the world vanished for her and there was nothing but our bodies and the lightning along her nerve endings. Then, slowly, she came back to herself, the world coming into focus and it was like waking from an amazing dream.

"Why is it," she gasped. "That we always seem to end up fucking each other's brains out?"

"Do I hear a complaint in there?" I asked, smug smirk firmly in place on my lips. She scowled and slapped my chest. "Ow," I said in a deadpan tone, though it really had hurt, a lot more than expected. She was still getting used to her new strength. We separated and I set her back down on her feet, leading her over to the middle of the clearing.

"Ready to head back?" I asked.

She thought about it for a moment, worrying at her lower lip, before she nodded. "Yeah, I gotta try and talk to Macy again, I think. She didn't take it well when she found out I was a Hunter. Gotta see if I can do something about that."

I nodded. I understood the sentiment but I wasn't really sure what she could do. "Not sure what you could possibly do about that one, to be honest. If she's going to hate you she's going to hate you. It's not fair but I'm not sure that it's your responsibility to try and fix that."

She shrugged and I had to smile. She had become pretty damned comfortable being naked around me. I wasn't a hundred percent positive that she was even consciously aware that she was just standing there, out in the woods, completely bare.

"Maybe not. But I think I have an idea that she'll respond to."

She wouldn't say more than that, no matter how I bugged her, so after a few minutes we shifted back, again with me rolling around on the ground like an idiot. It only happens when I go full wolf, I swear, and I have never been able to figure out *why*. It doesn't happen with my hybrid shift. I pushed the thoughts aside and Ava and I raced each other back to the house.

I'm proud to say that she beat me, but only by a tails length.

We slipped inside and showered. The temptation to fuck her again was strong, but she wanted to go talk to Macy and I needed to see Markus and William so we just showered quickly and dressed again in clean clothes. I found my pants and vest on our bed. They smelled like Markus so it appeared that he had collected them and brought them in for me after I'd left them out on the edge of the property.

Ava lifted up on her toes and gave me a deep, searing kiss, before she turned and sauntered away in search of Macy. For a moment I worried about letting her go alone, but I was confident my girl could protect herself, so I let her go and stalked off in search of my brother and his Arbiter.

I found them in the dining area again. Seated at the same table from the day before. No one else was around and as I approached I caught the tail end of their discussion.

"... seen anything like it before. I've never even *heard* of anything like it before," Markus was saying. "To make the change without the full moon to show her how to do it... it's unprecedented William."

"I get that, Markus. Really, I understand. You've only said it about thirty times now. But that doesn't really mean anything to me. Ok, it's unprecedented. Splitting the atom was unprecedented until someone did it. So was climbing Mt. Everest, swimming the English Channel and any number of things that normal humans have done over the centuries. What you haven't explained is exactly *why* that's got you chasing your tail like a lunatic."

Markus glowered at William. "I am *not* chasing my tail, Boy. But you have to admit this is strange, isn't it?"

"Who cares?" I asked and pulled out a chair next to William. "She did it; freaking out about it isn't going to change anything, right?" Markus nodded, reluctantly.

"I guess," he muttered and I had to smile, seeing the old man acting more like a petulant child than the aged Arbiter that he was.

"We've gotta settle on what we're going to do *after* the full moon," I said, interrupting William just as he opened his mouth to tease Markus. I could tell by the smug grin he was trying to hide that he was going to rib the old man, and while normally I would have been happy to join in, but there were more pressing matters to discuss.

"Well, we're all heading to Arizona to link up with the rest of the pack," William said. "We're at about 98% confirmed from the out of state members. Only twenty or thirty haven't yet responded."

"I haven't figured out what Ava and I are going to do yet, but we'll have to decide sooner rather than later."

"You've got an idea though, don't you, Boy?" I glanced over at Markus, not for the first time, impressed with his insight.

"A few thoughts have been circling," I admitted. And they had. Ever since Colorado I had an idea that had made more and more sense the longer I thought about it. "Got a few questions that could help settle it though. Got a minute Markus?"

"For one of you youngins to pump me for information again? Sure. Why not?" he muttered.

"Thanks. Ava is a Median. What does that mean, long run, for her?"

"Well, for one she's gonna keep getting these visions, dreams, whatever they are, and she'd better listen to them. They're trying to tell her something important when they happen."

I nodded and motioned for him to continue. "On top of that it'll be good to have her around when going into or even just through another pack's territory."

"Why is that?"

He hummed, pinching his lower lip thoughtfully for a moment before he shrugged. "I can't give it a solid explanation, really. Medians are sort of considered like priests, or priestesses in this case. Shaman type characters. There haven't been many and if she's with you, a pack will, more often than not, welcome you as honored guests. As long as you and your people are respectful and don't cause any trouble you've basically got an open pass to travel anywhere without stepping on any toes."

I mulled that over for a minute before a question occurred to me. "But how are we supposed to prove that she's actually a Median? I mean, anyone could come in and say 'oh, this member of my pack is a Median, we request a place to sleep for the night and we'll move on in the morning,' ya know?"

Markus shrugged. "Couldn't tell ya, Pup. But any wolf-kind worth their salt is gonna know something's different about yer girl. I could tell right away she was different, I just didn't know what it was until she mentioned that dream she had. That's when it all clicked and come together."

"What're you thinking, Remus?" William asked, staring intently at me.

"The Alpha Wolves gave me an idea. An excuse for us to move around, even a way to claim some territory. If I plan it right, we can grow a small pack and start taking the fight to the Hunters."

William and Markus both raised a brow at that one, giving me nearly identical incredulous stares. "You're going to *hunt* the Hunters?"

"In a manner of speaking. And I have a way to do it that'll keep us off official radar and legitimize our moving around the country." I turned to William. "When you branded me, you wanted me to find something new. Something of my own. I think I might have an idea how to do that."

"What're you thinking?"

"I'm going to build my own pack. Going to build a pack of wolf-kind misfits with nothing to lose. A crew that, like I said, can bring the fight directly to the Hunters. With Ava's knowledge and the right combination of strengths and skills, we could do a lot of damage to their power base here. Because, let's face it, we did some damage last week, but I'd be willing to bet that Mathias already has new labs up and running, humming along at full speed."

They both nodded, but William had a pensive expression on his face.

"I hate to say it," he started and I interrupted him.

"Then don't."

"I hate to say it," he said again, glaring at me and I sighed and leaned back in my seat, arms crossed over my chest. "But you're an Omega. There aren't going to be many wolf-kind that are going to be thrilled about an Omega as the pack's Alpha."

"That's why I'm only going to recruit *other* Omegas, or new wolf-kind if the situation arises where it's necessary."

I'll be honest. I took a slightly perverse pleasure in their dumbfounded expressions. Especially Markus. It wasn't often that I was able to surprise the old wolf and twice in as many minutes was an especially rare treat.

"An entire pack of Omegas?" Markus muttered once he'd managed to gather his wits. "That's actually a pretty brilliant idea, Boy. But at the same time, it's dangerous. Usually a wolf is made Omega for good reason. Some of the characters you're likely to run into won't be the kind you'd want to share a space with."

"And some of them made honest mistakes. Some of them are looking to redeem themselves for their poor choices. It's only fair I give them a chance."

Markus and William couldn't think of anything to say to that, so we just sat and talked about other things for a while. Unimportant things. It wouldn't be long before my family, my pack, was on their way out of here and I would be separated from them again. But I took some solace in the fact that I finally had something to look forward to. When I'd left Washington, I'd wondered if an Omega could ever outrun his past.

I finally understood that, no, you couldn't outrun your past; that was impossible. The past would always be there. All you could do, was run toward a future of your own making. And do everything possible to make sure it was a future worth fighting for.

For the rest of the day, people wandered in and out. Ava and Macy came in together about an hour later. Macy went to her table far away from us but I noticed that she sat a little closer than she had the day before. Ava slid into the seat next to me and said that she and Macy had worked some things out. She didn't have any new bruises so I figured that it had been done through conversation, not confrontation. She was going to train Macy to fight while we were here, get her into a better condition to handle and protect herself.

The next few days passed with a lot of the same. Chatting with my brother and Markus while Markus worked with Evan, trying to get the man to accept his new condition. It was tough going but it needed to be done or he likely wouldn't survive his first change. Ava and Macy worked together, day and night, and by the end of the week I have to say that Macy had become a rather impressive student. Her instincts, power, and determination made sure she learned quickly. She was still really rough around the edges, but she had enough to build on and I was sure in a few months she would be a pretty deadly opponent. I was glad that I wouldn't have occasion to fight her myself. Strong as I was, Macy was scary *fast*.

The day of the full moon was a quiet one. Everyone felt a certain degree of nervous tension, but no one wanted to do much. We ended up lounging in a media room on the third basement level, watching movies and pigging out. The new pups in particular needed to build up their energy reserves. The changes took a lot, burned a lot of calories, and with our already rapid metabolisms it could be dangerous.

As a group, the eight of us made our way out to the forest. Stripped of clothing we waited, just at the edge of the trees. Ava and Evan shivered slightly in the cooling air but the rest of us simply waited. When the moon came out and shone, brilliant and full upon us, I felt him stir.

The wolf was awake. He was wound up and anxious. He wanted to play, he wanted to fight. He wanted to *run*.

Ava made her change, swiftly, with minimal noise. Chloe was again preternaturally swift in her change and she padded over to nuzzle at my girl, the two of them bounced about a bit, playing as we waited for Evan. Evan still hadn't changed.

"Come on, Boy," Markus muttered in his deep growl. He was holding back the change focusing on his self-imposed charge. "You can't fight the wolf. You don't want to, trust me. Just let it go. Work with the beast. Open up, just a little."

Evan shook and trembled, his hands balled into fists at his sides, every muscle taught and quivering with tension. Sweat stood out on his face and for a moment I thought we'd have to knock him out, let the change happen while he was unconscious so it wouldn't kill him. But then it happened. With the usual sickening cracking and snapping that accompanied most of our transformations, Evan slowly vanished, and was replaced by a powerful red wolf. He stood nearly waist high on me, if I'd been a wolf he'd probably match me shoulder to shoulder. His coat was a deep tan with a cream undercoat, shot through with streaks of brilliant, gingery, red.

As each of the rest of us made our changes, I was the last to finally assume my full wolf and when I immediately started rolling on my back to relieve the maddening itch, many of the others started yipping and barking, laughing at my behavior in true canine fashion.

I rolled and leapt to my feet, growling at them and leapt at William, teeth flashing halfheartedly in his direction. He dodged the attacked, shouldered me aside, and barreled past me toward Ava who leaped out of the way and barked once at him. As if by some unspoken signal, we all turned and dashed into the woods.

Long into the night we ran. Eight wolves, howling at the moon, chasing the occasional big horn sheep, and generally terrorizing the local nightlife. It felt great to be part of a pack again. To run, and play, and interact with my own kind.

I hadn't realized just how much I had missed it during my time alone, and I was more determined than ever to build a pack I could love and be proud of. And with Ava by my side, I was sure that we could do it.

Epilogue

Macy

I kept to myself on purpose. I hated this, hated everything, hated that *lying bitch* and everything she'd stood for. I was angry, I was heartbroken, and there wasn't a fucking thing I could do about *any* of it.

I stared across the room, huddled in on myself, and watched Evan, who was watching me. He didn't understand, he couldn't, and he wouldn't *listen to me* so I avoided him, even when all I wanted to do was sooth the hurt that was raging just beneath his surface.

I'd taken up a corner in one of the media rooms down on the second basement level of the bunker we were all staying in. It was two stories up top, but down below, it went down three. I liked it in here, despite being closed up underground again. It was cozy, like a den, the smell of old books a comforting thing. When I'd been human, I had always taken refuge from my fucked up home life in libraries and used book stores.

I should have never let Miranda talk me into that camping trip…

The door opened, dispelling the memories, and I could smell her before I saw her. Jasmine and some underlying metallic scent, rancid almost, chemical and manufactured.

"Go away," I grated, before she found me in the stacks of bookshelves, huddled in the corner on a beanbag.

"Not going away, and not going to try and kick your ass again either. I have an offer to make you."

"I don't want what you're selling, bitch. So you might as well just go the fuck away."

"Macy, I'm trying to help you."

"Help me do what?" I demanded.

"Fight better for one. Let me train you. Let me make you useful, and then let's go get the sons of bitches."

"Why do you even want to help me?"

"Because helping you, helps me… duh."

"What are you on about?"

She rounded the corner and crossed her arms under her breasts, looking me up and down.

"You can't bring down an ages old secret society without a team of capable people."

I snorted, "You'd need an army to take down the Hunters."

"Not really, Sweetie. Honestly," again she looked me up and down, "I just need Remus, you, possibly that fellow that was in the cage with you, and maybe one or two more on the outside."

Something about the look she was giving me both thoroughly scared me, and gave me pause. She was absolutely certain that she could do this. Like scary certain.

I considered what she was offering and finally, I nodded slowly, "Okay, I'll drink the Kool-aide. When do we start?" She smiled and it was an icy thing that sent a shiver of dread down my spine.

"We've started already; I just need to get you caught up."

I eyed her mistrustfully, but I *did* need training. I needed to be far more capable than I was. They'd grabbed me too easily… I didn't know where else I could get the kind of training she was offering so…

"Okay," I agreed, and my wolf seemed pleased about it.

I thought at it, hard…

I hope you're right.

Of course it hadn't steered me wrong, yet.

THE MOON FORGED TRILOGY: BOOK III

HUNTER'S END

AJ DOWNEY | RYAN KELLS

About the Authors

A.J. Downey is the internationally bestselling author of The Sacred Hearts Motorcycle Club romance series. She is a born and raised Seattle, WA Native. She finds inspiration from her surroundings, through the people she meets, and likely as a byproduct of way too much caffeine.

She has lived many places and done many things, though mostly through her own imagination... An avid reader all of her life, it's now her turn to try and give back a little, entertaining as she has been entertained. She lives in a small house in a small neighborhood with a larger than life fiancé and one cat.

She blogs regularly at *www.ajdowney.com*. If you want the easy button digest, as well as a bunch of exclusive content you can't get anywhere else, sign up for her mailing list right here: *http://eepurl.com/blLsyb*

A California native and avid reader, for Ryan Kells, making the transition from reader to writer was simply the next logical evolution. He enjoys a number of genres from paranormal suspense to dystopian post-apocalyptic. All of his work contains a romantic spin with a decidedly erotic flair.

www.facebook.com/authorajdowney
www.facebook.com/authorryankells

Second Circle Press

Made in the USA
San Bernardino, CA
11 August 2016